I0714862

# MATCHMAKER MAYHEM

## SARA LAFONTAIN

Cover Design: Leigh McDonald

Editor: Rachel Hoff

Matchmaker Mayhem/ Sara LaFontain - 1st ed.

ISBN 978-1-958025-03-1

To my favorite artist,
Willow River

# CHAPTER ONE

There are numerous benefits to having a friend who 1) loves to bake; and 2) doesn't have his own kitchen. A dozen of those benefits are coming out of my oven right now.

"Cassidy, wait, let them cool first," Tanner warns me. He's holding his spatula in a threatening manner, like he thinks that's going to stop my quest for chocolate. Too bad for him that I'm fast, and I'm not afraid of burning the roof of my mouth. I dodge the weak plastic weapon and grab the cookie he just deposited on the cooling rack.

Ouch.

Maybe I should have listened. Molten chocolate is searing my finger, but I have to maintain a neutral expression and pretend it doesn't hurt. I refuse to show weakness, so I take a careful bite, trying to keep as much cookie as possible between my teeth, rather than touching any of my soft tissues.

Tanner is watching me in amusement, lips quirked in a grin. His annoyingly adorable dimple is showing. For some reason, that always irritates me. Partly because I don't like thinking he's cute.

"These are delicious," I assure him. "And plenty cool enough to eat." One of those two statements is accurate. I think. It's hard to taste the flavor while protecting my tongue.

"I'm not falling for that. *I* can be patient."

"Hey, cookies!" My brother wanders into the kitchen and takes one directly from the pan, sliding it off in a soft crumbly mess. "Ow! These are hot!"

"Good thing you took out an insurance policy for your fingers," I comment. I'm not joking; his hands are worth a lot of money, though not nearly what his voice is insured for. As a world-famous musician, he's rather dependent on both of those things for his career. And as his assistant, I'm rather dependent on them as well.

Powell drops the cookie on the marble countertop and wipes the melted chocolate chips on his shorts. "I'll eat it later. I'm really just here to share some exciting news." He pauses dramatically to ensure we're both listening.

"Well?" I ask when his pause becomes a little too dramatic. He craves attention, and it's been over a month since his last performance, so he'll take whatever audience he can find, however limited and unwilling it may be.

"I'm getting married!" Somehow, he manages to make the proclamation with a straight face.

"Congrats!" Tanner moves to give him one of those manly handshakes that turn into half hugs. My reaction is less celebratory. I cross my arms and lean against the counter.

"No, you aren't."

"Yes, I am." Powell widens his light golden eyes in earnestness, but he can't fool me.

"Powell, you aren't even dating anyone, and if you wanted an arranged marriage, wouldn't I be involved in the vetting process? So, no, you aren't. Tanner, stop congratulating him. He's a liar."

"No, Deedee, I am," my brother insists, using my childhood nickname as if that will convince me of the truthiness of his words. "I mean, not, like, immediately; there's no date set or anything."

"Who's the bride?" I ask because I'm pretty sure when you get married, another person is supposed to be involved, and as of the last time I talked to him—an hour ago—my delusional brother was still completely single.

"I don't know yet."

See, here's something annoying about Powell: he is wholly incapable of telling stories. He does well in media interviews because questions flow in a predictable order, and he normally has been given advance prep on those, as well as talking points. In real life, prying information out of him is like trying to ask a two-year-old where they hid your car keys. You might find out eventually, but it will involve cajoling, threats, and listening to a lot of extraneous details.

"Okay, Powell, we're going to start this conversation over again." I'm speaking to him slowly, enunciating every word. "You want to tell us that you would like to be married at some point in the future. What is your plan for going about this?"

He sighs, annoyed that I'm talking down to him, but he's aware of his conversational shortcomings. He knows my tone is justified. Or he should know—I've had to use it often enough.

"I signed up for a matchmaker service," he finally provides the information that would have been helpful at the very beginning. "Have you heard of Felicity L'Amour?"

"The millionaire matchmaker?" Tanner asks in surprise. I wouldn't have expected Tanner to recognize the name. Perhaps he's taken paparazzi shots by their offices before.

"Yeah, that's her. I met up with her when I was out in LA. She personally accepted my application. She's going to find me a wife."

Oh, I wish I could see that application. And I can't help but wonder how large of a check accompanied it. I should have gone with him on that trip—Powell should never be allowed unsupervised.

"A wife? Or a girlfriend? Because you sound like you're skipping an important step or two."

My brother takes another cookie—not the one he dropped—and pokes the top cautiously to test it, before shoving the whole thing in his mouth. We wait an impossibly long time for him to finish chewing before he finally responds. "I'm ready to settle down. I'm putting a ring on the finger of the next woman I fall in love with. Should be soon." He speaks with the utmost confidence, as though thousands of women are lined up, eager to rush to the altar with him. Truthfully, they probably are. I could post a notice on one of the fan forums, and he'd be inundated with photos of women in wedding dresses who have been praying for this opportunity.

This is not a new development either. Powell has been marriage-ready for years. Many men at his level of looks and popularity prefer to play the field, but he's always been a serial monogamist. Sadly, his last girlfriend cheated on him. Her infidelity didn't break his heart since that particular relationship was more publicity-based than love-based, but his feelings were hurt, and his resultant drinking binge led tangentially to the explosive murder of his close friend and former bandmate, Jace Monroe. So overall it wasn't a great situation.

I plaster a fake smile on my face. "That's wonderful! I'm going to call Mom and Hank and tell them. Do you want me to start planning an engagement party? Tanner, you're a portrait photographer. Can we hire you to do the engagement shoot?"

"I'll do it for free as my wedding gift," Tanner offers. "But I want to post the pictures online for my portfolio."

"Fantastic. I'll have Powell's attorney draw up a contract. Now let's talk venues. Those tend to book well in advance, so we should start making some calls. I'm thinking next spring? Maybe up in Sedona? Powell, will I be a groomswoman, or do you think your bride will want me on her side? I'm picky about dress colors."

"The wedding photography is a bigger job; I'm not up for that," Tanner jumps in on the planning with me. "I'll help you find someone though. You'll want at least three still photographers and two videographers, and maybe a drone? People are doing interesting things with those lately."

"Okay, enough," Powell interrupts. He would have stopped us sooner, but he'd shoved two more fresh cookies in his mouth. "I'm not ready to plan the actual wedding. Besides, my fiancée will probably want some input on that. And you two aren't funny! I was making an important announcement about some major changes in my life, and you're turning everything into a joke."

"We're happy for you, I promise. It's just all so sudden." I can't help but keep teasing him. I mean, he is trying to buy a bride. That's certainly a tease-worthy event.

"I bought you a membership too, Cass. Maybe we'll have a double wedding." My brother's grin is somehow menacing, and I no longer find any humor in this situation.

"No, you didn't." Surely enrollment in a dating service would require my consent. He can't just sign me up; he can't forge my signature. I mean, literally, he can't. He's tried before but can't get it through his head that just because I'm female doesn't mean I dot my i's with hearts. It's a giveaway every time.

"I sure did. I didn't get you the guaranteed package, but you're now a happy member of the LoveMatch Singles Network. Our intake interviews are the day after tomorrow, and our first event is next weekend. You're welcome."

Oh, how I want to throw something at him, but the only things within reach are too good to waste by bouncing them off his face. Damn Tanner for making delicious cookies.

"You're . . . you're looking for a boyfriend?" Tanner sort of stutters the question, and an uncomfortable vibe settles over the kitchen.

"Absolutely not. Powell, you had no right to sign me up for anything!"

"But you're single." He shrugs as though he's done nothing wrong and enrolling me in an expensive matchmaking service is a common and normal thing for an older sibling to do. "Why not make a positive change?"

"This isn't funny anymore," I protest. "You're the one looking, not me. I shouldn't have to hang out with a bunch of desperate people with ticking biological clocks."

"Is that what you expect? The parties are mostly going to be full of rich people who are too busy to bother with dating apps and want to outsource the work of finding a partner."

"That doesn't sound any better! I don't need to outsource my dating life."

"You haven't been doing a good job insourcing it either. Why not try something new? Cass, we almost died recently. Isn't it time to start living?"

"Powell!" I protest again, but he's not looking at me anymore. His eyes glaze over, he hums a few bars, mumbles something about 'time to start living' and abruptly leaves the kitchen. But he does grab a cookie on the way out, which causes me to yell after him. "POWELL! GET BACK HERE!"

"I thought you weren't allowed to disturb him when he drifts into songwriting mode," Tanner says. He's correct. When Powell gets that vague dreamy look, I'm supposed to make sure he has a notebook or recording device and clear the area, so he can write a hit and make another couple million dollars. However, that's not what my brother is doing.

"He's faking." I slam my hand down on the counter in frustration, which only results in a stinging palm and a greater level of frustration. "If he were actually writing, he wouldn't have paused for a snack. I hate when he does that!" He doesn't do it often, but this is how my brother ducks out of uncomfortable conversations. He's probably heading off to his bedroom to scroll through a catalog of LoveMatch bachelorettes.

"Was he really serious?" Tanner removes the final batch from the oven and carefully transfers them to the rack, keeping a cautious eye on my thieving hands. "About the dating service?" His voice is slightly higher than usual, as though making an effort to keep his tone light.

"Yep. When he makes a decision, he sticks to it. If he's decided he's getting married, you better make sure you have a suit that fits."

"You think I'd be invited?" Tanner seems absurdly pleased by his hypothetical invitation to a not-yet-existing wedding.

"Why wouldn't you be? If Powell didn't invite you, I would." And I'd buy him a tailored suit, too. Otherwise, who knows what ill-fitting rag he'd show up in? He spends all his time behind cameras, so he's not one to care too much about his own appearance.

"I don't know, sounds like you're getting a LoveMatch, too. Your new boyfriend won't like you bringing me to a family event."

"I'm not interested in dating," I remind him. I don't like talking about boyfriends with Tanner.

"But you're going to your intake appointment?"

"Yeah, I guess so. It's paid for." I'll go for Powell's sake though, not mine. I need to accompany him to the matchmaking events, help weed out the women who are after a piece of his fame and fortune.

"Of course, money is the reason. You certainly can't ask for a refund." Tanner turns his back on me and starts washing the remaining dishes. He usually cleans as he goes, so baking trays are all that's left. He's scrubbing rather harder than necessary.

"Stop being like that. You know this is my job. I'm Powell's assistant. Sometimes I have to do things I don't want to."

His shoulders tense for a moment, then relax. "Sorry. I was just caught off guard by the whole matchmaker thing. Jace's fans aren't going to be happy. They want you to stay single forever."

"Ugh. Don't remind me." When Jace died, his will identified me as the love of his life, and our 'story' has been thoroughly romanticized in gossip blogs and fan forums. The sad truth is that, while he may have been in love with me, he never made that clear in life, and I never reciprocated. But I'm media savvy enough to know what will happen to me if I ever admit that, so I smile and pretend. Only a few months have passed since the media got their hands on a copy of the will, and I'm already tired of the attention. I was tired of the attention about five seconds in, actually.

"Well, I guess I'm done here." Tanner dries his hands and begins packing the cookies into a couple of boxes. I don't honestly know what he does with all that he bakes, but he always leaves plenty behind as a thank you, so I'm not overly concerned with the rest.

"Are you okay?" I ask, because he's moving rather stiffly, and his cheerful mood of earlier has completely evaporated.

"I'm fine. I'm happy for you and your brother and how lucky you are to be offered the chance to find happiness with the special match of your dreams." I recognize that last part—it's the tagline from LoveMatch commercials.

"Sarcasm is unbecoming in a man," I inform him. Inwardly, I'm cringing. I don't want to join a cheesy club for singles. And I want to smooth this over; I don't like when Tanner gets all weird and rude. "Want to stay and hang out? Go for a swim?"

"Can't." He rarely turns down an opportunity to jump in my pool, so I'm surprised. I'm even more surprised when he gives his reason: "I'm on my way to a poker game. That's why I made the cookies."

"You can't play poker!"

"Why not? You and I aren't in a relationship, you can't tell me what to do."

Where did that sudden defensiveness come from?

"Tanner!" He possesses the singular ability to go from zero to offended in no time flat. He is so ridiculously prickly sometimes.

"No, Cass, I'm serious. You can't tell me what I'm allowed to do with my free time. Don't act all mad just because I don't want to swim with you."

"I meant you can't play because you can't bluff. Your stupid dimple gives you away all the time. But never mind. Go lose all your money, see if I care."

I hate the way his lips quirk and his ridiculous obnoxious annoying dimple flashes while he tries to think of a cutting response. But all he can come up with is "I guess I'll see you later," and he and his baked goods go out the door.

# CHAPTER TWO

Twelve dozen red roses have just shown up on my doorstep, accompanied by an impressively large gold-wrapped box of chocolates, and an envelope addressed to me.

"Powell, did you order me flowers?" I shout. I'm not stupid enough to bring them inside. We've been attacked enough lately, and even though the people who tried to commit murder-via-bombing are either in jail or incapacitated, I'm still wary.

"Red roses are for romance," my brother says, coming up behind me and looking over my shoulder at the extravagant display. "So, no, definitely not from me. Tanner?"

I have to laugh at that. "Why would Tanner send me flowers?"

"I don't know; you still haven't told me what's going on with you two. I just know that during the three weeks I was out of town, he was over here every single day." He arches a brow expectantly, like I'm about to confess to a torrid love affair.

"What makes you think he was here?" If he was spying on me through the security cameras, I'm going to enact revenge by leaking embarrassing photos. I have a whole file of them: bad hair days, drooling in his sleep, the unfortunate see-through pants incident.

"I recognize my own house." At my blank stare, Powell adds, "I follow him on SwiftaPic. He posts a lot. Plus, Omaha keeps me updated. He tells Mike, and Mike tells me."

They're playing a game of security guard telephone. I'm lucky that's all Omaha—our neighborhood gate guard—passed along. It's true, Tanner was over here nearly every day during Powell's trip. He even stayed overnight in one of the guest suites several times. But that's because I was almost murdered recently, and sometimes I don't like being alone. Some nights I was scared. I did crash at our parents' house a few times, but Mom was beginning to get concerned about me, and I don't like to worry her. Tanner is my friend. He doesn't mind staying up late and watching movies or spending afternoons by the pool. And he doesn't make me talk about uncomfortable subjects. He's content to sit in silence.

Powell nudges me. "So, who sent them? Check the card."

"I don't want to touch it in case there's a bomb." As soon as the words come out of my mouth, I realize how ridiculous they sound. I'm trying to overcome my paranoia, but it's only been a little over a month since our attack. My face may have healed, but my nerves haven't.

"Want me to call Mike and have him bring a bomb squad here?" Powell teases. No, I don't need his security expert to come out, cast a skeptical glance at the mysterious offering, and break down into hysterical fits of laughter. "Besides," my brother adds, "This is probably your welcome package."

"Welcome to what?" I reluctantly pick up the oversized bouquet to bring it inside. Powell grabs the gold box and rips off the outer layer of foil on the way to the kitchen—to see if they're melted is the excuse he makes.

"Read the label," I reflexively remind him.

"Peanut-free facility," he points to the writing on the package. The box is still factory sealed, so it should be fine. After his recent hospitalization, he decided he should enroll in one of those allergy desensitization programs, ones where doctors carefully feed little bits of the allergen to train the immune system to eventually view them as less of a threat. But since it's life-and-death related rather than music related, my slacker brother hasn't scheduled anything yet.

I'm too busy opening up the other envelope to argue with him when he starts helping himself to my chocolates.

"*Dear Ms. Cassidy Corbitt*—they got my name wrong—*welcome to the LoveMatch Millionaires' Circle*," I read aloud. "Powell, what the hell is this?"

"I told you I bought you a membership." His voice is garbled by stolen candy.

"Yes, but Millionaires' Circle?"

"Of course." He finally swallows and clears his throat. "You're a millionaire. That's where you belong, so that's the level I enrolled you at. It gets you admission to all the swanky events. They're very exclusive."

"Where's your welcome package?"

"I'm in the guaranteed match level, and they sent me diamond cufflinks. So there."

I don't know what that childish retort is supposed to mean. Wait. "Are you jealous that I got chocolates and you didn't? Powell, they gave you *diamonds*."

"I already have cufflinks; I didn't already have a box of chocolates. Try one of the round ones—they're caramel." Empty wrappers are piling up on the counter, even though he's only had the box open for two minutes. And I haven't had any yet! I swat his hand before he can grab another.

"Those are mine. If you're forcing me to join a matchmaker club, I'm keeping my benefits."

"So, you will join? Good. I wasn't sure, what with Tanner and all . . ." He trails off and looks at me expectantly. That's the second time he's managed to bring Tanner up in the past few minutes. Powell needs to get over this obsession.

"Nothing is going on there. We're just friends."

"Are you sure? Because I think—"

I slap his hand harder as he sneakily makes another attempt at my treats. I'm on to this game, using Tanner as a distraction. Nice try. Powell should know better anyway; Tanner's too much a relationship kind of guy, and I'm too much the opposite.

"I think you should shut up about Tanner." I pick up the letter again. "I think I should find my"—I scan the page—"soulful love match, who reaches deep into my heart and completes me. Powell, come on. What kind of crap is this? How did they sucker you in? You're smarter than that."

"There's a guaranteed level. Felicity promised she can find me true love. That's what I want. But I need your help. I signed you up so you can go to the events with me. You're . . . I hate to say this and please don't get a big head over it, but you're a better judge of character than me."

That's sweet but misguided of him since the last person I befriended tried to murder us both.

"I knew that about us. Why can't I go as your assistant? Why do I have to be matched too?" I'd rather follow him around with a clipboard, taking notes and checking off boxes. Pretty? *Check.* Maternal instincts? *Check.* Puts up with Powell's nonsense? *Check.*

"It's the only way. There are all kinds of non-disclosure agreements we need to sign. For the millionaire level and beyond, the events are very exclusive, and they don't want people gossiping about them. After I commit to someone, I'm required to do a couple of publicity statements and recommendations. But before that, nobody can know that I—that either of us, actually—are clients. Felicity doesn't want people signing up just to meet me." If it's meant to be a secret, maybe he shouldn't have mentioned any of this in front of a member of the press. Tanner won't tell anyone though.

Ah, my search through the paperwork uncovered those NDAs. A copy of the full contract is here, and I am appalled at how much my brother is shelling out for my membership. "If my level costs this much, what are you paying for your guarantee?" I ask, after I pop my eyeballs back into their sockets. This is absurd.

"About twice that, plus a premium when I become serious with 'the one.'" He shrugs, seemingly unconcerned with frittering away so much money. "It's worth it, Cass."

"At these prices, I should hope so. Your bride better come with her own engagement ring."

"I have to buy a six-figure ring," he admits, wiggling his own fingers as though imagining what a rock like that would weigh. "One of my choice, though."

Likely from an approved list of designers, all of whom provide kickbacks to LoveMatch.

"You had to sign a contract about what ring you purchase? That's ludicrous. Are you going to get a choice of woman, or is Felicity buying you one somewhere? This whole guarantee sounds kind of creepy and possibly like a very expensive prostitution scam."

"No, it's not like that. I'm starting to think your soul is utterly devoid of romance." He blinks and that familiar song-idea haze settles over him. But I'm not letting him run away this time, so I poke him in the chest.

"And I'm starting to think you're too gullible. Did you have your lawyer read the contract before you signed?"

"Of course." He glares at me indignantly, offended that I could possibly suggest that he may have made such an oversight. Then his eyes dart from side to side guiltily. "I mean, I meant to. I don't remember if he ever got back to me."

"Powell! What's wrong with you? You need to protect yourself and your assets! Is what Felicity doing even legal?"

"If it wasn't legal, she'd have been put out of business by now. LoveMatch Singles Network has been around for over twenty years."

"Really? I thought they were new." I've been hearing their ads a lot lately—so has Tanner, apparently—but I don't recall having heard of them prior to the past couple of months.

"They used to be only in New York and LA. Felicity is expanding to other cities. The Phoenix branch is the latest addition. That's part of why she's excited to have me onboard, and it's how I know I can trust her. If I give her a good endorsement, they gain a foothold over the cheaper knock-off versions. If she screws up with me, I plaster that all over social media. And then what happens to her business?"

While I'd like to tell my brother he's full of himself and not nearly as important as he thinks he is, he's actually right in this case. His name sells products. His endorsement will be marketing gold for Felicity. Conversely, he can destroy her with a single negative posting.

"That's true for you, but I still don't understand why you're roping me in. If you hit it off with someone at one of these events, I'm sure you'll see her outside of the events, too, and I can make my character judgments then. I don't need to be physically present at the start of the relationship."

"When's the last time you had an actual real-life boyfriend?" he asks but continues before I can answer. "Your freshman year of college, right before you dropped out. That's it. Other than that, what's your record? Three, maybe four dates? Maybe it's time you give yourself a chance to open up to somebody. I think you could be really happy if you had a boyfriend who loved you and cared about you. Since you reject everybody I ever suggest, you may as well try this method. You don't have anything to lose."

"Fine. But I don't like it." I slam the papers down on the counter, take *my* chocolates, and retreat to my room. Yes, I will end up going with him, and yes, I will subject myself to personality tests and whatever else the intake entails. But I won't be happy about it. And I won't share any more of my membership bonus.

Powell's allergies mean I have to get rid of all of the flowers, so after an hour of pouting and chocolate eating, I load them up and take them to Star Fitness. I figure they'll brighten up the front desk, and anyone who wants a bouquet can help themselves. I'll need to make a little 'free to a good home' sign, and I'm done with them. Plus, I can hop on a machine and work off all the calories I just consumed.

As I'm pulling into the parking lot, I spot Tanner's van. It's a rundown junky looking thing, but the dents are all strategically placed for cosmetic de-appeal, and the rust is fake. Since he lives in it, he keeps the outside camouflaged for safety reasons. His strategy works. Nobody has ever broken in, though he claims he had his tires stolen once, probably by someone who thought it was an abandoned vehicle. He's lucky he isn't towed regularly.

I park my cute little Boxster next to him, right as he's getting out and grabbing his gym bag. Perfect, I could use an extra set of hands.

"Are you here for the spin class?" he asks when he sees me. "Best put on some lipstick. I'm taking pictures before my workout today." We have a bartering arrangement: he takes photos for the gym's website and SwiftaPic account in exchange for a membership. It benefits us both. This is the nicest—and most expensive—gym in town, a place he could never afford. And he's building up my follower count and providing excellent marketing that I don't have to delegate to someone on my payroll.

"I was . . . but I don't want my picture taken. I'm glad you still have your van. I was afraid you'd lose it at your poker game."

Tanner laughs at me. "You think I'd gamble my van? I was playing with a group of photographers. The ante was a quarter, Cassidy. The largest pot was about eight bucks and a lens cap."

"Oh." Given his characteristic frugality, I should have assumed that.

"What kinds of poker games do you go to?"

"I once saw Xander lose his watch, a Jaguar, and a hyacinth macaw, all on one hand." To be fair, my least favorite of Powell's former bandmates had won the bird earlier in the evening and didn't really want it. He was mad about the vehicle, though. Not so much the watch, but that's because it was a well-crafted knock off. "I wasn't gambling, I was there to support Powell, and keep him out of the game. He's like you, he can't bluff."

Tanner's lips are twitching. He can't decide between criticizing the wealthy in general or Xander specifically. Personally, I'd go with mocking Xander. He's an easy target. Finally, he comes to a decision, runs his hands through his permanently disheveled hair and asks, "Jaguar the car, or the animal?"

"Use your imagination."

He's struggling to avoid making one of his disparaging 'rich people' comments, but it's still all over his face. "If Powell doesn't play, why did he go to a poker game anyway?"

"We don't turn down yacht parties."

"You . . . I don't know why I even ask." He slings his bag over his shoulder and starts to walk toward the gym, pausing when he realizes I'm not coming with him.

"Wait! Can you help me unload these flowers first?" I pop open my trunk to reveal the bundles of red roses, belatedly realizing I should have put them in boxes.

"Wow, somebody has a secret admirer," he says. "Or maybe not so secret? Who are they from?" There's a hint of something in his voice that almost sounds like jealousy. He's got no reason to be jealous. I'm sure he has admirers aplenty.

"These are from Felicity L'Amour, as a symbol of all the romantic gifts I am going to receive from my new boyfriend, identity to be determined at a later date."

"You're definitely going through with it? I thought you might have changed your mind."

"Only for Powell's sake. I can't send him out into a pool of sharks alone, can I?" I mean, I could, but I don't trust that he'd emerge unscathed, in either his heart or his wallet.

"You know what your problem is?" Tanner asks, a sure sign he's about to insult me.

"Lack of help unloading all these roses?"

"No, you've got that." He scoops up an armload, wincing as a few thorns find his unprotected forearms. "Your problem is that you're a pushover. You never stand up for yourself."

"That is categorically untrue." I gather the rest of the unwanted membership perk and use my foot to slam the trunk shut.

"It is. It's absolutely true. You present this façade of a strong independent woman. When I first met you, I thought you were completely emotionless and stony. But then I eventually realized that you hide everything deep down inside. And instead of asserting yourself or doing anything for you, for yourself, you just sort of . . . obey."

"Excuse me?" I'm about to find out if I can break a bouquet over his head. "I am not obedient. And I'm not a pushover."

"You are. Like right now, you're about to prostitute yourself out because Powell asked you to. It's not what you want, it's not what you need, but you're going to participate anyway. Everything you do is because your brother wants you to, or because it helps his career and enables you to stay in the background. When I helped out with that magazine photo shoot of you after Jace died and left you all his new music, I noticed something. You were just going through the motions. I don't know exactly what you were feeling because you don't believe in showing anything other than stoicism, but you clearly did the shoot out of a sense of obligation, not because you wanted to. You parroted whatever Powell's publicist told you to say, and I don't think any of it was real. Even later, after you were almost murdered and had your face broken, you kept every emotion locked down tight and did whatever the FBI and the publicist said afterward. Don't you ever want to be yourself? Make a choice for you, not Powell?"

"Tanner," I keep my tone even and firm, which he must love since it's further evidence of me keeping my emotions locked down. "Powell pays me a salary to be his assistant. Sometimes my work is easy. Sometimes, it's stupid. Sometimes I attend yacht parties filled with wild animals, other times I find myself at a matchmaker club trying to find a sister-in-law. It's all part of the job."

"I don't think it is. I think it's part of you going along with everything and doing whatever your brother asks. If he wasn't paying you, would you still go?"

"Of course. If I wasn't working for him, he'd still be my brother and my closest friend. Human beings do helpful things for the people they care about. Are you telling me that if one of your siblings asked you to please attend a singles event with them, where food and drinks are provided, you wouldn't go?" I had to throw in that reference to the food, because Tanner never turns down a free meal. He's frugal. He likes to go down to the Herberger Institute at ASU and sit through talks, just for the free pizza. Sure, he claims he's there to learn stuff, but I'm almost positive his primary motivation is not having to pay for lunch.

"I'm not the person any of my siblings would call," Tanner admits. "I would do something like that for my friend. But not all the time. And I wouldn't go to a singles party if I was interested in anybody."

"Okay?" I'm not following.

He stares at me for a moment, green eyes narrowed, before he lets out a long sigh. "Fine. Whatever. Let's take these flowers inside so you can show them off."

"I'm putting a free sign on them so people can take them to their loved ones. If you had anyone you cared about, you could help yourself, too."

"If only," he mutters, following me into the building.

Here's the joy of having an assistant, the kind of thing Powell takes advantage of: the assistant manager is at the desk, so I hand off the distribution of the flowers to her. "Can you set these out around the lobby with some free signs?" I ask. "I'd like them all gone today."

"Sure." As Adriana is bustling around, setting up a display, I am going to go hop on an elliptical. If I'm getting dragged to my LoveMatch intake, I'm going to sweat my frustrations out with cardio—but not in a spin class with an annoying and unnecessarily sullen paparazzo.

# CHAPTER THREE

The LoveMatch offices are in downtown Phoenix, in an outwardly generic brick office building. We arrive a few minutes late, because Powell is a celebrity and celebrities, even those who own watches worth more than the average house, are notoriously unpunctual. Time waits for them, and nobody even calls them on it. Well, I do. That's why I spent most of the drive over here pointing out that our appointment was supposed to start at one o'clock. Powell has never been late for a performance, but with everything else, he's flexible.

As I expect, nobody comments on our tardiness. Instead, we are welcomed with applause the moment we step into the lobby. Powell is in his element. Applause makes him glow with health and beauty and recharges his depleted reserves. He flashes his magazine-ready smile, raises his hand in a wave, and thanks them for their effusive welcome.

Meanwhile, I'm shivering and digging through my bag for my pashmina. One thing about summer: it's boiling outside, but businesses keep their air conditioning set to arctic chill. Once I'm wrapped in warm cashmere, I can look around at the crowd of employees and discover the horror of the building. Yes, the horror. The room we are in is . . . pink. Very, very pink. Like a semi-truck carrying Valentine's Day decorations crashed into a vat of strawberry ice cream, and the contents of both geysered out, drenching every available surface. For a company that charges such exorbitant rates, I would have expected they could afford something classier.

Felicity herself has flown out from the Los Angeles offices for this meeting. She practically dances out from the crowd of clapping employees and greets us both with double cheek kisses.

"Mr. Corbitt, I am so thrilled you are joining us. I assure you, love is in the air! And your beautiful sister! Oh, my poor Ms. Corbitt, I am well aware of your past heartache, and I am here to help you heal." She dramatically places a hand over her own heart, as if to show me where she plans to heal me. She is, of course, referring to the loss of Jace Monroe, and the mischaracterization of our relationship memorialized in his will. I swear, Jace's referral to me as the love of his life will haunt me forever. It doesn't help that the same people who killed him later made an attempt on Powell's and my lives as well. That just added more drama and intrigue to the whole thing.

"I'm not sure I'm ready to move on," I tell her, in as sorrowful a voice as I can manage, in an effort to use the pretend relationship to get me out of trying to find a real one. Powell shoots me an annoyed glare. He knows the truth, but he also knows better than to argue about it publicly.

"Don't worry, baby sis, I'm sure that in time, the right man will come along to teach you how to love again. I have high hopes for you. And if not, I support your choice to be a spinster. I'll even buy you robotic cats." He throws an arm around my shoulders in an affectionate hug.

"Robotic?" Felicity asks, not getting my brother's joke.

"Just because you're allergic doesn't mean I can't have real cats to keep me company and eat my body after I die alone," I remind him, with a sharp elbow to the ribs. "I've made my peace with that."

"No! No, no, no, no! Ms. Corbitt, I will not allow you to give up on loooove!" Felicity pronounces the word love as though she's imbuing it with magic, as though that word is the only thing that matters in the entire world. I am not going to enjoy this process. "Now, please, please, both of you come with me, let us begin this journey together."

She links Powell's arm in hers and leads us down a pink-walled hallway with pink marble floors to a conference room that is mercifully slightly less pink than the rest of the place. It is full of flowers, though, and Powell immediately balks.

"Don't worry, these are silk," Felicity assures him. "We don't use real flowers because they are dying, and what kind of symbolism is that? No, silk flowers, like the love you will find, will last forever! Please, take a seat. My assistant will bring you a drink." She claps her hands, and the lights dim. A screen lowers from the ceiling. I didn't see her hit a button, so I wonder if it is clap activated? I try to discreetly clap my hands under the table, but either that's not the trigger, or I wasn't loud enough.

A well-built man in a tight pink polo shirt and white pants enters with a tray of drinks. We are provided rosé champagne—to celebrate *loooove!*—and bottles of water. As Powell sips his champagne and I open my thankfully non-pink water, a video begins playing on the screen. The opening scene is provocative, to say the least.

"Whoa," Powell mutters. "If the rest of those clothes come off, I'm leaving." Good, I'm glad he doesn't want to sit around watching soft-core porn with his sister.

"Loooove," Felicity's voiceover starts. "That magical connection bringing two souls together. Loooove. What we all seek, and what only I can help you find."

The couple on screen fades out and is replaced by Felicity, wearing a swirling pink gown and a white fur stole.

"Greetings, seekers. I'm Felicity L'Amour, and I am here to bring you the love you deserve. Welcome to LoveMatch, where all of your dreams can come true!" Her accent wavers between American and something vaguely but generically European.

The remainder of the video has the production values of a mid-nineties made-for-tv movie. Felicity is introducing the different tiers of membership—something we don't need to see, since my brother paid upfront. Then it gets into descriptions of the various activities and events where we are sure to find our great loooove.

Here's what I'm learning: It is virtually impossible to meet someone and make a romantic connection in everyday life. Dating apps are exclusively for finding sex, not love, and if we rely on them, we will lead sad, empty lives. That's why we're so lucky to have the LoveMatch Singles Network. With their proprietary technology and top-secret algorithm, we will be connected with our perfect matches and—according to the video—our lives will be filled with strolling on the beach, sipping wine at sunset, and rolling around in white sheets that tastefully hide our nudity. I'm rolling my eyes, but my foolish gullible brother . . . he's all in.

The video ends, and Felicity does a double clap to make the screen roll back into the ceiling. I hope she says something worthy of me clapping, so I can make it come down again.

"So you see, my beloved Corbitts, loooove is out there. We will find you the perfect match. But in order to do so . . ."

And now we've reached the part I've been dreading: the paperwork. Personality tests. Interviews with our assigned matchmakers. Baring our souls so that they might be analyzed and digitized and matched.

Felicity claps her hands again, and the door opens. I saw the knob turn though, so it's not clap controlled. The screen doesn't come back down either, so I guess she's got a hidden remote. Too bad.

The women who enter are, to my relief, not wearing pink. My eyes are tired from all this rosy monotony. I want to hug them and their tasteful black dresses.

"I am so proud to introduce you to my daughters," Felicity's wide gesture encompasses the newcomers. The one on her right is her virtual clone, all straight lines and hard angles, showing what Felicity must have looked like thirty years ago. The other is a cheerful freckly redhead, whose coloring probably makes her grateful to be permitted to wear black rather than pink. "I am leaving you in extraordinarily capable hands. Ms. Corbitt, my cherished Lillian will be your guide on this most romantic of journeys. And Mr. Corbitt, this, this darling woman is Tabitha, your own personal matchmaker."

The younger version of Felicity, who has been shoved in my direction, glares back at her mother while Tabitha blinks in shock. It seems this distribution of clientele is a surprise to them both. Lillian composes herself and shakes my hand graciously.

"I'm so excited to assist you," she says, but she keeps shooting glances over at her counterpart talking animatedly with Powell. Way to make me feel like the sad little consolation prize.

The walls of Lillian's office are a muted shade of pink, but they are covered in enough certificates and framed photographs of presumably LoveMatched couples that the color isn't overwhelming. I sit in the comfortable chair across from her desk.

"Ms. Corbitt," Lillian leans toward me as she speaks. "I am thrilled to help you on this journey." She's repeating the same words her mother used earlier. I wonder if the employee handbook includes a list of mandatory phrases that must be uttered during every intake.

"Are you? I sensed a little sibling rivalry back there. It's fine, everyone would prefer to work with Powell." Because he's a famous attractive man, and there is no ring on my matchmaker's finger.

"You're perceptive. You strike me as someone who values honesty, so I'll be candid here. My mother"—she checks to make sure her door is closed before she continues—"has promised control of LoveMatch to whichever of her children most epitomizes the finding of true love. That's what she says, at least. But we all know her decision is based on matching the big money clients."

I'm amazed she's speaking so frankly and not spouting a bunch of euphemisms about soulmates and the like. The business side of things I can tolerate. The romantic platitudes, not so much.

"Is it down to you and your sister?"

"Tabitha is my stepsister. My mother married her father when we were in high school. There are five of us siblings, and she's been dangling company control in front of us for years. But now she's running on a deadline. My stepfather is showing signs of dementia, and she'd like to retire and travel with him while they can both still enjoy it. My mother's favor varies, so yes, today I thought I had your brother's account. It doesn't matter though, Ms. Corbitt. I promise you, I will do whatever it takes to find a perfect match for you."

She means it. There's passion in her voice and fire in her eyes. Now I'm almost afraid I'm going to end up forcibly married just so she can win against her stepsister.

"It's Blaine-Corbitt, actually," I correct her. "But please, call me Cassidy."

"Cassidy. I think we'll be able to work together just fine." She smiles, and I tentatively smile back. She might be a little too intense for me. But I'm already in this, so we'll see what happens.

*Sigh.*

What happens is testing. Lots of testing. I'm handed a tablet and forced to go through multiple personality tests, preference tests, and something where I'm rapidly shown pictures of two different people—A and B—and must quickly tap whichever I find more attractive. It's like a video game, but the characters are real people, and I'm not earning any points.

At the halfway mark, a cheese tray and glass of white wine is brought in for my consumption, by the same pink-poloed man who served the drinks earlier. He bows to us as he leaves. I am going to have to ask Powell if he got the same treatment. I imagine he's lounging on a couch in Tabitha's office being fed peeled grapes while a cadre of beautiful A and B selections are paraded in front of him.

Now, the tests are done. I set the tablet down next to the remains of the cheese and prepare to leave. But Lillian stops me because this nightmare is never ending.

"Are you ready for the interview portion?" she asks brightly, much more cheerful than she was earlier. That may be because while I took one or two sips of my wine, she downed at least two glasses of her own.

Ugh. I hate this sort of thing. I'm not big on talking about myself anyway, especially with strangers, and even more especially while being recorded and analyzed.

She starts with what kind of person I'm looking for. I want to say independently wealthy, because I don't want a sugar baby, but that makes me sound like a gold digger, so I use 'self-driven' and 'business minded' as descriptors instead. I tell her I want a man who is attractive, but not ridiculously so. Tanner's face flashes to mind, and I shove the image away. Someone like him would be nice, but since I'm not intending to participate in this process, it doesn't matter.

"Your first love was twice voted the sexiest man in the world. I'm glad that's not the standard we're trying to achieve," Lillian says.

Shoot. Maybe I should have said someone comparable to Jace. That would create an impossible goal, and possibly allow me to break this contract and get a full refund. After all, they can't deliver me the sexiest man alive. The current title holder just married his fifth wife, a barely legal actress one third his age. Plus, I'm not interested.

"I know Jace Monroe is gone, and I'll never be able to replace him," I try to squeeze out a tear, but fail. "In fact, I'm not sure I'm ready to try. He was so precious to me."

"Nonsense." Lillian is matter of fact in her assessment. "One thing I've found in this line of work is that men are interchangeable."

That is certainly not what I expected to hear from an overpriced matchmaker.

"How so?" I don't entirely disagree, but I'm curious as to her reasoning.

"Cassidy, you are here at the millionaire club level. You're a successful businesswoman and a jetsetter. You've had wealthy lovers and been romantically linked with celebrities. You're fully cognizant of your worth. What you need is a man who is not intimidated by you, one who looks good on your arm, who can make conversation at music industry events, but who is not so ambitious he sees you as a steppingstone for his own career."

I definitely prefer her evaluation of me over Tanner's snarky 'obedient follower' one.

"Maybe I should clarify that I want someone a little more complex than just arm candy who stays in the background.

But I still don't understand how you think you can find him." Particularly given my lack of interest in helping.

"That's what all those tests you took will help with. Our proprietary software will search our database for compatible companions for you."

"Not to be rude"—obviously, this means I am about to be rude—"but your services are expensive. How do you find enough potential matches? There can't be many single millionaires in my age range."

"My mother solved that problem years ago. LoveMatch International is a singles *network*. We work one on one with our exclusive, high-level clients like you and your brother. However, we have thousands of other club members too, all of whom have taken the same personality and compatibility tests as you."

"Yes, so? Do you run your scans and set up a date for me or what?" I hate blind dates. I always find myself struggling to come up with conversation while a complete stranger explains why Powell thought we'd be perfect together. Usually the reasoning involves the guy playing whatever random instrument Powell is currently obsessed with. No offense to my brother, but he has terrible taste in men. He claims he's trying to help, but really all he wants is a brother-in-law to jam with.

"No. One-on-one dates don't happen until you've met naturally. We can find someone for you who is perfect on paper, but if you lack chemistry, it will never work. Instead, after you RSVP to Millionaires' Circle events, we run through our system, and send requests to at least five eligible men who could be your perfect match. Our members who buy in on our open level receive special invitations welcoming them to mix and mingle with our exclusive members on a case-by-case basis."

"Then you tell me who they are, so I can meet them?"

"Of course not!" She's scandalized by the very suggestion. "You will attend the events knowing you have more than one perfectly matched gentleman in the room, hoping to be found by you. Neither of you will know which of the many guests you are looking for. That gives you a chance to form an organic connection, a chance to look for a man who captures your eye before he captures your heart." The last part sounds overly rehearsed. I like Lillian better when she's showing her practical business side, not when she's quoting lines from Felicity's video.

"And this is how it is for Powell, too?"

"This, and more. With your brother, we are not only working hard to find and introduce his ideal match locally, but we are going the extra mile, seeking out women through our vast network. Our search is not geographically limited, and while Tabitha is his dedicated staff member, every matchmaker in our office will be able to access his file and do our own independent searches. He will be married by the end of the year."

Given that it's late July, I doubt I'll be attending a wedding ceremony for him this year. I smile anyway and pretend I believe her. "Good for Powell, I guess." Once he finds someone, I'm out. I will never set foot in this pink monstrosity again.

Lillian hands me a stack of printouts, including lists of upcoming events. "You're confirmed for next week, so I will have some potential candidates there for you." She shifts in her seat and her voice becomes warmer and friendlier. "By the way, do you have any advice on what your brother is looking for? My sister may be his case worker, but like I said, we've all been encouraged to assist."

I know exactly what she's doing—she wants to steal the prize. Honestly, with management of the family business up for grabs, I don't blame her. But I never betray my brother's confidences.

"Powell lives his life as an open book. There's nothing you need to know about him that can't be found in a magazine somewhere." Seventeen years' worth of interviews and at least two documentaries have chronicled his every move. Lillian looks disappointed at my unwillingness to take her side in her battle for company control. Fine, I may as well let her in on one thing since it helps my brother. "Find a piano player. He'll never be serious about someone who doesn't play the piano."

When Lillian finally releases me, she escorts me to the lobby where I find Powell signing autographs, but not posing for photos. He's either already done that, or all the staff here are in compliance with the rigid non-disclosure agreements and won't risk losing their jobs by posting pics with him in their office.

"Well?" he asks when he drags himself away from his adoring fans. "What did you think? Are you open to finding your one true loooove?"

"I'm open to going home and swimming a few laps while you mix me an apology daiquiri for what you put me through."

"Did you ask for a daiquiri because they're pink?"

Oh, I hate the smirk he gets sometimes.

# CHAPTER FOUR

Our first LoveMatch Singles event is a cocktail party in a ballroom on the top floor of a downtown Phoenix hotel. There's a massive terrace overlooking the city, for those of us who don't want to sit indoors and listen to the jazz band.

"See, this is awesome," Powell says enthusiastically as we pause in the doorway to survey the room. Of course he's excited about it. I'd say the attendees skew female and late twenties, a demographic that appeals to him. Also, he likes the opportunity to dress up. It's funny, in the house he prefers old sweats and faded shirts, but when the chance to don fancy apparel comes his way, he gleefully opens up his suit closet. Tonight, he's chosen cobalt blue sharkskin, with a pale blue shirt and no tie. It's summer in Arizona, he's already sweating, but apparently, he thinks fashion is worth suffering for. Too bad he can't get away with light sundresses like mine—I get the benefits of looking good and feeling slightly less overheated. I mean, it is July. There's no such thing as actually feeling cool, only less hot.

"Sure," I say noncommittally. I'm watching how many women are turning to check him out, sizing up first Powell and then me, to see if I'm competition. I'm used to the appraisals—we're siblings via stepparent adoption, not blood, so we look nothing alike. He's made of gold—his tan, his hair, even his eyes are golden, whereas my summer tan has pink undertones, my eyes are blue, and my chestnut hair is way thicker and straighter than his wavy locks. In short, we are in no way identifiable as coming from the same family, which is why eyes are focusing on me, and speculating as to my connection. Are we strangers who just happened to arrive at the same time? Am I his hired driver, who will be waiting at the door when it's time to go? Are we a couple looking for a third? This is sort of an IQ test: anyone who thinks Powell arrived with a date to a matchmaking event is automatically too dumb to date him.

Before we can fully enter the event, we are given wristbands, I assume as a marker to keep the riffraff out.

"Silver is for our exclusive level members," the doorman explains as he fastens one around my wrist. "You'll see red on our invitees." Ah, so while I won't know which of the men have been algorithmically selected for me, at least there will be a hint.

"Why is mine the same as hers?" Powell complains. But he stops his whining when I dig my elbow into his ribs. I have to do that far too often. Maybe I should start kicking him in the shin instead.

"What do you want, rhodium? Let everyone know about the ginormous engagement ring on the line? They aren't going to advertise your guaranteed status."

We make our way into the ballroom, exactly the kind of stuffy pretentious event I hate. This isn't where I want to find my brother a wife; I'd rather find her volunteering at the food bank, or perhaps at a concert, where she's the one playing. At a place like this, there are two different types of red wristbanded women trying to entice the male millionaires. First there are the ones who make their own approach, tottering up in their high heels, tossing their hair and touching the men's arms, laughing and introducing themselves. Then there are the ones who are hoping to make the men approach them, standing around in bored poses, making sultry eye contact and slowly smiling, casting come hither looks at every silver-braceleted fellow who passes by. Men are outnumbered three to one, which doesn't bode well for me—if I wanted to meet somebody.

"Canapé?" Okay, perhaps there are some people I want to meet, and they're all circulating the room with loaded trays. I help myself to the cute little gouda and pear bruschetta the caterer is offering. Powell waves them off. His allergy prevents him from eating passed food or buffet food. He's missing out—these are delicious.

"So now what? Divide and conquer?" he suggests. His eyes are roaming the room, checking out the opportunities and competition. This whole thing is making me squeamish. This is a meat market, where the women are literally for sale.

"Are you sure this is the best way to find your one true love?"

"No. But I'm tired of dating around, and I'm tired of hoping something just happens. And I'm extra tired of people reaching out through my agent, as though I'm a publicity opportunity rather than an actual human being with feelings. I want what our parents have. Don't you?"

"Maybe someday." It's not something I spend much time thinking about. Our parents have had a perfect relationship, ever since they met at a Last Barons of Sound concert on my twelfth birthday. But while Powell might hashtag them as #relationshipgoals, a long-term romance is not something I've ever aspired to reach. Sure, I enjoy having a man in my bed occasionally, but I'm less interested in the whole sharing a life thing. It seems like too much work.

"Alright, here's the plan. I can't keep talking to you—nobody knows you're my sister. You scout around, search out anyone I might like. I'm going to sit down with a drink and wait to be approached."

"Fine. You owe me for this."

"You'll get a niece or a nephew out of it," he promises, not realizing that threatening me with babysitting is the farthest thing from an incentive. If mom were here, she'd be walking around with a clipboard asking probing questions until she found the perfect future daughter-in-law who was ready to pop out babies right now.

I don't usually drink at events like this, but I'm going to make my way to the terrace bar anyway. Maybe I can find a quiet corner, and tip one of those passing waiters to keep checking on me with various hor d'oeuvres. I can sit back, relax, and observe. That counts as helping Powell, right?

Before I can maneuver all the way through the crowd, a man with a red wristband stops me. He's tall, dark, and handsome in a small-time television actor sort of way. "Excuse me, are you Cassidy?" he asks. I nod. "Lillian told me I should look for you."

"She did?" So much for not identifying the matches. I suppose she took my 'attractive but not Jace-level' suggestion seriously.

"Yes. She thought we'd be a good match. I'm not quite as perfect as your late lover, but"—at this point he drops to one knee and with one hand over his heart and the other in the air sings—"I-iiiiiiiiii-iiii am willllllllinnnnnngggg to tryyy-yyyyyYYYYY!"

Now I need to think back over the contract and try and remember if there were any clauses about this being filmed for a prank show, because this cannot possibly be real. The man is kneeling in front of me still, proud of his vocal skills and the attention we've garnered.

"No, thank you," I reply politely, because I'm genuinely too shocked to think of anything else to say. I walk around him to reach the bar.

"Didn't enjoy the show, miss?" the bartender asks. I recognize him from my visit to the LoveMatch offices. He's the buff man who wore a pink polo shirt and silently provided us with beverages and cheese plates.

"Oh, is that what that was?" I dare to glance over my shoulder. The singing interloper has risen to his feet and his ego is being soothed by a woman in a skin-tight gold dress.

"We get all sorts here. What can I make for you?"

"Something sweet and alcohol-free, please."

"Ah, not a drinker?"

"Not in situations like this."

"Smart." He pulls out some ingredients and talks me through the watermelon juice with mint and sparkling water that he shakes and pours into a martini glass. "And nobody will know."

"Thanks," I squint at his nametag. "Isaac?"

"Yes. Best of luck tonight." He goes to serve other customers, and I take a sip of my frothy pink beverage. Delicious. I'm going to text Tanner this recipe later. He's always interested in trying new things. This would be refreshing out by the pool, maybe with added rum.

"I have to ask," a dark-haired man in an expensive Italian double-breasted suit takes the stool next to mine. A thin sheen of sweat on his forehead shows that, like my brother, he cares more about looking good than being comfortable on a warm night. "What the hell was that out there?" he nods in the direction of the impromptu singing.

"I think it was supposed to impress me."

"Did it?"

"I was amused, at least."

"I suppose that's something. I'm not hitting on you, by the way." He holds up his wrist to show me his silver band, proof that he's one of the elite and not one of the invitees provided for our pleasure.

"Silvers aren't allowed to hit on each other?"

He smiles widely, showing perfect teeth. "I haven't seen you at one of these before. Are you new?"

"First event."

"If you'd been matched with a silver, your matchmaker would have discreetly made an introduction, with a wink and a nudge. I'm surprised one of them isn't shepherding you around tonight. At my first party, mine introduced me to every single person."

Is that what they normally do? I'm happy to avoid that—Lillian would quickly realize I'm not participating properly and would forcefully make me interact with every remotely attractive man in the room.

"No luck finding your perfect soulmate?" I ask.

"Not yet. Someday, maybe. Jackson Shih," he extends his hand to shake.

"Cassidy Blaine-Corbitt."

"Corbitt as in you're related to Powell Corbitt? I thought I saw him inside."

"He's my brother. And he's the reason I'm here. He decided we both need to find spouses."

"You seem unconvinced."

I shrug. I don't want to trash talk this service at an event, especially with someone who paid the exorbitant fee himself. He probably believes the hype.

"It worked for a friend of mine. He used LoveMatch out in California," Jackson says. "He met his wife, had a whirlwind romance. I just moved to Phoenix, so I thought I'd try it too, see if it works for me."

"Well, I wish you luck."

"Thanks, you too." Jackson finishes his drink in one gulp. "It was nice meeting you. I should go circulate amongst the red bracelets, though I doubt anyone will look in my direction while a celebrity singer is on the premises."

As soon as Jackson strolls off, a woman claims his barstool. She drops down next to me, her gauzy skirts flying out around her. Her hair is so matte black it can't be real, and her eyes are rimmed in black, but her multi-layered dress is all the colors of the rainbow.

"Greetings, my fellow silver sister." Instead of trying to shake my hand, she taps her wristband against mine. "I'm Aurora Ridge."

"Cassidy," I respond. "First time here."

"Yes, I thought you looked new. I'm Aurora Ridge." She repeats her name and raises a penciled-on eyebrow.

"Pleasure to meet you." I'm not sure what other type of response she wants.

She sighs. "How long have you lived in Arizona? Are you new?"

"Seven years."

"You must not follow the arts scene. What is it that you do?"

"I own a fitness center. And also, I provide lifestyle assistance to a world-renowned singer." I could have described my job as babysitting that same singer, but I'm trying to talk myself up. And, I do 'follow the arts scene.' My mother is a prolific art buyer who is always getting invited to gallery openings, and I often accompany her. Mostly to try to tone down her spending, per Hank's request. It's not about the money; they're running out of display space in their home.

"Hmmmm." Aurora's frown suggests she's never before met someone who doesn't immediately fawn over her. But I've honestly never heard of her. "I am an *artiste*."

From the way she pronounces 'artiste' I assume she pictures herself wearing a beret and a striped blouse and frowning at an easel, a pallet in hand, with a view of the Eiffel Tower out her window. I'm about to ask her what specific form her artistry takes, when we are both distracted by loud singing—thankfully not my brother. The troubadour from before found a new victim.

Women have a universal agreement, one we don't discuss, but all participate in. If you are out somewhere in public, and another woman comes to you with desperation in her eyes and is pretending she knows you, go along with it. She is most likely being harassed, and you need to welcome her into the fold, protect her from whomever is chasing her, and later go your own way, content with knowing you made a contribution to the wellbeing of the sisterhood.

So, when the blonde woman pursued by the now-drunk singer makes desperate eye contact with Aurora and I, we instantly respond.

"Dearest darling, there you are!" Aurora calls out in her expressive voice, and we stand to invite the woman into our small circle. I encourage her to take my stool and position my body in between her and Mr. Sings-too-much.

"You again?" He leers at me. He's had a lot to drink since our last encounter, which wasn't that long ago. He must have been slamming shots. "Well, hello beautiful. I knew you couldn't get enough."

I use a line I've had to firmly deliver many times in the past: "Walk away before I call security." The line works on teenagers trying to sneak into backstage areas, it works on nosy reporters, and it works on this drunken fool, perhaps because of my sharp take-no-prisoners tone. Or my death glare.

"Thanks," says the blonde, shaking her head and watching her pursuer retreat. "That guy kept singing at me. Is it always like this at these events? This is my first one."

"I don't know. It's my first one, too. But I was subjected to his music earlier."

"It's not always like this," Aurora assures us both. "I'm not sure what set off this level of musical madness tonight."

The newcomer holds up her wrist, showing her red band. "He had one of these, too, so he picked the wrong target. I suppose he's trying that on everyone. I'm sure he was doing it because he's intimidated by the boyband singer inside." She laughs, but I don't. If Powell is in there performing, I swear I'm going to . . . do something. I don't know what. Probably lecture him on how spontaneous acapella is not a mating call, and flaunting his fame is certainly not the way to find a 'nice normal girl to settle down with.'

"The one from the Last Barons of Sound?" I ask, on the off chance a plethora of former teen idols are congregated in the main room.

"Yes, did you see him? According to some ladies in the restroom, he's the catch of the night."

"And you aren't going to head in, try and make that catch?"

She laughs again. "Not worth it for a Last Baron. Now, if it were Miles from FormulaFive, that might be a different story."

"Miles is bald and wears a hairpiece," I respond, my knee-jerk reaction to protect and promote my brother over his former competitors.

"Really?" Her eyes widen at that scandalous bit of gossip. "How do you know?"

"It fell off at a party last year. He didn't buy the kind that is sewn on."

"Hair or no hair, I don't think the thirteen-year-old girl who lives inside me cares. It's *Miles*."

Aurora has watched this exchange with interest, and now she gasps. "I recognize you! You were being modest before. Lifestyle assistance to a singer? Please. You're Cassidy Corbitt!"

"Blaine-Corbitt, actually. And yes, Powell is my brother." I wait for the inevitable demands for an introduction, but they don't come.

"Oh, you poor dear!" Aurora practically has tears in her eyes. She takes my hand and pats it gently. "I read the profile of you in *Media Matters*. You were so haunted by the loss of your lover. Oh, my darling, next time you are experiencing any such sadness, you simply must come to my studio and allow me to paint you!"

Well, that's not an invitation I've ever received. Or one I'm likely to accept.

"Thanks, I'll consider it," I reply, and she opens her bejeweled handbag to pull out a business card for me. It is a glossy black rectangle with @auroraridge in raised gold letters.

"That's how you find me on every platform." She folds my fingers around the card to ensure that I won't ever lose her contact information. As an afterthought she offers one to the blonde as well, though she doesn't go so far as to forcibly wrap the other woman's hands around it.

"Um, thanks. I'm Emily, by the way. And I feel terrible for joking about your brother," the blonde finally introduces herself. "I didn't mean what I said about FormulaFive being better."

"Don't apologize, that was the highlight of my night."

Aurora is still stuck on my love life.

"You're so brave," she croons. "Putting your heart on the line again after a love like Jace Monroe."

"Jace Monroe? Isn't he the guy who recently . . ." Emily trails off, her eyes filled with horror when she realizes who we're talking about. She clasps her hands over her mouth, as though to block the words. Come on, it's not like I don't know Jace is dead. I can talk about him.

"Yes, he passed away a couple of months ago. And I'm not sure I'm ready to be with someone new, but my brother thought this dating service would help. What about you two? Who are you hoping to find here?" I know exactly how to deal with drama-mongers like Aurora. The kind of woman who introduces herself with the assumption everyone has heard of her already is also the kind of woman who is happy to dominate a conversation with her own life story.

"Me?" Aurora puts a hand on her chest dramatically. "Much like you, Cassidy, I seek my soulmate. I need to find someone who matches my passion for art, but he must be one who complements me, not one who competes. A poet, perhaps, or a photographer, a man who enhances my work and speaks to my soul."

I do believe Aurora has bought in to the LoveMatch hype. Fortunately, Emily has not.

"Wow. Are you both really here for soulmates?" Emily asks. "Do you think it really works? I just moved to town from St. Louis, and to be honest, I joined to meet people, but I'm not holding out a lot of hope for finding a husband. I'll be happy if I manage to make friends at all."

"Of course it works. You must trust the process. Which I do. Now, I must be off. I am going to seek my poet. Cassidy, contact me when you're available to sit for a portrait." Aurora disappears into the crowd, presumably in search of a red-wristbanded hipster, preferably one holding a book of his own pretentious poetry.

"She was . . . interesting," Emily comments.

I nod in agreement and help myself to a caprese salad bite from a passing waiter. He offers the tray to Emily as well, but she waves it off.

"I never eat at these sorts of events," she tells me, almost apologetically. "I'm deathly allergic to peanuts, so I avoid anything I can't be sure is safe. I can't imagine the embarrassment of being carted off in an ambulance from a fancy soiree like this."

That's so much like Powell I almost laugh. And then I examine her a bit more closely. She's a pretty cherubic blonde with innocent blue eyes. She's wearing a short-sleeved black dress. It's designer, but from the Bezley Rose collection four years ago, and a couple of loose threads dangle from the hem. This is either her favorite dress she wears often, or she picked it up used. Judging by her practical black flats that look freshly polished but still show wear, I'm going to guess both. A thrift store find that she loves.

"So, what do you do, Emily?"

She blushes. "I'm sort of unemployed at the moment. I was taking care of my grandmother, but she passed away. That's why I moved here. I always felt a connection to the Southwest, and grandma left me enough money so I could go start over somewhere new. I'm thinking of going back to school."

Personally, if I were unemployed, I wouldn't spend my limited funds on a dating service. But I bet she sees it as networking, too. After all, here she is at a millionaire party.

"If you went back to school, what would you study?" I'm betting she says business or law, something she can use to impress the targets here.

"Musical education. I used to teach piano for extra spending money; I'd love to be able to teach middle school music classes. That's the age where children are starting to discover their skills and passions."

Okay, now I know exactly why she received an invitation to this event. Her wristband is for my brother. A mild-mannered piano teacher who isn't interested in sucking up to celebrities? Plus, she's a curvy blond. She's the kind of woman I would have conjured up, had I the ability.

If I can introduce them, I no longer have to attend these events.

"So, Emily, would you like to meet my brother?"

The face she makes is not one of enthusiasm.

"Umm, I could, I guess. But I'm not . . ." Her cheeks are turning pink again, and she looks like she's about to make a run for it. I appreciate that she's not ready to throw herself at Powell. He needs someone who isn't impressed and obsessed.

"Never mind. You don't have to." Except she does. I'll just have to be more subtle when I make it happen. My phone buzzes in my purse, and I pull it out to check.

DON'T GET MAD.

I read Tanner's message, and, while I don't immediately get mad, I do get annoyed. "Excuse me a moment," I tell Emily and text Tanner back: THAT'S NOT A PHRASING TO KEEP ME HAPPY.

I'M OUTSIDE.

OUTSIDE WHERE? ARE YOU FOLLOWING US???

NO. A TIP CAME THROUGH AND I GOT A CALL TO COME DOWN HERE AND SNAP SOME CELEBS LEAVING A SINGLES EVENT.

SOMEONE CALLED YOU?

MY AGENT, OBVI. I JUST FOUND OUT POWELL IS THE ONE WE'RE WAITING FOR. A COUPLE OF US ARE AT THE FRONT OF THE HOTEL, 2 IN PARKING GARAGE NEAR HIS CAR, AND 2 AT REAR ENTRANCE.

Is there seriously nothing else going on in this town tonight? We don't ordinarily have that many paparazzi operating in this area. Usually it's just one contractor—like Tanner. At least he thought to warn me. But in order to maintain a modicum of privacy, I'm going to need to smuggle Powell out.

THANKS FOR TELLING ME, I send him. He responds with a grinning thumbs-up selfie.

BTW: IF POWELL DOESN'T WANT PEOPLE TO KNOW WHERE HE IS, HE SHOULDN'T HAVE PERSONALIZED LICENSE PLATES.

I read the latest message and roll my eyes. Of course. My brother's security expert has delivered numerous lectures on this topic, but why would Powell listen? No, instead he continues to only purchase vanity plates saying POWELL1 or POW3LL or whatever combination of letters and numbers needed to place his name on his nine vehicles.

We need a plan to smuggle him out of here unseen, and so I think Emily is going to be meeting Powell after all.

"Emily, I may need a tiny favor. Did you drive here?"

# CHAPTER FIVE

Sometimes Tanner stops by for breakfast, claiming he was 'in the area.' Since his house is on wheels, that's plausible. It's equally plausible he just likes my espresso machine and will travel any distance for a free caffeine fix.

"Did you have fun last night?" he asks, and I'm not sure I appreciate the smirk on his face. But at least he's making two café lattes.

"It was okay."

"Did your heart find it's one perfect match that fills your spirit and soul with blissful joy?" At my snort he hastily adds, "That came from a LoveMatch ad. You know I don't really talk that way, right?"

"I know. And no, alas, despite being serenaded by a complete stranger, I did not find true love. I spent most of the evening sitting on the terrace and waiting for Powell to finish flirting. Or rather, finish having women flirt at him." When I dragged him out, he was in the middle of a crowd of beautiful women vying for his attention. And they weren't subtle either—necklines were lower and hemlines higher than they were at the start of the evening.

"Fun. Speaking of Powell, nice evasive maneuvering. Where was he, in the trunk?"

"I'm not going to tell a paparazzo our secrets."

Of course, someone else has no such qualms.

"The trunk? No room. I store my emergency guitar in there. I was laying down in the backseat of someone else's car." Powell plops down on the stool next to me and reaches for my coffee.

"Dare I ask about the emergency guitar?" Tanner says, as I deftly move my mug out of my parasitic brother's reach.

"If you make me a latte, I'll tell you all about it," Powell promises, but that's not a fair deal for Tanner. Literally, the guitar is only there in case Powell decides to put on an impromptu performance. No emergency in the history of mankind has ever required a guitar to resolve.

"Don't make him anything. He doesn't deserve it." But Tanner doesn't listen to me, perhaps because he's a guest in our house. He's back at the espresso machine, grinding more beans.

"Thanks for the warning, by the way," Powell says to Tanner when the grinding noise stops.

"No problem. Though I didn't necessarily expect you to hide. Don't you think you'd get hundreds more possible matches if people knew you were at a LoveMatch event?"

"Hundreds of women who lie on their applications and say things they think I want to hear. Do you know who I met last night, already, without anyone knowing I would be there? Aspiring singers, aspiring models, aspiring actresses. I just want a woman without aspirations. Is that so difficult?"

"A woman with no aspirations? Sounds boring, Powell." I elbow him in the ribs.

"That's not what I meant, Deedee. The only remotely interesting person I met was that girl Emily who smuggled me out."

"Really?" Ha! I knew it! Since I introduced them, I assume this means I've gained control of LoveMatch, wresting the company away from the L'Amour sisters. My first act as CEO is going to be to hire an interior decorator.

"Her car is so old it still has a cassette player, so while I was hiding under a blanket, I looked through her collection."

"Did she have any of your music?" Tanner asks as he slides a mug to my brother. He's getting better at latte art—he managed a flower. Usually he just makes hearts, because those are easier.

"No! So that hurt a little. She mostly had classical. And she had Argerich and Maisky playing Bach. That was my favorite album as a kid. It's perfection. Can you believe that?" His face has become animated, and it's not because he's been ingesting caffeine. Our LoveMatch membership may be ending soon.

My phone rings, and Lillian's name shows up on the screen. I'm going to take this call outside.

"She's going to yell at you for not flirting enough," Powell shouts at me as I walk out the door. He's probably right, which is why I'm not answering in front of him.

"Hello, Lillian."

"Good morning. I'm calling for our post-event debriefing." There's nothing friendly about her tone. This is clearly a business call, and she's going to want raw numbers, stats, and a comprehensive listing of every red-braceleted man I spoke with.

"It was fine," I respond automatically, while desperately trying to remember what the pamphlets said about this part.

"You didn't speak with many of our invitees. I heard you spent most of the time sitting at the terrace bar, with other members of our Millionaires' Circle. Don't worry, that can be a positive thing."

"It can?" I'm already cursing Isaac. He's more than a bartender, he's a spy.

"Yes, in your case. You received a request."

"What does that mean?"

"A request is when someone is interested in getting to know you outside of LoveMatch official events. It is an invitation to the requisite first date, before you can exchange phone numbers."

"Oh." It had better not be the singer. I never even got his name.

"Do you recall talking to a Jackson Shih?"

"Briefly. We chatted for about thirty seconds. And he told me he wasn't hitting on me."

"Perhaps that was a test. He filled out a request with his matchmaker this morning. I'd like to schedule a meeting for you tomorrow afternoon."

"Is he a match for me?"

"He could be. He's a wealthy investor, so he's not after your money. He's attractive; he'd photograph well."

Money and looks. Great. Who cares about his personality, or the fact that he made it quite clear he wasn't hitting on me?

"Cassidy?" Lillian prods when my silence has gone on too long. "You may as well try this. On paper, you could work. And if you don't like him as much in person, he'd still be an advantageous connection. Networking matters."

"All right," I agree. "You can set something up." Here's my theory: if I agree to one now, I can reject many others in the future. I'm demonstrating my openness, so later I can point out that I tried, I tried so hard right from the beginning, and it can't possibly be my fault when I end this whole thing still single.

When I return to the kitchen, Tanner is cooking up a panful of scrambled eggs while Powell makes toast. I am in shock—he got my brother to do some actual work? Powell isn't sitting around waiting for others to do his bidding? Why has Tanner never revealed these magical powers, and can he use them to make Powell stop leaving his shoes in the living room?

"Well? Was I right?" Powell asks. "Are you in trouble with your matchmaker?"

"No. In fact, I have a request for a coffee date tomorrow." *In your face, Powell.*

"You do?" Powell's eyes are incredulously wide.

"Don't act so surprised. I'm a catch."

"You're going on a date tomorrow?" Tanner doesn't turn around from the stove. "I thought you weren't taking this seriously."

"I'm not. But Lillian thought I should at least give it a try, so why not?"

"I wonder if I got any requests?" Powell turns the conversation back to himself. "I wonder if I got one from Emily?"

"I think as the higher status match, you're the one who has to make the request. Talk to Tabitha later, see what you're supposed to do."

"Maybe I'll call her now." Powell sets down a piece of toast, half-buttered, and wanders off. I knew him working was too good to be true.

According to the contract I signed, the first date is always coffee, no meals, no alcohol. Honestly, that concept shouldn't be unique to LoveMatch. It's a smart idea for any single woman. Coffee is quick, you can guzzle one cup and leave; you don't have to suffer through course after course if you can tell right away the relationship isn't going anywhere. And no chance of a spiked drink or beer goggles getting you into bed with someone unworthy of your time, attention, and body.

The assigned location is a quirky little indie coffee shop where there is a reserved table, decorated with the swirly LoveMatch logo. Ugh. We're going to do this very publicly. So much for those non-disclosure agreements.

Jackson is waiting for me, and he's more nervous than I'd expect. He's looking around and kind of . . . twitchy. He keeps lifting the LoveMatch sign and examining the bottom and checking under the napkin holder. Fidgeting is not the way to my heart, but from the moment I got the interest notification, I haven't thought my heart is what he is after.

I order an iced coffee—it's hot outside; I don't know why an ice cream shop isn't a first date option—and join him.

"You actually came," he says in surprise, as if he'd already decided I was going to stand him up. Given that I'm five minutes early, I'm a little bothered by that. Unlike my brother, I do understand the concept of 'on-time.'

"Of course. I am trusting the process, as Lillian keeps ordering me to do."

"You're with Lillian? She seems kind of intense. I'm with Tabitha, the one with the enormous rock on her finger and extremely high levels of enthusiasm."

"Tabitha is my brother's matchmaker. And yes, I noticed the diamond." According to Powell, Tabitha used her own company's services and is always willing to turn the conversation to how amazing it is to be in love. She might be better as a spokesperson than a matchmaker.

"She's engaged to Isaac."

"The bartender?" I'm impressed he could afford the ring she keeps flaunting around. I assumed Tabitha's fiancé was some wealthy man that she claimed for herself when his file hit her desk.

"He does other things too."

I'm aware of that: other things like parade around in tight pants and deliver cheese to new clients. Maybe Tabitha is onto something. Eye candy that provides delicious food . . . maybe I do want a relationship. A very specific limited relationship. A *catered* relationship.

"You know more about them than I do."

He shrugs. "I like doing my research. I looked you up before this date."

"And?"

"I think it's cool that you own a gym. I've driven past it before, looks like a nice place. Why don't you use social media yourself?"

"Because I don't need to keep strangers informed as to my life." Other than the requisite gym accounts, I do have personal ones, but not for posting. They only exist so people can tag me, and I can keep track of how gossipmongers are talking about me online.

"In your position," he begins, and now I see what's happening. His interest in me is purely business. He's going to attempt to sell me something or try to convince me to become an 'influencer.'

"In my position," I interrupt, "I'm quite happy. If this is you about to talk to me about marketing myself better, I'm going to walk out the door right now."

He smiles ruefully. "I was going to say most people would take advantage of your brother's fame. It's both admirable and refreshing that you don't."

"My brother is my best friend, and I will do anything to protect him, which includes not letting people use me to gain access."

"I understand. And we seem to have gotten off on the wrong foot. I'm sorry, but I don't think this is going to work out. I'm going to cut this short. But maybe I'll see you at a future event."

That stings a little. Granted, I wasn't particularly interested in dating him, but I don't appreciate being rejected so quickly.

"That's fine, Jackson, I'm not feeling this either. Best of luck to you in your search."

He leaves without a backwards glance; I stay and finish my coffee in the air conditioning, though I do move to a different table. I'm not going to be the woman sitting alone at a table marked with a swirly heart logo and obviously decorated for a date. Lucky for me, I brought my e-reader. I'm halfway through a fascinating book.

When I finish—the beverage, not the book—I buy Powell an iced coffee to go and head out to the parking lot. And there's Jackson, leaning against my car.

"Finally. I thought you'd be out sooner," he greets me, while wiping sweat from his forehead. "I wish you'd parked in the shade."

"What do you want?" I'm not inclined toward politeness now.

"To talk to you, but somewhere else."

"We were just talking inside. You were the one who left." Abruptly, I might add.

"I don't trust anything set up by LoveMatch. There are things I want to say, but not with them listening in."

"Seriously? You think someone was eavesdropping?" The barista did keep staring at me, but I assumed it was in recognition. I'm not famous, but I'm not entirely unknown.

"I think the table was bugged. I don't think anyone near us was listening. You said you want to protect your brother, so do I. For real, can we go somewhere private?"

Recent experiences have taught me that there can be long running conspiracies against Powell and myself, so of course I'm fascinated and eager to learn more. But I'm not reckless enough to follow a conspiracy theorist who I just met to an undisclosed alternate location. Movies are made about the women who do that, and usually it's a true crime documentary where everyone sadly shakes their heads and murmurs that 'she should have known better.'

"I don't think that's a good idea. Let's talk here." In this hot parking lot, under the punishing sun. The heat should entice him to get to the point before he dies of heatstroke.

"You and I have a mutual friend, Percival Von Sharkington. He would tell you to trust me."

That name is enough to make me curious. Yes, let's go someplace without hidden listening devices, and then Jackson can explain to me how he found out the joking nickname I gave to an FBI agent a few months ago, a name that was shared nowhere, and the only person I told it to is now in a federal prison cell.

I guess Powell isn't getting an iced coffee after all.

In the past, people have strongly implied that I may have trust issues. They'd be correct. That's why I tell Jackson we can meet up at Tempe Beach Park, a ten-minute drive from here. It gives me enough time to make a phone call.

"Hello?" My favorite FBI hacker sounds half-asleep when he answers.

"Percival! Did I wake you?"

"Cassidy." It's both an acknowledgement of my call and an exasperated correction. "Yes, you did. Why?"

"It's afternoon, you should have been up for hours. Come on, aren't you happy to hear from me?" Agent Walters was assigned to our case when we discovered someone had been embezzling money from my accounts during the bombing investigations. He was reticent to admit we shared a first name, so he had insisted having me calling him by his title. So of course, that means he forced me to assign him an unasked for and intentionally ridiculous nickname.

"You're calling on my personal phone, on the weekend." He's a lot less whiny in person. Though I suppose I've only seen him fully awake, during the workday.

"You gave me the number. Anyway, under the circumstances, you should have expected my call. Who is Jackson Shih?"

"I have no idea."

His words make my blood run cold. How did Jackson know that very specific nickname?

"Okay, Agent Walters, we have a problem. Because I just talked to a man named Jackson Shih who claims we share a mutual friend named . . ."

"Wait!" He cuts me off before I can finish. "Sorry, yes, I know him. Asian guy, gets manicures, obsessively interested in kombucha, is a fan of shiny shoes?"

"Ummm . . . I'm not sure about all of those details." I did notice how neat his fingernails were, all trim and glossy. I'll have to somehow sneak kombucha into the conversation and examine his shoes for reflectivity when I see him in the park.

The agent lets out a long sigh. "You woke me up. I don't think well when someone wakes me up."

That's when it hits me.

"Jackson isn't his real name, is it? Does he work for the FBI?"

"I just didn't recognize the name right away. That's not what I call him. And no, he's not FBI."

"Why did you tell him about me?"

"He asked. He knew I worked the Monroe bombing case. Is this really important? He said he met you at the LoveMatch thing and wondered if . . . I don't know how much he told you."

"Nothing yet. Is my brother in danger?"

"Not everything is about your brother. Powell is fine. I—" He's interrupted by a woman's voice in the background. "I gotta go. But I promise you can trust the guy."

"Wait! Can you tell me anything more? Or is your girlfriend getting jealous of you being on the phone with me?"

He snorts at that, rather insultingly. "Ms. Blaine-Corbitt, I assure you, she's not jealous. She knows I prefer women who make complex alpha-numeric passwords."

"Ouch, Percival. I have complex passwords *now*."

"Right, I'm sure you do. And if you need anything else you can call me. But during the work week, on my work phone."

"Some things can't wait for the work week." I hang up, slightly closer to trusting Jackson, and infinitely more curious as to what is going on.

Jackson is parked and rubbing an imaginary smudge of dirt from his car door when I pull in. He drives a black Audi R8 Spyder—I recognize it because Powell bought the same model in yellow. Pricey vehicle, leading me to wonder who exactly he works for. I also wonder if his bosses will be paying for the speeding tickets he's sure to accumulate.

The sun is blistering hot, so I pull my enormous sunhat from my trunk, and help myself to Powell's iced coffee. If I didn't, it would just end up warm and watered down, and he would complain and ask me to go buy another one. But if he never knows it existed, he won't miss it.

"I thought you'd pick a place with shade," Jackson complains, so I offer him the Last Barons of Sound baseball cap that I keep in the glove compartment. I drive a convertible, so it comes in handy. He grimaces as he accepts it—it does not suit his image. The faded denim clashes terribly with his linen shirt, designer chinos and, yes, very shiny shoes.

"I picked a place nobody could overhear us, but public enough you can't get away with murdering me," I tell him honestly. I have another secret reason as well—the heat is a weapon. It's become quite clear Jackson is not from around here, and he hasn't acclimated yet. The oven-temperature air will keep him uncomfortable and make it more likely that he'll make a mistake if he's lying. This is a tactic I just invented, but I'm going to be sure to tell Powell. If he ever retires from music and we open our own detective agency, we'll question our witnesses in the Phoenix sun, as they melt and suffer.

We walk down to the waterfront and find a bench shaded by a large tree. Drat. I wanted to keep Jackson sweating.

"It's hot," I say, angling the brim of my hat so I can see him better. "I can't wait to head home and have a big bowl of kombucha." Okay, yes, I worked that in awkwardly. And no, I don't actually know what kombucha is.

He looks at me askance. "You drink it from a *bowl?*"

Shoot, I was guessing it was soup. But I keep my dignity. "You and I travel in different circles. Celebrity culture, you know?" I wave my hand vaguely, as if to indicate all the famous people with kombucha bowls that I try to emulate. I hang out with supermodels; they do strange things.

"Anyway," I continue, needing to change the subject and get down to what we're here for. "You know Percival? Should I assume you are colleagues? You're with the FBI?" This is an important test, even more important than making sure he matched Walters' description: will he lie right away?

Jackson takes off the cap and fans himself with it. "We're not colleagues, not in real life. We're in the same collective, though. We do raids, that sort of thing."

Oh yes, raids and whatnot. Of course.

"Who do you work for?"

"I've been freelancing the past couple of years, so whoever pays me. That's how I met Walters. I found some discrepancies in a company's IT systems, and it turned out to be a massive money laundering scheme. It was pretty cool." He's glowing with enthusiasm and pride for his role in that investigation. Or glowing with sweat. Even in the shade, the heat is brutal out here.

I'm intrigued as to what one of Agent Walter's technical collaborators has to do with LoveMatch. More money laundering? Identity theft? Matching up married people? Is conspiracy to commit adultery a crime?

"Are you investigating a threat against my brother?"

"No. Well, maybe. Not an active one. Tell me why the two of you signed up for LoveMatch."

Since Jackson's gaze is so intent, I take a long slow sip of my coffee. He licks his lips, and his eyes have moved from my face to the condensation dripping down the side of my cup. I wonder if this counts as torture.

"My brother is interested in meeting someone, and he decided to drag me along with him," I finally admit, giving the barest of details.

"Did he pay for a guaranteed match?"

"Isn't there a non-disclosure agreement about such things?" Though I doubt I'm bound to honor someone else's contract.

"Yes, there is. But I'm not on LoveMatch's side here. I won't tell them you told me."

"Whose side are you on?"

In reply, he pulls a picture up on his phone and shows the screen to me. It's a smiling man, probably early thirties, sitting at a computer and giving finger guns to the camera. "This is Lester Zheng. Do you recognize him?"

"No. Was he at the event?" Now I'm wondering what we've gotten mixed up in. This Zheng guy appears nerdy and amiable, but he must be an assassin or a drug lord, using LoveMatch to . . . I don't know what. Perhaps I was right when I told Powell it sounded like an expensive prostitution scam.

"He's dead. It was all over the news a few months ago, but you may have missed it, due to another high-profile death."

"Jace Monroe?"

"Yes. That one consumed most of the media attention. I'm sorry for your loss," he adds belatedly. There's an awkward pause before he continues. "Lester was a successful app developer. At the time of his death, he was worth nearly a billion dollars."

"What's this got to do with Jace?" His killers have been caught. Unless there are more. Oh, please don't let there be more. I'm tired of getting attacked.

"Jace? Nothing. No, that was a coincidence, a timing thing. Lester purchased one of LoveMatch's guaranteed packages, met the perfect woman and married her, all within four months. Then this happened." He passes me his phone again, now with a news article headlined *Groom Killed in Tragic Honeymoon Accident*.

I skim the article. Six months ago, Lester Zheng, founder of the Bop di Boop app (I've heard of that; my mom is addicted to trying to bop the falling balls before the timer goes off) drowned while scuba diving on the second day of his honeymoon. The wife, Angelica Zheng, survived, but was distraught and was quoted as saying all the usual platitudes about her husband being taken away too soon, this was supposed to be the happiest time of their lives, she'd never love again, etc.

"And you think LoveMatch had something to do with this?"

"His family does. All of Lester's money was tied up in an ironclad trust, so it wasn't considered marital property. The wife is now suing them for it, trying to claim a marital share under estate law. She's saying it's what Lester would have wanted. But would he? He married a woman he barely knew, paid seven figures for the privilege, and died that weekend."

"Do you think she murdered him?"

"The more I look into this, the more I'm sure of it. But there's no proof. Yet." There should be *dun dun dunn* music accompanying this pronouncement. Where's Powell's emergency guitar now?

"None of this happened in Phoenix. Why aren't you investigating Felicity's Los Angeles office?"

"Because Lillian L'Amour was his matchmaker, and she's out here."

Oh, that's *my* matchmaker. Is she going to find a man to marry and murder me? No way, she's too focused on the bottom line.

"That doesn't make sense. Lillian would have earned a massive bonus for finding the match. She doesn't stand to gain anything if the guy dies, especially if she was counting on an endorsement."

"You make a valid point. That's why this investigation is ongoing. It's entirely possible that his death was an accident. But have you ever done an Internet search for groom dies on honeymoon?"

Of course, I haven't. I've run some strange searches, mostly in the interest of proving Powell wrong about something, but never that particular phrase.

"If you do," he continues, "You'll find a surprising number of wealthy men who die within a few days of getting married. Some of them I could rule out, like when both parties are killed in car crashes. But there have been a couple of other diving accidents, or grooms going missing while hiking in a remote location, or dying of terrible food poisoning—one man was accidentally served improperly prepared fugu, and another sampled a wild mushroom while on a romantic hike, and passed away in agony two days later."

"And they bought guaranteed matches?"

"Possibly. You know how these write-ups go, they always talk up how the couple got together, so I eliminated the ones that had been childhood friends or met at work or through shared hobbies or whatever. But when their initial meeting wasn't described or they claimed someone set them up or they met online, those ones I checked out. And I found five who connected through LoveMatch. That's too big a number to be coincidental. Not all of their relatives were positive about whether the grooms paid for a guaranteed match, but at least two did. And all of them had very short courtships."

His theory is intriguing, and I can't help but agree that these deaths are suspicious. But at the same time, I can't imagine they'd target Powell. He's too high profile. If LoveMatch finds him a wife, the publicity they'd get would be far more valuable than the money they earn for the match. I tell that to Jackson, and he mulls it over.

"True. He might not be at risk at all. Or maybe he meets and marries someone and survives the honeymoon. But how much longer after that? Can you trust that he's marrying a woman who is who she says she is, or is it more likely she's going to use him?"

Honestly, I've always assumed whatever woman he meets is going to use him anyway. That's my realistic—or some might say, cynical—side coming out. I don't want him to be set up to be killed though. Haven't we been through that already?

"Should I warn Powell?" He's likely to dismiss it, especially from me since I've been sort of down on this idea the entire time. Plus, he's known for not being concerned with personal safety. He tends to assume everything will work out, and he'll come out the other side just fine. It's always worked for him, so I don't know why it wouldn't this time. Oh wait. It wouldn't because perhaps he's paying a lot of money to bloodthirsty monsters who want to drain his accounts under the guise of community property or spousal inheritance rights.

"No. I don't want LoveMatch tipped off to what I'm doing. I just want you keeping an eye out for your brother, and for anything suspicious. And maybe you keep me informed of what's going on with his matches."

I don't like hiding things from Powell. I don't make a practice of lying to him or misleading him. Well, sometimes I do. Like when his stylist and I disagree about something, I defer to the expert and don't say things like, no, Powell, that's an ugly shirt, and you look terrible. I leave that form of honesty to the

SwiftaPic-sphere. And then I lie to him and tell him I have no idea why so many people hate his clothing choices.

"I won't tell him now, but I reserve the right to tell him in the future." That's the most I'll agree to.

"And don't mention any of this at LoveMatch events. I'm serious when I say I think they're bugged."

"I will keep that in mind and tailor all discussions appropriately."

Jackson raises an eyebrow at that. If he's a highly trained secret agent, he can read between the lines, and he's probably regretting confiding in me.

"All right, Cassidy. Text or call me if anything happens with your brother. And next time we meet up, I'm bringing you kombucha. Real kombucha. That you can drink from a cup."

# CHAPTER SIX

I am sixty minutes into an intense cardio workout when Adriana, my new assistant manager interrupts.

"Cassidy, I hate to bother you, but a woman is at the desk looking for you. She says it's something about your brother."

Ugh. That means it's likely a reporter, but not one we've worked with or leaked to in the past. If the visitor were someone we trusted, she would have given her name. Adriana hasn't been here long enough to be well practiced in throwing those kinds of people out, so I give my machine a quick wipe down and head to the front desk to handle the expulsion myself—and maybe demonstrate how it's done, so next time this happens I don't have to cut my cardio short.

But the woman nervously drumming her fingers on the lobby desk is not a reporter. It's Powell's current love interest, Emily. And she's not in exercise clothes, nor is she holding a gym bag, so I doubt she's here to try to cage a free membership. Though I wouldn't be surprised if she were to inform me that on their recent date my brother promised her one. He does that sometimes.

"I am so, so sorry to interrupt your workout," she apologizes as soon as she sees my sweaty face. "I'd hoped to find you here, but *working*, not *working out*."

"I was almost finished anyway," I lie to be polite. "What's going on?"

"There's something I wanted to talk to you about. In person." She straightens her spine and squares her shoulders to project confidence, but her hands are trembling. Is she afraid of me? She shouldn't be. I'm perfectly friendly and kind, until someone gives me a reason not to be. And she hasn't given me a reason yet.

Since she's gone on two LoveMatch sanctioned dates with Powell so far, I should treat her like a potential sister-in-law. Besides, if I'm rude to her, word will get back to my brother, and then he's going to spend hours moaning about how I'm ruining his relationship. Being nice to her now saves me a lot of hassle later.

"Okay, let's grab a smoothie and talk," I gesture toward the large glass refrigerator in the lobby and invite her to help herself. I select my current favorite, a Blueberry Restoration Delight. She takes a Chocolate Energetic Bomb. I stop her before she can crack the lid. "Not that one."

"Sorry." I should keep track of how many times this woman apologizes. "I misunderstood . . ."

"That one isn't peanut-free," I explain because I think she's worried I stopped her based on the price—the brand she chose is more expensive. "It's not safe for you."

She blinks slowly and then the realization hits. "Oh my gosh! I can't believe you remembered my allergy! Thank you!"

If she were Powell, she would be subjected to a very long lecture right now, one he's received a few times about safety and reading skills, and not acting like a careless idiot with a death wish. But she's not Powell, so I just smile and shrug and say, "No problem."

After she chooses a Vanilla Peach High Octane Buzz—and carefully reads the label—I lead her back to my office, so we can speak privately.

I'm still damp from my workout, so I perch on the edge of my desk—don't want to contaminate my chair. Emily sits on my small couch, her hands in her lap twisting her purse strap. I'm starting to feel stressed out and agitated just watching her.

"I'm sorry"—she leads with an apology again—"I know it's weird coming here like this. It's just . . . I lied to you."

Now my interest is piqued. We've had exactly one conversation before, and it wasn't that deep. "When? What are you talking about?"

"The night I met you, I lied. And I've been feeling just terrible, especially after spending time with Powell. And then I started to worry you'd tell him what I said, and he'd think less of me."

I'm scanning my memory. She recently moved here, her grandmother died, she wants to go back to school, she plays the piano. That was about the extent of our conversation. Well, there was one other thing.

"You didn't have a crush on Miles? Or you don't prefer FormulaFive to the Last Barons?"

My joke does not lighten the mood. She's going to wear a hole in her purse strap, or perhaps gnaw through her lower lip.

"I did, I swear, that part was true. Mildly embarrassing, and I regret admitting anything about my teenage obsession, but true. No, I just . . ." She pauses to let out a long quavering sigh. "I was talking to you and Aurora, and you're both so glamorous and interesting and sophisticated. I was intimidated, so when you asked why I joined LoveMatch, I lied and said I signed up to make friends. I didn't want to admit that I wanted to find a husband, with the goal of settling down and having children. I thought you'd judge me. For being so mundane, you know, with my trivial desires to be someone's wife."

"Why are you telling me this now?" I'm trying not to laugh. She's being so earnest about something that was nothing more than a blip on my radar.

"Because I've gone out with Powell a couple of times, and I really like him. My lie has been haunting me. I was so afraid you would tell him what I said, that I was looking for friends, and he would think I wasn't serious about him, or about us . . ." She trails off and puts her head in her hands.

If she wants to be in a long-term relationship with my famous brother, she's going to need to toughen up. She will be under scrutiny in the media, she will have to attend publicity events, and she'll have to stop being so nervous and apologizing for everything. Plus, I had assumed at the time she didn't mean what she said. Nobody with limited funds spends money on a matchmaking service if they aren't seeking a committed romantic relationship. There are plenty of free options for making friends. I figured she'd said it to make herself seem less desperate.

"Emily!" Her name comes out more harshly than I intend, so I try to soften my tone. "Emily, it's fine, I believe you. And it's not a big deal."

"Really?" Her smile is tremulous. "Oh, thank you, Cassidy. I'm sorry I interrupted your workout today. It's just been preying on my mind. When we were at the cocktail party, and you asked me to sneak him past the paparazzi, I thought it was going to be one of those funny stories, the ones people use in ice breakers. I'd be able to say, 'I once ran a blockade of photographers with a celebrity hiding in my backseat,' and people wouldn't believe me right away. That's all. But he and I spent the ride talking about music. Music!"

"Well, he is a musician," I point out diplomatically. And that is his favorite subject. Besides himself. And his car collection.

"Yes, but I thought . . . I thought all those boybands were just made up of pretty boys who could sing, guys who only cared about being famous. I didn't realize any of them actually loved the musical aspect of it. Maybe that's me being naïve or cynical, but I assumed fame was the goal. But Powell, he's got music in his soul." Her eyes are shining with love and wonder, and I kind of want to throw up.

"When I got the request to meet him for coffee," she continues, "I could hardly believe it! What would an amazing talented man like him see in someone like me? I almost turned him down. But my matchmaker, Lillian, convinced me to go. And I'm so glad I did. Powell is, well, he's a dream come true! I couldn't believe how much we had in common!"

"I've heard him say the same about you." He gushes like she does. *Emily is so amazing. Emily smells like springtime. Emily would like to learn to play the harp. Cass, where can I buy a harp? Emily is so sweet. Emily* . . . blah blah blah. I tune out a lot of the effusive compliments, but the overall gist is that he's happy, especially since she seems to like him for him, and hasn't tried to exploit access to him in any way. She may be the only person he's ever met that doesn't use social media. She has not once requested a selfie with him, and when he offered her a photo, she was surprised and flustered by the gesture. According to him, she didn't even know where to look when he took a shot of them together, and he had to show her where the camera was. Personally, I find that strange, weird, and possibly a pretense, not refreshing, but I'm not the one dating her.

"He talks about me, too?" Her whole face lights up when she smiles, and I can see a little bit of what Powell sees. She is pretty. And I want to like her. I want this to work out, and not because I'm selfishly trying to get this matchmaker stuff over with. My brother is a kindhearted man who deserves to find happiness. If he weren't famous, Emily would be absolutely perfect for him. And even though I worry that she's not strong enough to stand in his peripheral spotlight now, she can learn. If twelve-year-old me could figure it out, I'm sure grown-up Emily will do fine.

"He sure does," I reassure her. My mind is already planning ahead—she likes him, he likes her. And there's a matchmaker event tonight that Powell RSVPed us for. When I get home, we're going to have a talk. Maybe I'm free tonight after all. Pajamas, popcorn, and Crime TV, here I come!

"Thank you!" She throws her arms around me, not caring about my gross sweaty state. I smell disgusting. She smells exactly as Powell describes her, like springtime. Or more specifically, like honeysuckle. It's interesting: Tanner is also from St. Louis, and he also frequently delivers scented hugs. I prefer his cinnamon.

WHAT ARE YOU UP TO TONIGHT?

The text from Tanner reminds me I need to have a serious conversation with my brother.

PROBABLY ARGUING WITH MY BROTHER FOR A FEW HOURS AND THEN AVOIDING A LOVEMATCH EVENT. YOU?

CAN'T SAY. NDA.

ARE YOU KIDDING? DID YOU MESSAGE ME JUST TO SAY THAT? The smugness oozing through the phone is almost tangible. Tanner must have been hired to photograph a fancy party. Or an orgy. Those also require NDAs, or so I've been told.

NO. JUST WONDERING IF YOU WERE GOING TO FIND YOUR 'ULTIMATE SOULMATE AND LIFE COMPANION' TONIGHT. YOU SKIPPING IT?????

Oh, I want to. I turn my head to the side, where Powell is dozing next to me. We're out by the pool, both too lazy to swim, but taking advantage of the shade and the misters to stay cool.

"Hey Powell, about tonight . . ."

"Still going."

"But what about Emily? It seems to me that you getting matched with other people puts a damper on the whole evaluating her as a prospective wife thing." Not that I want him to marry her immediately. In my mind they should date at least three years before making such a monumental decision. I don't believe in insta-love, even if I did witness it once, when my mom met Hank. That sort of thing is rare, and doesn't work when one party is wealthy, famous, and easily flattered.

"Yeah, but Tabitha says I still have to go. She says I need to be open to all possibilities and while Emily and I are a great fit, I still need to explore whoever else might be out there."

"Will Emily be there, too?"

"Nope. Which is good because I don't think she'd like to watch me flirting with other women."

"Or you could not flirt."

Now he finally turns to look at me, lowers his sunglasses and flashes his magazine-worthy smile. "Cassidy, babe, you know I can't *not* flirt. It's in my nature." He winks, and I laugh. He's kidding, he's quoting his god-awful former bandmate Xander. "Besides, Emily and I discussed it. She says she wants me to go, so I can be sure of what I want."

"Or she's testing you."

"If she's the kind of person who likes to test relationships, then I'm not interested. I don't play games, Cass. You know that." He pushes his sunglasses back up his nose, and reclines, because apparently, he thinks this conversation is over.

"Powell!" He ignores me this time, so I splash some ice water from my cup onto his bare stomach, causing him to jump cursing to his feet, stumble, and almost fall into the pool. Too bad his dance training kicked in and saved him the plunge. "Powell, I don't think we should go to any LoveMatch events while you're trying out your relationship with Emily. It feels like cheating. If you marry her, do you want her to one day find out you were dating or making out with other women after you started seeing her?"

"I haven't even made out with Emily yet," he replies, using a towel to dry his stomach. "There's no sexual contact permitted until date seven. Seven! I thought conventional wisdom was date three. But since I'm not allowed to put my lips on anybody, and talking isn't cheating, we're still going. Cassidy, this is for you, too. It's not just about me."

"Why? Why are you so determined to find someone for me? And why are you suddenly so obsessed with getting married?"

"Sonit can pull himself up."

Typical Powell, and his annoying non-sequiturs. Bringing up his former bandmate's baby is not going to get him out of this conversation. Though admittedly, the kid is adorable.

"Yeah, I saw all five videos Mason sent this morning. Don't change the subject."

"I'm not. Cass, look at what's happened in the past six months. Mason had a baby, and Jace died. And you and I, we almost died too. Doesn't that make you rethink how you're living? Doesn't it make you reflect on the fragility of life? How can you look at Sonit and not want a child yourself? Jace left behind nothing and no one. All his talent, all his skill, all his everything is erased, gone forever."

My brother is passionate, intense, and wrong.

"Jace left behind his music. That's all the legacy he ever wanted. He wanted to be known for his songs, and he was. His music will always live on." That's not all, either. There's going to be an enormous stone monument. It hasn't been completed yet, but I've seen the sketches of Jace, sitting cross-legged with his guitar, perched atop a pedestal. Not to mention the Jace Monroe Memorial Foundation that Devon Malloy is running in Jace's honor. Those millions of dollars are funding music education across the country. Plus, there are Jace's two un-recorded albums that everyone is clamoring for. I inherited the rights to those, and I'm going to make sure they help cement his legacy. When I finally hire someone to record them, they'll go platinum.

"Yes, but there's nothing left of *him*. He's a name on a paper, nothing more. Kids are . . . kids are a path to eternal life."

"I swear, Powell, if you try to use that line in a song, I'm going to smash your studio so that you can never record again."

"But it sounds . . . no, you're right. It's awful. But seriously, Cassidy, I'm ready. I never thought I'd be this old and not be a dad yet." He's full of earnestness, which would be endearing if he weren't also trying to convince me to feel the same way. Fine that he's sick with baby fever; I'm not there yet, and it's not as contagious as he thinks.

"Yes, thirty-two is ancient. Your sperm probably doesn't work anymore, you should give up."

"You're my sister, you can't talk about my sperm. Gross, Cass. I'm getting a drink to wash those words out of my mind."

He heads to the wet bar, and I lean back against my chaise and ponder. I don't feel a powerful biological urge to procreate, but if he does, shouldn't I support him? Powell would be a good father, when he's not on the road, and some stars take their children on tour with them. He could be active and involved, and he'd be—

*Sonofabitch, he's not going to live long enough to reproduce.* He just dumped a bucket of ice on me.

Now I have an excuse to throw him in the pool.

Well, I couldn't escape the commitment, even when I tried the argument that the well-deserved pool dunking messed up Powell's hair so badly that he shouldn't be seen in public. Here we are, arriving at the LoveMatch Millionaires' Circle Level event. Fortunately, instead of a stuffy cocktail party with random drunk singers, this hotel ballroom has been converted into an indoor carnival, complete with games, wandering performers, silk dancers suspended from the ceiling, and even a tiny rollercoaster. Powell is casual in khaki shorts, flip flops, and a T-shirt that looks like his stylist pulled it from a dumpster, but actually cost four hundred dollars. It's the height of fashion. I chose to stick with my summer uniform—a light sundress. It was this or workout clothes, and I'm not parading around an event filled with horny red-wristbanded millionaire seekers with my ass on display.

"This should be fun," Powell says enthusiastically, as he always does when he's dragging me to something I don't want to do. But okay, I should stop being a party pooper, because this does look like fun. I am the reigning family Skee-Ball champion, and, while Powell's insurance will forbid him from riding the rickety contraption, I'm willing to hop on the roller coaster.

One of the first things we find as we start exploring our options is the Dance Dancercize video game. It's a screen hooked up to a platform with square sensors, and you're supposed to follow along with dance moves, tapping the correct lighted squares with your feet.

"Oh, Cass . . ." Powell calls in a sing-song voice, and I know I'm in trouble. "They have *Right For You*." He points to his own picture, his seventeen-year-old face grinning in the pack of Last Barons, right there on the side of the machine.

Oh, no. No, no, no. Was this a set up? Someone from LoveMatch had to have been supervising when all of this was being assembled. They lured Powell in, knowing he wouldn't be able to resist giving a performance.

Despite my shaking head, Powell grabs my hand, drags me up on the platform, and selects the song, one of the Last Barons of Sound's biggest hits. All right, fine. If we're going to do this, I'm going to make it look good. I kick off my sandals and take up the starting pose, legs spread, one arm down, one pointing at the ceiling.

When I was a teenager, Powell taught me every single Last Barons dance. He did it because he liked having an in-house practice partner, and honestly, it's fun. I would never go on the record saying that, but it is. I even appeared as a backup dancer in a couple of their videos, though I always lie about my involvement if asked. My real-life hair is thick and straight, but in the videos, it's a wild mane of curls. Those three-hour sessions in a stylist's chair gave me plausible deniability. I won't be able to deny it tonight though.

The music starts, and my feet pick up the rhythm. Powell and I dance as naturally as ever, as though we'd just rehearsed this morning. The machine only awards points for feet placement, but we've got the hands and shoulders down too. Step step, lean, cross arms, nod. Jump back, arms out, shake that ass. I can still hear the old choreographer shouting at the boys throughout rehearsals. *Sexier Mason, be sexier! Jace, perfect, everybody watch him! Devon, can't you tell right from left? Powell, stop grimacing and show me that smile! Xander, I said swivel your hips! Not shake! Swivel! Why do I bother with you graceless oafs?*

By the end of the song, we're both laughing. Or I am, until I turn around and see the crowd gathered behind us. We're surrounded by starry-eyed fans gazing rapturously at my brother. He's not going to have any trouble finding someone to 'try out' in Emily's place tonight. They surround him as he dismounts from the game, a seething mass of attractive women ready to pounce on their prey.

I would rescue him but, shock of all shocks, there's someone there for me, as well. Tanner is at the edge of the gal-pack, grinning and holding out a frothy pink cocktail.

"Tanner!" I slip my sandals back on and jump down from the platform. "What are you doing here?"

As he hands me the martini glass, he twists his wrist to show me the red wristband. "I was invited. I would have told you before, but NDA."

"You joined LoveMatch?" I'm shocked that he decided to pay for a service when he has tons of dating options—I've seen the number of messages he gets on SwiftaPic. Granted, many of them are 'influencers' who want to invite him to take pictures of them 'for exposure.'

"I figured everybody else was doing it, why not me? Cheers!"

Since he's smiling and charming and far more interesting than any of the other men here, I clink my glass against his and say, "Welcome to the meat market."

A cautious sip reveals that my drink is the same watermelon mint concoction I had last time. Not that I thought there'd be anything wrong with it, I just don't want anything too strong at an event like this. Someone has to keep an eye on Powell.

Tanner nods toward the glass. "I told Isaac I wanted to order a drink for you, and that's what he recommended. Only he thought I was hitting on you. I didn't tell him we already know each other." His words cause me to glance around quickly. Jackson is convinced there are listening devices everywhere, so the staff can gain information and use it to their advantage. Though what they stand to gain from a conversation like this is beyond me.

"Who's your matchmaker?"

"Isaac, actually. I met his girlfriend too. She was helping him out with some of the paperwork. I think he's new."

I sort of thought of Isaac as a glorified intern, so yeah, he's probably new. They wouldn't make the experienced matchmakers parade around in tight pants and serve water on gilded trays in the offices.

"Fiancée. That's Tabitha, Powell's matchmaker."

Tanner frowns. "No, I think he called her Lillian."

"Dark hair, narrow face? That's my matchmaker. She's his future sister-in-law, not his girlfriend. What'd you think of the intake?" I realize I hadn't told him details about mine, so I bet he was unprepared and horrified by the hours of testing.

"Intense. They sure ask a lot of questions. Did you . . . did you have to take off your shirt for yours?"

"No, are you sure you went to the right place? Did you accidentally go to a job interview for male strippers?"

"Okay, so it was weird, then. Isaac made me take off my shirt and he took a picture for my file. And he sniffed me." Tanner runs his hand through his unruly hair, a gesture he always makes when he's uncomfortable.

"Can you check the address you went to? Cause that didn't happen at my appointment." If Lillian had gotten her nose anywhere near me, I'd have walked out the door.

"Did you do a bunch of personality and preference tests?"

"Yes. With all my clothes on. And with no sniffing."

"Did you have to answer questions about your kinks?"

"Kinks like . . ."

"Yes, like"—he drops his voice even though everyone around us is only paying attention to a certain boyband star—"sex kinks. It was so invasive."

"What did you say?"

"Why do you want to know?"

"I'm just surprised you answered. I totally skipped most of that section." I did mark my deal-breakers though. For example, men who call me mommy and ask me to punish them. Unwillingly tried that, hated it, never happening again.

"I didn't know we could skip sections." He's staring off into space, perhaps wondering what exactly Isaac thinks of him. Personally, I'm wondering what he told Isaac. Is there some dirty secret Tanner has never shared? Not that it's my business, I don't want to picture him or anything, I'm merely curious. That's all.

"Well, whatever you put, it got you here, right? Somebody must be into it."

He grins. "True. Want to walk around and check this place out? Hit the midway, play some games?"

"And search for your match?" I suspect I know who he's been chosen for, a certain millionaire *artiste* who wants a photographer to 'collaborate' with.

The smile drops from his face, and he mutters, "Sure, yeah, whatever." I don't know why he's not more enthusiastic. He's the one paying to meet someone, may as well get his money's worth.

Every imaginable carnival game has been transported into this ballroom. We pause at one, to watch a man make multiple attempts at knocking down a pyramid of milk bottles with a softball. Each miss causes yet another new swear to fall out of his mouth, until the silver-braceleted woman he was trying to impress rolls her eyes and walks away.

"Want to take a turn?" Tanner suggests, as the previous loser wanders off to try his luck on something and someone else.

"I don't know if I'll be any good at this, but I suppose I could try." I'm lying, this is totally my game.

Tanner goes first and manages to take the top of the pyramid down, but there are still five bottles. The barker resets the stack, calls me "hot stuff," and encourages me to take a shot. They're both watching, and it's clear from their expressions they expect me to fail. But here's something they don't know about me: I spent an entire Last Barons of Sound tour as a merchandise girl. And one of my jobs included throwing T-shirts into the crowd. My supervisor didn't think I was old enough to use the T-shirt cannon, so I was in charge of the section within throwing range of the stage. I liked selecting targets, usually teenage girls who reminded me of myself, and by the end of the tour I had developed great aim. Plus, I happen to know the trick to this game. The bottom layer of milk bottles are heavily weighted, and the only way to take out the pyramid is a solid hit to the center bottle in the bottom row.

"Gosh, I'll try. But don't laugh at me!" I lightly bounce the ball in my hand, trying to get a feel for it. *Think T-shirt*, I tell myself, and the center bottle is a teenage girl who desperately wants a souvenir she can't afford, because her mother isn't flirting with the father of one of the stars at the concession stand.

The bottles tumble down with a satisfying crash, but what's more satisfying is the surprise on everybody's faces.

"I didn't know you could throw like that," Tanner says, and so I give him a smug grin. And when the games operator offers me a choice from the small prize selection, I pick out a glittery pink keychain with a smiley face.

"I won this for you," I tell him, forcing it into his pocket when he proves reluctant to accept. "Don't underestimate me next time."

"Never again. Now come on, let's find a game I'm good at." He takes my hand and leads me off through the crowd, scouting both sides of the midway. He finally finds what he's looking for at the water gun races. This one's a competition, shooting a stream of water into a clown's mouth. There's some kind of sensor inside that makes a series of bulbs light up, with the win going to whomever lights their final bulb first.

We sit down on the stools along with another duo who have been walking around longer than us—I can tell because they're carrying an armload of stuffed animals.

"I didn't realize you were a gun person," I tell him as I finish my drink and set my cup out of the way.

"I'm not, I'm a photographer."

"Yes, Tanner, I've heard that rumor." And I bet he's going through withdrawal right now, since cameras are prohibited at these events.

"Photography requires a steady hand. So does this. Watch and learn."

As it turns out, he's right. He's the steadiest of all of us as he trains his water rifle on the clown mouth and stays perfectly still, beating me by three light bulbs.

Then he takes an inordinate amount of time choosing from the many prize offerings. This is an exclusive event, so the stuffed animals are much nicer than the cheap sawdust- filled ones at most carnivals. He ends up selecting an adorable soft little duck.

"For you," he presents it to me with a flourish.

"Why a duck?" I'm curious as to his reasoning, given how long he took and how much thought he put into it.

"Because you like to swim. And it was cute. My second choice was the lion, because you're fierce, but one of the eyes wasn't sewn on properly."

"I love it," I tell him because he's so proud of his prize. This is fun. I'm no longer regretting coming to this, until I hear a voice behind me.

"Cassidy, darling, you came, I'm positively overjoyed to see you again." I suddenly find myself exchanging air kisses with Aurora Ridge. Then it gets worse because she sets her sights on my male companion. "And who is this luscious creature? Your eyes are gorgeous, are they real? I would so love to paint them."

"Like with make-up?" Tanner asks uncomfortably, and Aurora lets out a laugh that sounds posh and rehearsed.

"Oh, you dear sweet boy. I am Aurora Ridge—" but before she can pretentiously describe herself, Tanner interrupts.

"The artist? I've photographed some of your murals."

And now I think I've lost him. Aurora embraces him, her gauzy silks flying out all around. "Yes, yes, that's me, the *artiste*. And you . . . you're a photographer?"

Yep, he's gone. Aurora is holding his arm and gushing now, and I have been effectively excised from the conversation. May as well slink off to find my brother, see if someone is going to defeat Emily in the battle for his affections.

Powell hasn't made it far from the Dancercize machine, still surrounded by women, each vying for his attention in a different way. There's hair tossing, and forearm stroking, and giggling, and an awful lot of cleavage on display. As soon as he spots me, he makes a gracious exit, grabs me by the elbow and steers me away.

"Thanks for the rescue, finally."

"Weren't we planning to stick together tonight? You ditched me early."

"You were in good hands. I saw you with Tanner. How'd he get in?"

"Via special invitation."

"Yeah?" Powell smirks. "Bet I know why."

"Me, too." I glance back over my shoulder. I can just spot them in the crowd, Aurora laughing at something Tanner said, her hand gently caressing his bicep. We all know exactly why he came. I tuck my new stuffed duck into my purse before my brother can ask about it. Tanner can win one for Aurora now.

Tabitha comes to check on us as I am sampling the cotton candy. This isn't just any cotton candy—that wouldn't do for a millionaire level event. No, this is gourmet spun sugar with strands of edible silver made by a professional dessert 'performer.' Or at least, that's what his sign says, and given the way he's dancing around and pretending to be a magician conjuring the sugary treat, I guess it applies.

She greets Powell with a hug and a double cheek kiss. "I'm thrilled you came tonight, Mr. Corbitt!"

"I've asked you to call me Powell," he corrects her, and a faint blush colors her cheeks. His engaged matchmaker is not immune to his charms. "Cass and I are having a wonderful time."

"Good. But there seems to be a problem." She pokes his arm affectionately, a gesture at odds with the formality with which she addressed him. "You're supposed to be talking to potential matches, not your sister. Same goes for you, Ms. Blaine-Corbitt. You have some wonderful eligible men wandering around with red bracelets seeking your heart."

Gag. Does she really talk like that? Or is it an act she performs for clients? Does she go home and watch gory horror movies and write fanfic about break-ups and anti-love matches? With her and her sister competing for control of the company, I don't know how much of what she says is to stay in character and win the CEO position, and how much is her personality.

"I did meet a wonderful man, but Aurora Ridge swooped in," I tell her in a mock sorrowful voice. "I can't compete."

Powell snorts, but Tabitha is sympathetic. "Don't worry. You have three possibilities in this crowd. I'm not allowed to say anything to identify them, but let me assure you they are all attractive, athletic, and . . . well, two of them are intelligent. I know things didn't work out on your date with Jackson, but to be honest—we usually don't reveal these numbers—he was only a 62% match for you. I still can't believe Lillian even bothered to tell you about that interest card."

"How many matches does Powell have here?" I ask, to deflect attention from me.

"Nine. His personality is easier," she says. That hurts. I'm not actually looking, but I'd like to think I'm a pleasant enough person that people would want to be with me. At my expression, she reassures me. "But that doesn't mean much. Not as much. We use our proprietary algorithm to find personality compatibility, but it doesn't do any good if someone has an annoying laugh, or chews with their mouth open, or picks their nose in public. Powell is easy to match *on paper* because he's easy-going and optimistic. It's harder to find someone he can mesh with in person though, since he needs someone . . ."

Tabitha hesitates a bit too long, and Powell, who has been scanning the room and looking at red bracelets, becomes interested again. "Someone who what? Has perfect pitch?"

Of course, he'd go there, like musical ability is the only thing that matters. If it were, he'd have married the country singer he briefly dated three years ago for publicity reasons—the woman was a goddess at the mike. Too bad she was the most offensive person either of us have ever encountered. And we know Xander, so that's saying a lot.

"Powell, I say this with all the love in the world," Tabitha tells him gently. "You're focusing on the wrong thing. You need a life partner, not someone to sing a duet with."

"I know. If I wanted to sing a duet, my agent would—"

"Stop," Tabitha interrupts him, something most non-family members aren't brave enough to do. "Focus. Your perfect woman doesn't need to be musical. Look at Cassidy here."

"Look at the one non-option in the room?" I ask skeptically.

"No, that's not what I meant. Powell, you told me your sister is your best friend, the person you care about most in the world. And what instrument does she play?"

"Well, I've *tried* to teach her several," Powell gives me the same glare he did when I failed to learn the ukulele, the piano, and the harmonica, and later refused to 'help him out' by banging a tambourine in one of his videos.

"Right, you tried. And she has not one iota of musical talent. Yet you enjoy spending time with her, you trust her, and you listen to her. She's your assistant, your travel companion, and your roommate."

"So, you're saying I need someone like Cass? Except not related to me? And maybe nicer and more ready to have babies? And willing to make a commitment? And—"

"You don't have to keep listing my flaws, Powell."

"And maybe someone who doesn't elbow me in the ribs every time they're annoyed?" He dramatically rubs his side, even though I didn't dig my elbow in that hard. This time.

Tabitha laughs at us. "I wish my siblings and I got along as well as you two. We're in constant competition with each other. But yes, I am saying you need someone like Cassidy. Someone who stands up to you and challenges you. Lillian and I disagree on this; she thinks you'd be better off with someone you can coddle, a princess who makes you feel needed. But I think you'd be happier with an equal partner."

I'm going to side with Tabitha over Lillian here. And I realize that's what bothers me about Emily. She's too passive and nervous. Sure, she awakens Powell's need to be protective. It probably makes him feel strong and manly. But he would be better off with someone tougher, in my opinion.

"I just want someone who loves me," he says simply, and that's it. That's the truth that speaks to the core of Powell's being, his fundamental emotional wound. Deep down inside, he's the same person he's been since I met him: a sad boy who misses his mother. My mom, no matter how hard she tried, could never fill that aching gap for him, and neither can I. He still needs the tender loving care of a maternal woman, but one who will also have sex with him. I mean, let's be realistic here.

"There are millions of women who love you," Tabitha assures him. "You need to find someone who you love back. And you aren't going to find her talking with your own sister. Both of you, get away from each other. Go out there and mingle!" She waves her hands at us in a shooing motion before she takes her own advice and goes off to, presumably, harass another one of her victims. I mean clients.

"Tabby's word is law," Powell informs me, so I guess I'm abandoned. Before I even make it a few steps away, I hear a female voice behind me, introducing herself to Powell and telling him that she's not supposed to know this, but she's one of the nine. I'm not too impressed with the secret-keeping skills and discretion in this place.

I suppose I should go try and find my three options. I wish Tanner wasn't so busy talking to Aurora—they're still over there laughing together about something. I'd rather hang out with him and ride the tiny roller coaster than go looking for my possible matches.

I let Lillian's call go to voicemail. She can leave her lecture in message form. I can anticipate what she's going to say: I sabotaged myself by not mingling enough, I have no coffee requests, I'm ruining this process and possibly costing her the family business.

Powell, on the other hand, did throw in a match request. This was for Lexa, the curly haired beauty who accosted him the second I stepped away. Apparently, she doesn't play the piano, so I would never have thought he'd be interested. But learning piano is on her 'list' of things she'd like to do one day, as is skydiving, traveling to Antarctica, and saving a dying language, whatever that means. According to Powell, she's full of life and vibrancy, and he digs it. Yes, he said exactly that, "I dig it," which made me roll my eyes so badly I may need to schedule a surgery to unroll them.

"Did you send in any requests?" Tanner asks me. See, the guy can disappear on me one night, but then show up at my place with donuts begging for espresso bright and early the next morning.

"Of course not. If I did, it would mean I was taking LoveMatch seriously. I told you, I'm just in this until Powell gets engaged." I take a bite of my donut and powdered sugar explodes everywhere. Messy, but my favorite kind. Sometimes, when I was a kid, my mom would buy a small package of them at the gas station as a rare weekend treat. Those had a more processed taste than the fresh baked ones Tanner brought—though he bought the box this time; he didn't make them himself.

"Oh." He frowns down at his mug.

"What about you? Did you request a future encounter with a potential match?"

"No. I thought about it but figured it would probably be rejected."

"I doubt it. You and Aurora seemed to hit it off." Every time I saw him, she was attached. I had to ride the roller coaster with a red braceleted woman who only wanted to talk about how fun it must be to live with the amazing Powell Corbitt, superstar. Blech.

"Yeah, I know. We're doing a LoveMatch coffee date tomorrow."

I almost choke on a mouthful of donut, and even more powdered sugar sprays everywhere. Tanner sighs and gets the sponge from the sink to start wiping up my mess. But I take it from him. I can clean up after myself. At least, on the days when our maid isn't here.

I shouldn't have been so surprised. Obviously, something would happen. After all, he was clearly her intended suitor. Whatever, I don't care. They can have fun together. It doesn't bother me in the slightest. Maybe he'll get married before Powell. Maybe I'll be the last single person standing. And maybe that's what I wanted anyway.

# CHAPTER SEVEN

Sometimes everything in life sort of falls into place—for other people. Powell is happy and getting ever nearer to date seven and potential intimacy with Emily, while simultaneously ticking off the date list with Lexa. He likes them both for "different but equally compelling reasons," he said, and I told him that better not show up as a song lyric.

Meanwhile, I am staying busy, because we are just under two months away from the launch of his big double album, and three months from the accompanying tour. I don't have time to deal with romance and LoveMatch and everything else.

And because I'm so busy, I don't care that Tanner has totally disappeared on me. He's gone. I haven't seen him since the day after the LoveMatch carnival. He hasn't been at the gym—even though his membership is contingent on taking pictures for me. He hasn't texted, he hasn't called. But I don't mind. I'm *busy*. I don't need to waste time sitting around wondering why someone who was rapidly becoming my closest friend no longer seems to care about hanging out with me. It's fine. He has his life, and I have mine. So what if they rarely overlap anymore?

I have plenty of time to do other things that don't involve dealing with him. I'm working right now, aren't I? I'm too busy covering Adriana's break to bother thinking about being abandoned by my friend.

Speak of the devil, who happens to show up, strolling casually across the lobby? Yes, Tanner himself. So, I guess he is still alive.

"How's it going?" he asks cheerfully as he swipes his membership card, acting as though he hadn't disappeared from the face of the earth recently. I squint at the screen. That's what I thought, this is only his second visit in the past week and a half. It's summer in Arizona, and this is where he showers. He's far too clean looking to . . . yep, he and Aurora hit it off better than I expected. No ring on his finger yet, but that's probably coming.

"Fine. I guess Aurora finally let you out?"

He frowns. "What do you mean?"

"Last time I talked to you, you told me you were meeting her for coffee. You've only come in once since then. You've obviously showered somewhere, so I can only assume you've been holed up with your new lover."

He laughs in response. "You're kidding, right? I'm showering at my new apartment."

"You moved into an apartment?"

"You didn't know?" There is actual pain in his voice, and I've never seen anyone transform from confident adult male into little-boy-who-dropped-his-ice-cream-cone-while-watching-his-puppy-get-dog-knapped so quickly. "But I posted updates all week. I thought . . . I thought you followed me on SwiftaPic."

I want to both hug him and laugh at him. He's completely heartbroken. Men and their social media.

"Hashtag BabyJace," I reply, while biting my lip to keep from giggling. Maybe it's cruel, but he's adorable when he's crushed.

"Huh?"

"Haven't you seen it? Apparently, a rumor is going around that when I found out Jace died, I was so upset I miscarried his baby."

"You did? Cass, I'm so sorry, I had no idea." Seriously? How is this man so internet savvy that he can run multiple successful SwiftaPic accounts, but he can't figure out everything online is made up for likes?

"Tanner, don't be ridiculous; I've never been pregnant. It's not true. But the lie triggered a new hashtag, and people are making digitally altered images of what Jace's baby might have looked like. I'm being tagged like crazy. I haven't been on Swifta lately; I have thousands of notifications and I can't handle reading them right now." It's horrifying how far Jace's fans will go in their fantasies. Also, while I may consider having children someday, I don't need to see what a never-possible child with my eyes and Jace's cheekbones would have looked like.

"Oh. Oh! I saw some of those. A lot of people don't know how to use simple photo editing software. I could make better fake baby pictures." His eyes go distant, and he starts nodding to himself, already lost in the imaginary manipulations he's considering. Isn't he the one who always brags about being a photographer so focused on crafting the image and managing the lighting such that he doesn't need to do any post-shoot editing? Based on the way he talks about his skills, I would assume he has zero experience with any photo software.

"Not the point. You have to actually tell me about your apartment if you want me to know it exists."

"Sorry, I just assumed you'd seen my posts, and I was a little hurt you never congratulated me. Why don't you come over tomorrow night? I'll make dinner and give you the grand tour. Or rather, the not-so-grand tour. It's a studio."

"Only if you also make dessert."

Now his dimple appears. "Cassidy. I *always* make dessert."

If I were to take a moment to imagine what Tanner's new apartment would look like, I would picture one of those old warehouses that developers are converting into trendy artists' co-ops. High ceilings, concrete floors, splatterings of paint everywhere, artsy hipsters wandering around aimlessly. But no, he's renting a place in a luxury high rise near the Salt River. The building is glossy and modern, and Tanner's van is an eyesore in a parking lot full of newer, sleeker vehicles. And those are the ones who aren't paying extra for the underground garage. I bet the cars down there look like part of Powell's collection.

However, Tanner is still Tanner, despite the trappings of luxury. When I knock on his door, he answers, barefoot, wearing his usual faded jeans and T-shirt, with a dishtowel draped over his shoulder.

"What's with the fancy digs?" I ask as I walk past him into his apartment. The interior is as sleek and modern as the exterior, with hardwood floors, shiny white kitchen cabinets, and chrome accessories. The furniture doesn't quite fit in—a comfortable dark blue couch, a chipped coffee table, and a massive table in the corner covered in what looks like framing supplies.

"Trying to impress a girl."

"Did it work?" I can't imagine he did all of this in ten days just for Aurora. She'd prefer the warehouse style that I expected Tanner to have.

"I don't know yet." He waggles those caterpillars he calls eyebrows at me, and that's when I realize he's teasing me.

"Very funny. Maybe I don't want to give you these."

He looks down at my hands and his eyes widen. I shove the bag containing two bottles of wine at him.

"You didn't need to bring anything," he says, but he pulls one out to read the label anyway.

"One bottle is for dinner, because it's rude to show up empty-handed. The other is a bonus." I stole them from Powell's collection, purloining the bottles from the cases he acquired when he was showing off for the sommelier at an auction house a few years ago. "And these are your housewarming gifts." I try to offer the other bag to him, but he isn't moving.

"Housewarming gifts?"

I don't know why he's being so hesitant. I mean, Tanner can be a strange guy sometimes, but he's acting like he's never seen a gift bag before. Maybe he has a tissue paper phobia.

"Do you want to open it first, or give me the tour?" I could stand in the center and spin in a circle, and that would cover it. But I'd prefer an official tour, mostly because I want to know more about the art on his walls, and where this furniture came from.

"Tour," he decides. But the tour merely consists of him waving his arm around. "Kitchen, living area, balcony, bathroom is through the door over there." That's the extent of it. I notice he left off the sleeping area, as if I can't see his bed behind a three-panel bamboo room divider screen.

"Wow, thanks. You should work at a museum." I plop myself down on his couch and set the gift bag on the coffee table, careful to avoid the plates and silverware—I guess this is where we're eating. "Where's this couch from? This wasn't in your van, was it?"

He gives me the strangest look. "It was in my storage unit."

"You had a storage unit?"

"Yes." He says it slowly, as though he's speaking to an idiot. "That's where I store my stuff."

"I thought you kept everything in your van."

"I have . . . wow, you really thought I was poor, didn't you?"

"No, I thought you were a minimalist. There's a difference." I never once judged him for living in a van. That would be hypocritical of me since my mom and I lived in a station wagon after my dad died.

Rather than joining me and opening his presents, he heads over to the kitchen—about four feet away—to fetch a corkscrew and two glasses. I wonder what he was like as a child on Christmas morning. Did he sleep in and then leisurely meander his way to the tree, maybe having breakfast first?

When he finally ambles his way over to the couch, I nudge the gift bag towards him. "Do you need instructions? Reach your hand in the bag."

"Sorry, this feels weird. Nobody ever gives me gifts." Tanner is reacting as if I'm offering him a live rattlesnake. Or a bunch of spiders—he's terrified of those.

"Not even for Christmas or your birthday?"

"Last Christmas I was in the middle of my divorce, and prior to that, my ex-wife was the only one who ever got me anything. I told you, I'm not close with my family."

My heart breaks for him. I don't know what I'd do without my family. My stepfather is my mentor and my guide. My mom is my rock. And Powell? He's not only my brother, but my best friend, and my roommate. And my employer. And the jerk who keeps dragging me out to singles events, so maybe I do know what I'd do without *him*.

"Well, in the time I've known you, you haven't had a birthday. Believe me, I go all out."

"Yes, I have." He uncorks the wine instead of touching the gift and starts pouring.

"What? When? You never told me!" Hopefully it was around the time we met, before we became friends. Otherwise, I'm hurt he never mentioned it. I may not be able to bake, but I can *buy* some amazing birthday cakes.

"I spent my twenty-ninth birthday in federal prison, thanks to you."

That's not a funny joke.

Wait, his dimple isn't showing. Is he serious? Oh, no, that makes me feel terribly guilty, since it was possibly kind of my fault he was in there, since I was sort of the one who told the FBI he was a crazed bomber trying to blow up a concert. In my defense, the evidence against him was . . . well, circumstantial at best. I'm an awful person.

"Tanner! Your birthday was the day of the concert?" He should have mentioned something earlier, like maybe when I gave him the tickets. That would have been an appropriate time to bring up his birthday. Then we would have celebrated before he was hauled out in handcuffs.

"Day after. I spent all of it freaking out and wondering if I was going to prison for life. So . . . it wasn't the most fun day ever." That's an understatement. The poor guy wasn't released until hours after Powell and I were attacked by the real killers. The FBI kept him locked up because they still had to make sure he wasn't a co-conspirator.

"Why didn't you tell me? Even slightly late. At a minimum I'd have gotten you a delicious cake and had a very famous superstar sing to you." And apologized sooner for the whole arrest fiasco.

"Just what I've always wanted, a birthday serenade from a male sex symbol. Thanks, but I don't celebrate anyway."

"Fine. No birthdays. You can't complain about a housewarming gift though." I nudge it toward him, and he reluctantly reaches into the bag, bursting into laughter when he pulls out a fire extinguisher.

"Seriously?"

"In case your house gets too warm. Laugh all you want, but someday it might come in handy." My stepfather used to work in real estate development, and the housewarming baskets he would send to new home or condo owners always included a fire extinguisher. It's the one thing nobody thinks about until it's too late, he says. And since Hank is usually right about these kinds of things, and I don't want Tanner to burn to death, I went with that.

Next, he discovers the scented candle and laughs again. "I get it. You bought me a candle but think I'm not responsible enough to use it properly."

"Yes. That about sums it up." Also, the candle smells like cinnamon, so it reminded me of him. Oh, that reminds me, while I'm here, I should raid his bathroom, sneak a peek at his cologne, find out the brand. If it is cologne. It could be his natural aroma.

"And . . ." he reaches in again for the final item. "A phone case? That doesn't match your theme here. Unless this is likely to spontaneously combust."

"Consider that one a belated birthday gift. It's waterproof, shatterproof, and would probably survive an atomic bomb, so I think it's not flammable. Mike recommended this case awhile back, and I ordered one for you. The package came last week; I've just been waiting for the chance to give it to you." Mike Ochoa is Powell's security expert, so I trust his judgement. And I've heard Tanner's worries about sweating through his current phone case, though it's possible he intended that to be a hyperbolic complaint about our summer weather.

Tanner stares at the durable case, not saying a word. The silence is making me uncomfortable.

"Cass," he eventually says, "I don't know what to say. This is awesome, I've seen these advertised, but this is too much, you shouldn't spend this much on me."

"You can make another rich person joke if you like. Besides, you use your phone to take pictures at my gym, so technically this is equipment for work. I can even have my accountant write it off."

"Of course. That's how everything is with you, isn't it? Never any emotions, always business." He continues turning the case over in his hands.

"Why are you suddenly being nasty? No wonder nobody buys you presents; you just insult them afterwards." I'm tempted to take all the gifts back. Why give him something special if what is intended as a kind gesture just triggers his snarky side?

He stares at me silently for a moment, green eyes unreadable. And then he apologizes. I never would have expected that.

"I'm sorry I snapped at you, Cass. I sometimes don't know what to say . . . I never know where I stand with you. Am I an employee? A friend? An annoying guy you call when you need a favor?"

"Can't you be all three?"

"Can't I be more?" he responds, and I feel it again, this crackle of electricity in the air between us. It manifests sometimes and makes me nervous. Fortunately, the shrill beep of the kitchen timer interrupts before he can expand on his question, and before I am required to answer. He knows we can't be more. It's impossible. He's a commitment-oriented paparazzo, and I'm a commitment-phobic anti-paparazzo who would break his heart. And then we wouldn't be able to be friends anymore, and that would break my heart.

"Vegetarian lasagna," he calls, as he rushes to pull the gloriously bubbling cheesy dish from the oven. I want to grab a fork and dive in. "I hope you don't mind eating on the floor. My table is occupied right now."

Wearing a dress is not ideal for kneeling next to a coffee table, but I manage. As Tanner carries over two bowls of salad for a starter course, he explains his other table is a mess because he's working on framing some pieces for an upcoming gallery show. I did know about the show, because I *do* follow him online, just not when I'm being buried under a mountain of tags. His career is taking off, something he partially attributes to me, or so he says. I suppose I can claim some credit, since I did introduce him to a world-famous supermodel with over a hundred million followers, and she sometimes mentions him in her posts.

"Are you taking Aurora to opening night?" I ask. He hasn't mentioned her yet, and I'd like to find out where things stand with them. Not that I care, or it's any of my business. I'm merely curious about LoveMatch's success rate, that's all.

"Would you stop bringing her up? Our date was awful. And it wasn't even a date, it was me drinking hot coffee as fast as I could and looking for an escape while she told me all about how wonderful she is as an *artiste*."

"Did she offer to paint you again?"

"No, but she offered to graciously allow me to photograph her work to share with my followers. It all seemed more like a business transaction for her, when she wasn't droning on about herself. I think her interest in me was entirely related to the size of my SwiftaPic account."

"I'm sure there was something else," I assure him. He was an invitee to the event, so there was a match waiting for him, and who better than Arizona's self-identified most successful artist?

"She's seeking a collaborator to put her name out there more. That's all. Also, for your information, she's not as successful as she pretends to be. She's a trust fund kid whose daddy buys all her pieces at highly inflated prices."

"Really? Scandalous!" And that explains how she affords the millionaires' club.

"Anyway, you've had a failed LoveMatch date too. Or was it? You never told me anything and I didn't want to bring it up, in case . . ."

"In case what, I had secretly eloped? My coffee date was interesting. Actually, now that you're a member of the singles network, maybe I should fill you in." Jackson said not to tell Powell; he never mentioned not cluing in a different potential victim. Not that Tanner is wealthy enough to be targeted, but still. A warning should be given.

As we consume the wondrously cheesy goodness of the lasagna, I tell him about Jackson's theories, and my own later fruitless research. Many dead grooms on honeymoons, few explicit LoveMatch connections.

"Have you checked social media?" Tanner asks, because as a SwiftaPic obsessive (yes, the lasagna and the salads have already been featured on his story tonight), he immediately jumps to that sort of thing.

"To look for the dead guys' pictures on LoveMatch's Swifta feed? The non-disclosure works both ways."

"Right, but you can see if any of the deceased followed or liked LoveMatch anywhere. A lot of profiles get memorialized, but some families keep them active, so we'd be able to view their likes still. Email me a list of names, and I'll look into them later."

I'm glad I brought Tanner into the conspiracy fold. He's just as addicted to Crime TV as I am, so I should have thought to tell him sooner. At the very least, even if nothing is going on, and Jackson is wrong, we can amuse ourselves with theories and investigations.

After dinner, I help Tanner clear the dishes. And then he opens the fridge and brings out the real reason I'm here: dessert. For tonight's special treat, he's made chocolate mousse. I perch on the counter, and he stands next to me while we savor it.

The mousse is light and fluffy and sweet, the perfect end to our meal. "I had no idea you could make this. This is what you should have made when I couldn't eat solid foods." While my broken cheek was healing, he made me lots of pudding and a few sorbets. This would have been a tasty addition to the soft foods menu.

"This is my first attempt. I'm happy you like it. But you have a little…" he indicates a spot on my lip. I start to reach up to wipe it away, but he intercepts my fingers. When his hand touches mine, I feel that terrifying surge of energy between us. It always scares me, forces a retreat. This time I don't move.

His face is getting closer, and his eyes flick back and forth between my eyes and lips. It's like he's waiting—expecting—me to push him away, but I don't. There's something inevitable about this moment. The kiss is soft, hesitant, and far too short.

He draws back to rest his forehead against mine. "You have no idea how long I've been wanting to do that."

"How long have I had mousse on my face?"

"Why do you have to turn this into a joke, Cassidy?"

He's so intent his eyes are almost glowing, and I don't know what else to do, so I fumble for my dessert dish, take a swipe of chocolate with my finger, and dab it on my lips. "You missed a spot."

Tanner is talented. I learned that months ago when he angrily kissed me outside a restaurant. And I'm being reminded again now, as he wraps his arms around my waist and pulls me from the counter. He starts off aggressive, as though he's been holding back for too long, and now that he has the chance, he's going to take it. And I … well, while I wouldn't say I've been holding back, I have watched his hands and forearms as he kneads dough, and I have wondered what it might feel like to have those strong hands on my body. So, I'm responding well to his ministrations.

But we can't do this, can we? Even while my body is engaged, while my hands are exploring, while I'm gasping with pleasure from the way he's nibbling on my neck, a small corner of my mind is screaming at me. *We can't do this; we have to stop. What happens to our friendship, what happens to us if I let this move forward?*

I'm ignoring that voice in favor of listening to my body, to my cravings, of allowing myself to give in, for once, to let myself think about my needs, my own urgent needs.

We're stumbling toward the bed now, Tanner propelling me or me dragging him, I can't tell which. All I know is his shirt is off, and I am so grateful that I gave him that gym membership because it sure is benefitting both of us right now.

No, no, this is wrong. It's so wrong. It has to end, no matter how good it feels. He's tugging at the straps on my dress, about to tear the stitches when he can't slide them over my shoulders.

No, for real this has to end. We're too close to the point of no return. I force the words out: "The zipper is on the side."

Oops. That's not what I meant to say. I meant to say *pardon me, sir, but perhaps this entanglement is going too far, and I must flee.* But no, instead, I accidentally gave him instructions, and he follows them, and my dress is on the floor, and we are falling onto his bed together.

Why do things that are wrong feel so good?

Why do I want this so badly? Why can't I get myself under control?

He's on top of me, his weight pressing me into the mattress as his aggressive hands travel and . . . no. I have to put a stop to this.

This is going to change too much.

"Tanner," I finally regain control over my vocal cords.

"Yeah?" He momentarily pauses his oral explorations and looks at me with those burning eyes, and every inch of skin on my body protests what I'm about to say.

"We have to stop."

He pulls back, bracing himself on his forearms. "What's wrong? I have condoms in the nightstand."

"No, Tanner, we can't do this. It's going to make things too weird."

"Seriously?" He doesn't move. His chest may be off me, but his lower half isn't, and he's showing no inclination to change that. I never figured he'd be one of those guys who doesn't take no for an answer, who thinks a woman saying stop actually means *hey, let's negotiate.*

"Yes, seriously. We can't do this."

"You mean that?"

He still doesn't move, and now I know the kind of person he really is. Luckily, I've been taking self-defense classes after my last attack, so I'm pretty sure I can take him in a fight. But I'm going to give him one last chance.

"I do mean that. Get off of me. Now."

"Then unwrap your legs," he snaps, and that's when I discover that while I may have control of my mouth, I don't have complete control of my body, and my legs are still wrapped around his waist, holding him against me. I unhook my ankles and lower my legs, and he practically throws himself sideways.

We're both staring at the ceiling, trying to calm our breathing. My skin is too sensitive, too tingly, like every cell has been stretched too tight. I'm going to have beard burn all over my torso, reminding me of this mistake.

"I should have known you'd be back," he says, in a voice that somehow manages to convey frustration and defeat.

"What's that supposed to mean?"

He won't even turn and look at me. "You have two sides Cass. Part of you is warm and fun and open, and we get along so well. And then there's . . . well, the cold version. You shut me out. You always do this. We start to connect, and you slam up this wall of ice."

"See? I said this would make things weird, and you proved me right within two seconds. Thanks, jerk." I'm done with this. I don't need to listen to his insults and his assessment of my character. I need to find the rest of my clothing and get the heck out of here.

"I don't know why you think *I'm* making things weird, when this is obviously what you came over for in the first place."

"No, I came over for dinner. We've had plenty of dinners that didn't end with you on top of me." I hurriedly step into my discarded outfit and yank up the zipper.

"Cassidy, be honest, for once. You brought wine, you shaved your legs, you're wearing a matching set . . ." He gestures at my bra and panties, now re-covered by fabric that suddenly feels too thin. "The only reason women do that is if they're expecting someone to see it."

Oh, now he's the expert on all of womankind?

"It's tradition to bring wine to dinner, and I'm a courteous guest. I didn't shave; I had laser hair removal years ago. And my undergarment choices have nothing to do with you, or any man for that matter. Tanner, I dress the way I do because I like it, I feel pretty, and I *always* wear a matching set." By the end of the sentence, I'm yelling. How does he manage to make me so angry?

"You . . . why would you tell me that?" He covers his face with his pillow and lets out a muffled groan. "Just go. I can't deal with this right now."

I knew this kind of thing would happen. This is why I don't get involved with anyone. Tanner was my friend, then he tried to seduce me, and when he failed, he kicked me out. That tells me there was only one thing he's been after this whole time. Well, maybe two since he also uses me for his career.

I think I hate him.

# CHAPTER EIGHT

Powell's dates have all been chaperoned, and they've all taken place at the LoveMatch office, in the creepy LoveMatch suite. It's apparently what they use when they have famous people to protect, celebrities who can't make public appearances with significant others until they establish a serious relationship and clear it with their publicist. According to him, the suite is like a fancy hotel room, complete with bed—that he's not allowed to use yet—and an eating area catered by a local chef.

He's already on date three with Lexa, and five with Emily, a number he repeatedly tells me, as he gleefully looks forward to rushing through number six and arriving at the special touching-permitted one after that. Personally, I think he should decide between them before taking that next step. I don't think whoever wins the ring is going to appreciate him sexually auditioning his other potential fiancée. But I keep my mouth shut. Beyond making sure there are condoms and non-disclosure agreements available on his tours, I have no desire to glean any more knowledge of his sex life.

I am happy he's making progress—with the tour starting soon, I don't want him distracted by dating multiple women. He needs to pick a favorite by the time we hit the road. Or sooner. Like, now would be good, before he forces me to more matchmaking events.

Meanwhile, I'm going to focus on my own work. I'm currently sitting at my desk, going line by line through the riders for his upcoming tour. The labor is tedious, but necessary. Except how can I focus, when my brother—who has his own prep to do—barges into my room?

"You busy?" Powell asks, not bothering to knock. He strolls in like he owns the place—which, in fairness, he does—and makes himself comfortable on my reading chair.

"No, Powell, not at all. I'm certainly not changing the tour riders to demand that all venues set up a spa room for any members of your entourage that share your last name."

"You could do that. I don't mind. Hey, did you make sure there's a professional piano tuner available for all the acoustic shows? Traveling is hard on my baby."

He seriously has no faith in my organizational abilities. "No, I'm going to save the record company some money and do it myself. I just use wire cutters and clip the strings that sound out of pitch, right?"

Powell snorts out a laugh. I'm not actually allowed to touch any of his instruments on the tour. Nobody is, besides him, the head sound tech, and the instrument handler whose sole job is to make sure every guitar is perfectly tuned and ready at all times.

"Can you also add . . . wait, what's that?" He unsprawls from my chair to examine an object on my shelf. Oh, no. It's that damn stuffed duck. I should have thrown it away.

"It's nothing."

"Hmmmm." He looks back and forth from me to the duck, then does a scan of my bedroom looking for any other additions. My room is my Zen sanctuary, all light wood and white walls. As a jerkwad photographer once described it, it looks like a peaceful spa, beautiful, calm, and devoid of all personality. The stupid duck stands out, perched next to my childhood stuffed chickadee, the only personal objects in sight.

"It's nothing," I repeat through gritted teeth, before elbowing him away from my shelf, grabbing the toy, and tossing it into my less-than-Zen messy closet.

"It looked like one of those carnival prizes," Powell says, watching the trajectory of the bird as it lands in a pile of clothes, and I slam the door shut.

"Was there something you needed? I'm working."

He thinks for a moment. "Oh, yeah, I did come in here for a reason. Can you call Tanner?"

"What do you need a picture of?"

"Nothing. We're going out with Lexa tonight, and it's less awkward if you bring someone, too. Otherwise, I'm the weirdo who brought my little sister on a date."

"*We're* going out with Lexa? As in, me too? Don't you think you should clear these things first?" I'd like to inform him that he's not the boss of me, but he technically is. Though dating someone for his benefit seems slightly outside the scope of my duties.

"I put it on the calendar this morning. Aren't you the one who says I'm supposed to use that?" Oh, of all the times he remembers he has a documented schedule to follow.

"Yes, but so *you* stop forgetting *your* obligations. Not so you can impose obligations on *me*. I'm in charge of the calendar." And I should remove his editorial access.

"Just call Tanner," he says, as though I'm going to jump to obey. Which I would, if this were related to something important, like Powell finishing looking over the liner notes for his new album—the ones he was scheduled to submit two days ago. Or if this were in regard to a publicity event. But I'm not calling Tanner for any kind of social occasion, especially after what happened last time I saw him, a night which I will never disclose to my brother, or anyone else for that matter.

"Actually, I have someone else in mind."

Jackson was eager to accompany me to dinner with Powell and Lexa. When I called, he started to tell me he had important plans already, but then I uttered the magic words, "he met her at a LoveMatch event." I feel secure with a secret agent there, someone who can investigate Lexa and ascertain her propensity to murdering husbands.

Besides, we are meeting at the LoveMatch offices, another bonus for Jackson's investigation. He may try to sneak off and access some computer files. Perhaps I should dress all in black, so I can join him on his illicit explorations. Though that's probably a bad idea. I assume there are security cameras everywhere.

We cruise up to the building in the Audi. I had mentioned to Powell that Jackson also drove one, so of course he has to show off. And how fortunate we arrive at approximately the same time, so the men can examine each other's vehicles, admire each other's leather seats, and make mildly passive aggressive remarks about the merest hint of scuff marks on the shiny exteriors. *Sigh.*

Tabitha—I can't bring myself to call her Tabby—welcomes us and waits patiently for the peacocks to cease their preening. When they've established that both models have their perks, but yes, Powell's has a better sound system, they are finally ready to come into the air-conditioned building and get this over with.

This is my first time experiencing the LoveMatch dating suite. Much like everything else I've encountered here, the room is an example of how a young girl with a pink obsession might decorate. One end is dominated by the largest, laciest king-sized canopy bed I've ever seen. While I acknowledge this is probably no different than a hotel, in that sheets are changed between guests, I still find this set-up to be a little creepy. Why couldn't they let us eat in the conference room? But no, we'll be eating in the dining area of the suite, in full view of the ostentatious bed, where the tablecloth is unexpectedly white. The napkins though, are the same rose color as the curtains, the bedspread, and the flowers on the gaudy old-fashioned wallpaper. Even the gold edged charger plates have a pinkish cast.

We have to wait for Lexa, so when Tabitha goes to check on what's delaying her, the first thing Jackson does is look under all the plates. Then he starts moving the LED candles and shaking them gently. Powell watches in amusement but doesn't say a word. Jackson's behavior, while unusual, is not the strangest thing he's ever seen. He spends enough time with eccentric celebrities that he's willing to ignore almost any weird behavior, as long as it doesn't harm anybody. I'm sure he'll ask me to explain later, though.

Just as Jackson gets down on his knees to start checking the bottoms of the chairs, Tabitha pops back in.

"Do you know the craftsman?" Jackson asks, continuing to examine his chair as though it's the most normal thing to do. "I think my aunt would like these."

"I can find that out for you," she answers cheerfully, but she's also looking at him like he's an idiot. This furniture is mass produced and likely came straight from a restaurant supply store. "Lexa is running late, but Isaac will be in shortly to offer you drinks." Then she makes meaningful eye contact and crooks her finger in a summoning gesture at me. I consider ignoring her, but unfortunately, Powell caught the movement.

"Girl talk time," he says brightly, and when I glare at him, he laughs. "Actually, you're probably in trouble for something. That's the same expression Tabby had when I asked Emily for her phone number before I was contractually allowed."

As it turns out, yes, I am in trouble. Apparently, since Jackson was not a successful match, and since I failed to ask Lillian's permission to bring him tonight, I violated the terms of my contract, but sadly not in a way to trigger an immediate termination clause.

"He's not technically a date," I protest. "I'm not interested in him that way."

"Then why invite him? You should have called Lillian, and we would have provided a date for you." She whips out a phone as if she's about to start dialing numbers and lining up other possibilities for me right now. *Hello, we have a dating emergency. Report to the LoveMatch offices immediately! Wear a tie!*

"I thought I was supposed to see them first and develop an attraction."

"That's the way we do it when people are open to the process."

Ouch, that was judgmental. Accurate, but judgmental.

"I'll ask for an appropriate match to be provided next time," I promise, because I'm confident there won't be a next time. Powell's next date with Emily is already scheduled for this weekend, and it's at our house. The L'Amour family can't control what I do at my own house. I think. I'll need to review that damn contract.

"If things aren't working out with Lillian, you can always transfer to my caseload. Powell takes up a good bit of my attention, but I'm happy to handle you as well," she offers, with a smile I can only interpret as predatory. And there we have it—her real reason for talking to me. These sisters are devious in their competition. First Lillian hunts down the perfect pretty piano teacher, and now Tabitha is trying to steal me.

While I was being lectured by Tabitha, Lexa arrived, so dinner is ready. I follow Isaac back into the room as he is bringing in a tray containing the first course. The omnivores at the table receive a seared scallop on a tiny bed of delicate greens. I am given an enormous bowl of garden salad, with at least a dozen cherry tomatoes coated in a heavy creamy dressing perched precariously on top.

"Is this meant to be for everybody?" I ask, searching for more reasonably sized bowls to serve it up.

"This is what the chef made," Isaac either misunderstands my question or is deliberately ignoring it. Maybe he's covering up his embarrassment for forgetting the salad dishes and serving utensils.

Powell snickers and tells me to enjoy my salad. And of course, the second I try, a dressing covered tomato rolls off the pile and into my lap, somehow missing my napkin. Great, now I'm wearing food. This does not bode well for the rest of the evening.

"I'll come with you," Lexa bounces to her feet when I get up to go clean myself. "Ladies always go to the restroom in twos, don't they?"

Ugh.

And double ugh, because the bathroom attached to the 'dating suite' is also a pink and gold nightmare. It's huge, pastel, and horrifying. My main problem is with the central feature of the room, a tile pedestal two steps high with a heart shaped bathtub. The faucets and claw feet are gold, but the tub itself is gleaming pink porcelain. Is this supposed to be romantic? Does my brother plan on using it? Ew.

"Wow!" Lexa exclaims and immediately climbs in for a selfie. Maybe she'd be a better match with Tanner. He'd probably do the exact same thing, and gleefully post it: #tubfortwo #heartbath #IamajerkandIusefoodtoseducepeople. Okay, maybe he wouldn't publicly use that last one.

I'm almost hesitant to use the towels in here. Someone crocheted gold lace on the edges of all of them. They're the kind of decorative towels people put in guest bathrooms that aren't meant for actual mundane uses, such as drying one's hands. Same as these little heart shaped soaps in a dish on the thankfully not heart-shaped sink.

"Can I help at all?" Lexa asks, as I carefully dab water on my dress. I'm sure the stains will come out at the dry cleaner, but I don't want to smell like creamy garlic all night.

"It'll be fine." It's not like I'm the one trying to impress anyone tonight.

"So . . . your date is cute," she says, bringing us into the gossipy portion of our shared bathroom trip.

"We're just friends," I reply. "How are things going with Powell?"

"Great!" she chirps. "He's wonderful! He's soooo funny!"

Alarm bells are going off in my head. Powell is most certainly not funny. That's not an adjective anyone has ever used to describe him. It's not that he doesn't possess a sense of humor; he does get jokes. But he doesn't make them. He's dreamy and lazy, with bursts of intensity, but he's not *funny*.

"Yes, he's hilarious," I lie. "Do you see yourself getting serious with him?" And maybe murdering him? Perhaps while honeymooning together, a diamond encrusted ring weighing down your finger?

"Of course! We'll travel the world, explore everything! There are so many things I want to do!" Her face is glowing with expectation and joy.

"Will you take the kids with you?"

"What kids?"

"Don't you want to have children?" Like, didn't my brother tell you his number one priority? Ticking biological clock and all?

"Someday, sure. But we're young. I want to backpack South America, and road trip through Australia, and maybe take a stab at climbing Mount Everest first. Kids can wait."

And there she reveals herself . . . she's not looking for a husband, she's looking for a funder. She's after Powell's money. I didn't think it'd be this easy to uncover her true motives. Now to find out if she wants that money free and clear of Powell.

Lexa and I return to find Jackson and Powell immersed in a discussion about horsepower, engines, and whether German cars hold their value better than American ones. My eyes are glazing over, but Lexa is fascinated. Her fascination increases when Jackson makes an offhand comment about not caring how much a limited-edition Bugatti costs, as long as the model is exclusive and red. Because, yes, he's considering picking one up, but he's not fully committed yet.

Her eyes perform a reassessment of my dining companion. Designer clothing, check. Polished shoes straight from an Italian showroom, check. Sleeves casually rolled up to reveal an Audemars Piguet on his wrist, check. I don't know how a secret agent affords one of those, unless it's a fake.

"So, Jackson," she twists in her chair to better face him. "You haven't told me, what is it you do exactly?"

"A little of this, a little of that," he says evasively. Then he shrugs and gives his cover story. "I used to be in tech; now I'm an investor."

"And that entails?" she purrs. Yes, she did, she purred. She is flagrantly flirting with Jackson in front of Powell. She's now trailing Emily in the race for his heart, at least as far as I'm concerned.

"I take small amounts of money and turn it into a lot of money." Spoken like a true undercover agent who doesn't actually know what his character does.

"Hey, me too! So does Cass!" Powell pipes up. He's not quite accurate. We have people to do that for us.

"You convert music into money," I correct him. And he should be converting a lot more soon, when the new album drops.

"Then you take the money and convert it into . . ." Lexa prompts. Are her pupils shaped like dollar signs?

"Mostly investments and charities. I'm not a big spender." My brother shrugs modestly, pretending to be just a regular guy with regular guy spending habits.

I turn my snort into a cough. He only claims he isn't a big spender because he doesn't keep track. He decides what he wants, I charge it to his black card, and the bills all go to his accountant. Though also, a ton of free stuff magically appears on our doorstep, like designer clothes, shoes, bags, jewelry. Anything SwiftaPic friendly that needs a celebrity endorsement. Maybe Powell considers his acceptance of free gifts as a sign of inherent frugality.

"And you?" Lexa asks breathily, turning her focus to Millionaire Bachelor #2.

"I don't know," Jackson replies, because his undercover persona is unimaginative. "I'd like to do some traveling someday when I finish taking care of some other things. Maybe pick up a beach house in Malibu for when I'm not off having adventures."

Did he tailor that to Lexa? Was there a listening device in the bathroom broadcasting our conversation out here? Or is he just that good at reading people? Lexa's brain is almost audibly whirring as she runs calculations in her head right now.

Isaac comes to clear our salad plates and expresses immediate concern that I've barely made a dent in mine. He leans over to whisper to me that I'm allowed to keep eating; he can delay the main if I want to finish.

But before he has the chance to force feed me a mound of lettuce, the chef himself arrives. He's carrying a carefully balanced tray to serve us the entrée.

I've been a vegetarian for ten years, so I'm used to receiving less appetizing foods at functions. Uninteresting pasta thrown together by a sous chef as an afterthought is standard fare at weddings and formal events. So, I'm not surprised when the chef places three beautifully plated fish dishes in front of my dining companions, and I receive a bowl of broccoli fettuccine alfredo. But I am surprised—and horrified—by the volume of this thing. Everyone else has a reasonable amount of food, but I have a massive dish the size of my head, and it is filled to the brim. If I couldn't eat the salad, I sure can't choke down all this pasta.

We all express our gratitude for the meal, and Powell kindly tastes his cilantro lime tilapia and declares the first bite 'perfection,' but the instant Isaac and the chef leave, I am met with three incredulous stares.

"Wow, that's a lot of food," Jackson comments.

"Did you . . . did you order that?" Lexa asks.

Powell tries hard not to laugh but fails. "I dare you to eat all of it. Every bite. I dare you, Cass."

"I couldn't eat this much in a week! You guys want some?"

Jackson slides his plate away when I try to scoop pasta onto it. "Sorry, lactose intolerant."

"Too many carbs. Fettuccini isn't on my approved list," Powell puts his hands protectively over his own plate. He's such a hypocrite. He messily devoured a slab of chocolate cake last night and did not tell his nutritionist about it. Maybe I will.

"Lexa?" I point to the bowl enticingly.

"You're on your own," she replies. "Maybe you can ask for a to-go box. Or several. How many people did you RSVP for, Powell?" She places a hand on his forearm, caressing the skin gently, as though she hadn't been blatantly flirting with another man in front of him.

"Powell." I've decided on a tactic to expose Lexa for what she is. "Check it out, this bowl is big enough to use as a baby bathtub." I span the porcelain with my hands and tilt it toward him—without spilling—to demonstrate the volume.

His eyes light up. "Did you see that picture of Sonit? The one with his hair spiked up?" The image in question, of chubby little Sonit covered in bubbles with shampoo-styled hair, arrived this morning. Powell had been literally cooing over it.

"Who is Sonit?" Lexa asks politely, still stroking Powell's arm instead of, I don't know, eating her meal.

"Mason's baby. He's adorable," Powell produces his phone and starts flipping through the gallery to show her. Mason and his Bollywood star wife are keeping his child's image out of the press, with the exception of a few limited professional pictures. But that doesn't stop Mason from assailing his former bandmates and me with daily updates.

Lexa is trying to be polite, but her eyes are wandering. Powell saved an entire album on his phone, and he expects her to look at every single picture and exclaim with delight, and she does . . . not.

"You don't like babies?" he asks when he picks up on her disinterest.

"They're fine. I mean, that one's cute and all," she equivocates.

"Are you interested in having children?" His posture changes. He's leaning away from her, and he's become serious.

"Someday, sure," she says, just as flippantly as she had in the bathroom. "But not any time soon. I'm young, I want to travel. Don't you want to travel with me?"

"I'm going on tour in November."

"Right, but I want to see the world. Not just concert venues around the United States." Lexa is speaking as though she's been invited on the tour. I suppose if Powell gets serious about her in the next couple of months, she will be. However, her chances of receiving that invite are slipping through her non-maternal fingers.

"I'm doing another international tour sometime; it isn't booked yet. A *real* world tour, not just the English-speaking countries. But touring the US is fun, right Cass? Most of the shows are sold out." That last line is directed at Jackson. Powell's not stupid. He sees the way Lexa's actions are calculated to keep the attention of both men.

"Almost all of them are," I confirm. I've been getting regular updates from the tour manager, and I follow ticket scalping sites. Powell is deviating from his normal tour by adding in some small-scale acoustic shows. We held some of those seats back for fan club member giveaways, but the remaining tickets sold out in minutes, and I've seen them going online for ten times the face value.

"Right, but afterwards. You'll need a break after all that performing. Wouldn't it be fun to have some adventures? We could go backpacking but stay in resorts rather than hostels. That'd be so exciting, don't you think?" Lexa's greed shines from her face. She's misread my brother so badly.

Powell looks at me and raises his eyebrows, so I answer for him, "You know Powell is recognizable, right? A trip like that would require a whole team of bodyguards shadowing you constantly." Also, I can't imagine him wanting to travel that way. We've gone on family vacations where we've done the touristy things like visiting Roman ruins, climbing all the stairs in the Eiffel Tower, and walking along the top of the Great Wall of China, but those were all Hank's ideas. Powell prefers pure relaxation. His ideal trip involves oceanside accommodations, snorkeling, playing guitar on a balcony overlooking the waves, and going to bed early, so he can take quiet walks on the beach at sunrise. That's another reason we get along so well; I am also a fan of beaches and opulent relaxation. Not so much the guitar on the balcony part—that's where I like to read while sipping fruity cocktails.

Lexa tosses her hair. "I don't mind an entourage." She primps, perhaps imagining herself running the photographer gauntlet, a cadre of servants trailing along behind carrying her steamer trunk, hatbox, and matching leather suitcases.

"You would need a nanny, too, wouldn't you?" I'm bringing the conversation back around to showing Powell why Lexa is a bad match. Besides just her gold-digging attributes, that is.

"Not for years. I'm too young to worry about kids now. Children would interfere with my dreams." Her hand is under the table, and I think she's sliding it up my brother's thigh—gross!—but the movement doesn't distract him from her words.

"You don't want kids soon?" He moves his leg from under her wandering hand and sits up straight, looking at her with disappointment. All potential interest has evaporated. Emily owes me one.

Although the date ended the moment we finished dessert—sadly, the one meal component that was not giant-sized for me—Powell doesn't arrive home until nearly midnight. I'm still awake, making notes on the invitation list for Powell's album launch party. Maybe I'm being petty, but I take pleasure in drawing a black line through Tanner's name.

"What took you so long?" I ask as he staggers into the living room, toes off his shoes, and collapses on the couch. He stayed behind after dinner, under orders to debrief with Tabitha. Jackson gave me a ride home, and the entire time we discussed whether Lexa was likely a gold digger *and* a murderer, or just a gold digger.

"Talking things out with Tabby," he explains, yawning. It's way past his bedtime. He tries to stick to a healthy sleeping routine, especially when he's preparing for a run of shows. "Did you know that after you two left, Lexa slipped Tabby a request card for coffee with Jackson? She was openly flirting with him right in front of me, and then she did that?"

"And you broke it off with her immediately?"

He sighs. "No, Tabby is going to handle it for me, more diplomatically than I would have. Lexa kissed me on the cheek and told me she couldn't wait for our next date. Can you believe her nerve?"

"What I can't believe is that she was a match for you."

"She wasn't."

"Obviously she wasn't, based on tonight, but didn't the so-called infallible algorithm put you two together?"

"Turns out, she lied. She must have overheard Tabby telling me I had nine matches and decided to make her move. All she saw was my fame and my wallet. And you should warn Jackson."

"I'm sure he can handle her." Also, I'm sure she'll be very disappointed when she finds out that he's not some super wealthy investor after all. I bet his real car is a beater, and he has to return the designer wardrobe to his agency and go back to wearing off the rack discount clothing. I'm basing that on how Agent Walters dresses, and assuming all spy agencies have similar pay scales.

"It doesn't really matter. I was leaning toward Emily anyway, and this just cemented it for me. Honestly, I think I might be falling for Emily. She's so sweet and caring, and we would make such beautiful babies."

"How much do you have to pay LoveMatch if you knock her up before getting engaged? Did they run fertility tests as part of your guarantee? Or does that cost extra?"

I'm lucky Powell's so tired. When he grabs a throw pillow and aims it at my head, he misses.

I should have been suspicious when my brother developed a sudden craving for a mid-morning croissant, which had to be from a particular French bakery over in Paradise Valley rather than the one five minutes from our house. He couldn't pick it up himself, no, not when he was finally planning to approve the liner notes. And he didn't want to pay a delivery service, not when his assistant—i.e., me—was available.

Yeah, that nonsense should have tipped me off, but it didn't, and so when I walk into the bakery and run into Tabitha, it takes a moment before I recognize that I've been set up.

"Oh, good, you came. I ordered you a"—she consults her phone—"café latte, easy on the milk, with a splash of hazelnut flavoring and absolutely no whipped cream. To be honest, I wasn't sure Powell would be able to talk you into meeting with me."

"It was more of a command." I'm not going to admit I was tricked into a croissant mission, one that I do not intend to fulfill. Don't lie about your cravings to me, buddy. I might buy *myself* a croissant and spite eat it, but I'm certainly not bringing one home with me. I join her at the table, and refrain from pulling a Jackson-style search for listening devices.

"Either way, I'm glad you're here. I'd like to keep this off the record though, so maybe don't mention this to Lillian."

"Are you trying to poach me?"

"I'm trying to help you."

A waitress brings over our drinks and a small assortment of pastries. Since there are vanilla financiers on the plate, I suppose I can be convinced to listen to her pitch. Honestly, I don't care who my matchmaker is; it doesn't affect my opinion of the process, nor does it inspire me to want to be matched.

"Alright, I'm listening. Explain to me why I should transfer to your caseload."

She laughs. "It's not about that, Cassidy. Your official matchmaker doesn't matter. We all have access to the same database. What matters is you opening yourself up to the opportunities we're offering. Powell is concerned that you aren't willing to try."

"Powell doesn't understand that just because he wants something doesn't mean everyone else does, too. He wants to get married, so he assumes I should want to as well."

"That's not why we're here." She reaches across the table and takes my hand, patting it as though consoling me. "Your brother worries about you. He wants you to be happy, and he's afraid you won't let yourself open up to others. You dedicate too much of your time to other people's happiness, at the expense of yourself."

"My job is to take care of him," I object. "And I do also take care of myself." Not to brag, but I'm in peak physical condition. I work out daily, I eat mostly healthy, and I get plenty of sleep. Plus, there's a day spa I visit every other week for some extra pampering.

"I lost my first love, too," Tabitha says. Wow. She is exactly like my brother. He's the king of non-sequiturs, making conversations often difficult and confusing. I guess she's the queen.

"Sorry to hear that." She's using Powell's annoying conversational techniques, so I'm going to have to wait until she gets to whatever point she plans to make. And I'm going to eat this financier while she does so. The little cake is delicious enough to make me amenable to sitting here for a few minutes. I'll listen until I finish it. And maybe while I have one more.

"I met him in college," she continues. "His name was Kent Clark."

"Is this a real story, or something you use to sell LoveMatch memberships?" I can't help but interrupt. If she's going to create fake stories, I'm going to give her a little advice about choosing realistic names for her characters.

She laughs, but with an edge of sadness. "His parents were comic book fans. Believe me, he was teased his entire life. When we married, he planned to take my last name."

"He wanted to be Kent L'Amour?"

"No, that's my stepmother's name. I do use it professionally at our business, but my real last name is Trent, which should give you enough of a clue as to how much he hated Clark. But anyway, like I was saying, we met at Stanford. When I moved to Tucson for my MBA at Eller, he decided not to come with me. He had just gotten his dream job, and we knew we could make our relationship work. I didn't mind. I'm a little like you in that regard. I need my own space."

My prediction for where this is going: the future Mr. Kent Trent cheated, she learned long distance relationships always fail, then she met her fiancé and life is magical and good and everyone needs to get married.

"One weekend," she continues, "he was planning to visit me. But I had a major presentation due, so I asked him to postpone his trip. One week wouldn't make a difference, right? Not when we had the rest of our lives together. Since he didn't come out to see me, he went hiking with some friends. They were down by the Tule River, when some children fell in. He managed to rescue two of the three. Unfortunately, he and the other child were swept away, and it took days to recover his body."

"Oh. Oh!" That's worse than my guess. That's tragic. Now I'm feeling a little bad about being so flippant with her.

"I know what you're going to say; I've heard it all. He was a real superman, what a hero, he would be proud to make the ultimate sacrifice in order to save lives. That's what everyone says. But me, I blamed myself. If he had flown to Arizona, he never would have been at the river. And he'd still be here today. But those two children wouldn't. So, I think you and I have a lot in common. I know about Jace. I know you're the one who called and asked him to take Powell's place on that helicopter."

"Powell told you?" Not that it's a huge secret, but my involvement in the matter is not gossip I necessarily want to have spread. I will never stop feeling guilty for making the call, though at the same time, I'll never stop feeling relieved that I inadvertently saved my brother from being blown up that day. Someday I should probably talk to a therapist about all these conflicting emotions. But my modus operandi is to smother it all, hide it away deep down inside, and that's what I do again. My emotional lockbox is bursting at the seams, but it won't break.

"He did. Powell told me you made that phone call and now you're letting it eat you up inside. You are not at fault for the loss of your great love, just as I'm not at fault for the loss of mine. We've both been wounded by our losses and the guilt that accompanies them. But we owe it to them to go on living. We owe it to Kent and to Jace to move on and find love and companionship with someone else."

"Which you've done."

"Yes, thanks to LoveMatch. I found Isaac using our system. He's a 94% match for me, which is as perfect as can be. We are solid on the mandatory elements, and so close on the optional ones. Plus, he's an absolute sweetheart." None of what she describes sounds like a romantic connection to me, but I suppose good-on-paper is enough to help her over the loss of Kent.

"Mandatory elements? I missed that in the contract."

"It's not in there. Pretend I didn't mention it; they're part of our algorithm. You can't have a successful long-term relationship if you don't agree on certain fundamental issues." She ticks them off on her fingers. "Money management, reproduction, division of labor, and empathy levels."

"You left off politics and religion."

"Believe it or not, those both fall under empathy levels. We look at those core issues, plus basic personality traits and preferences. I can't tell you too much more; it's confidential. Regardless, our system works. I can see it working for your brother, because he is open to the idea of finding someone. He's trying. You, not so much."

"In my defense—" I'm about to argue that I am unwillingly involved in this whole ordeal, and I am not a candidate to be matched with anybody.

"No." She holds up a hand in a throwback to the nineties 'talk to the hand' nonsense—a move incorporated into a stunningly cheesy Last Barons dance for their song *Ain't listening No More* —and cuts me off. "Cassidy, you have a choice here. Lillian and I, our job is to find suitable matches for our clients. My stepsister will find someone for you. He will be passive arm candy with low ambitions because that's what she's decided you need. You will end up dating him, if only to shut your brother up. And you will suffer through a boring bland relationship until at long last you decide to give up the charade and dump him, and then you will be stuck going through this whole thing all over again."

"I'm not at your guaranteed level. I'm pretty sure I can walk away at any time, boyfriend or no boyfriend." Pretty sure, but not absolutely sure. Why didn't I have an attorney look over that ten-page contract? Most of it was such flowery nonsense that I just skimmed the words. I should probably stop chastising Powell for not reading things thoroughly.

"You think you can. But it seems to me that once Powell fixates on something, he always gets his way." She's insightful and completely correct. Damn it.

"We're leaving for a tour soon." I'm grasping at straws here, because she's right, my brother will constantly harass me and may even bump my membership up a level for increased pressure. "I can't see myself starting a relationship when I'm about to be on the road for months."

"Oh? I didn't realize phones no longer existed." Tabitha crosses her arms. There's a small smile on her face—she knows she has me.

So maybe it's time for the truth. Or semi-truth.

"Tabitha, when Powell gets engaged, I will be withdrawing my LoveMatch membership. I am not interested in dating at this time." I try to soften it with a minor lie. "Jace has only been gone from this world for a few short months. No amount of pressure is going to speed up my mourning. My brother is doing what he thinks is best for me, and I appreciate it, but he's wrong."

Tabitha leans back in her chair, studying my face. She's smarter than she came across at our initial meeting. I thought Lillian was the cold-blooded one, but I suddenly feel like I've made an error in judgment.

She nods slowly. "I understand, and I will stop pressuring you. Lil won't; you're her ticket to inheriting the business. She knows it's supposed to go to me—I was the one who successfully opened the Chicago office while she failed in Miami. She will not back off of you. Also, I should remind you, you are obligated to a twelve-month membership. But we can put it on hold until you're ready."

"That's all I can ask for." It's not. I'm going to find a way to buy out my contract. For now, though, at least I've got one of the aggressive matchmakers off my back.

# CHAPTER NINE

We have a maid that tidies up twice a week, but apparently, that's not enough. Yesterday Powell had a team of people come in to deep clean the entire house, inside and outside. Why? Because Emily is coming over today for date number six, and he wants to impress her. Her lack of enthusiasm for his fame is really getting to him. His ego is wounded.

Right now, we're sitting in the music room, and he's fussing over exactly which piece of sheet music should be displayed on the piano. Something he wrote, or is that too show-offy? What about something he's working on right now, so he can subtly demonstrate his creative process? Or would it be better to go with a classic? But not something too mainstream. Like, he wouldn't want *Clare de Lune*, why, that's practically Hot Cross Buns. He could set up the famously difficult *Gaspard de la nuit*, but again, what if she thinks he's being pretentious? And yes, he *can* play that, but maybe not if he's nervous, and how is he going to feel when she's watching him? Sure, he's performed thousands of times, but not for the woman he might marry.

"Enough!" I yank all the sheet music out of his hands and lightly bop him on the head with it, careful not to muss the golden waves he spent an hour sculpting. "Powell, you're working yourself into a frenzy. Close your eyes, right now."

"That doesn't help," he protests, but he obeys.

"Okay. Now think back. Who is Emily's favorite composer?"

"Prokofiev. I remember because he was my mom's favorite, too. She taught me his Children's Pieces for my very first recital." A smile appears on his face at the memory, and his fingers are twitching as though playing the opening notes.

"Perfect. Put up something by him. But maybe a little more difficult than what you played when you were four."

"And this is why I love you, Deedee. You always know the right thing to do." He goes to his filing cabinet to find an appropriately difficult yet beloved piece, and I stack up the discarded pages.

The doorbell rings, and Powell shoves a music book in my hand and sprints off to welcome her. Is this the seventh date? He's sure acting like it. Just in case he decides to violate the rules, I did check his bedside table to ensure he had condoms, and I kindly left a non-disclosure agreement on his bed—though if he finds it before Emily does, I suspect I'll receive an angry text, and the paper will disappear.

I shake the book gently and let it fall open to its most used page and set that up on the piano. Perfect, the room is ready. And now I can go greet Emily, but when I reach the foyer, it's not her. No, it's someone far less welcome.

"What is Tanner doing here?" I ask Powell, not him. Because I don't want to talk to him. He used cheese and chocolate to manipulate me and seduce me the other night and then, as predicted, got weird. The only things I've heard from him since then are work related: Ms. B-C, PER THE TERMS OF OUR CONTRACT, PLEASE FIND ATTACHED THE PHOTOS FOR STAR FITNESS. MS. B-C, I HAVE DRAFTED A POST FOR THE SWIFTAPIC ACCOUNT. PLEASE LOGIN AND APPROVE.

"He's my St. Louis connection," Powell proudly informs me, as if it's difficult for a wealthy man with all his resources to track down someone from one of the Midwest's largest cities.

"I brought the goodies!" Tanner announces, but he's not even looking at me as he holds up a Styrofoam cooler and a large cake box. "The rest is still in my van."

"Cass will take that to the kitchen." Powell helpfully transfers the contents from Tanner's arms to mine. It takes all of my willpower to not accidentally drop them on the floor. *This is for Emily*, I remind myself. Also, selfishly, *this is to get out of LoveMatch events.*

I courteously don't slam the cake box down on the counter, because, again, this is for Emily. And it was thoughtful for Powell to want to surprise her with a taste of home. At least, given the picture of the Gateway Arch on the box, I assume it contains a local delicacy. I hope it's not some kind of Mississippi River fish.

"Are we going to be able to get through today without fighting?" Tanner asks when he brings in the grocery bags. I don't appreciate how he's treating me like *I'm* the problem. Isn't he the one who told me to leave his apartment, when he didn't get what he wanted?

"I'm a mature adult. I can tolerate you," I inform him. "If you insist on behaving like a whiny little child who was denied a lollipop, that's on you."

"Whiny? I'm being polite and professional, which is precisely how you want me to treat you." He's not being professional though, not with that snide tone, and not with the way he's glaring, brow furrowed, unkempt eyebrows drawn together.

"If you're going to act like this, just drop off the food and go. Do you need me to pay for it? I can give you cash."

That manages to make his face turn an interesting shade of red. He's furious.

"Ms. Blaine-Corbitt, your brother paid a courier to deliver most of these. The rest I'm happy to contribute. That's what friends do sometimes, they provide food with absolutely no expectations of getting anything in return." He steps closer as he harshly enunciates each word.

"No expectations from my brother. I know what you wanted last time you provided one of us food."

He's right up in my face now, and he's so mad. He's probably going to kiss me. He's done that while angry before. I'll stop him, of course. Maybe not immediately. Maybe after a few minutes, like after he's pressed me up against the wall and is pulling my hair. Then I might maybe probably stop him.

But he stops himself, spinning on his heel and going to the counter instead, picking up the cooler and carrying it to the fridge to unpack its contents. He's not talking to me at all, and the back of his neck is still bright red.

I'm glad he's far away and cooling off because I never heard the doorbell, and all of a sudden Powell is bringing Emily into the kitchen which would have been embarrassing had Tanner gone through with what his angry eyes indicated he wanted to do. She's brought something as well, a pan of homemade brownies. Guess we're getting multiple desserts tonight. That's not something I'm going to complain about. Powell might need to consult his nutritionist, though.

"This is the kitchen," Powell is saying, just in case Emily doesn't know what a room with a stove, double oven and enormous refrigerator might be used for.

"Oh, this is amazing. You can cook anything in here!" She's nodding and smiling as she looks around the room. She's correct that anything can be cooked in here, but if that 'you' was meant to refer to Powell, she's going to be sorely disappointed. He can barely make his own sandwich. But I'm not going to bring up the great over-mustarding incident of 2010 right now. No, I'll save the embarrassing stories for later. Maybe after dinner. Or during. I'm flexible.

"And this," Powell continues the tour, "as you know, is my baby sister Cassidy, and her friend . . ."

"Jackson! Of course, it's so nice to meet you," Emily is a hugger, so that's how she greets Tanner.

"Um . . . I'm not . . ." he tries to say when he detangles from her embrace.

"It's okay, I heard all about your double date the other night," Emily assures him. "I don't mind. Like I told Powell, we're looking at a potential lifetime commitment. I know he has other options. I want to be sure that I'm his choice, not just someone an algorithm picked out for him."

Powell intervenes to save the conversation. "Emily, actually, this is my friend Tanner, the one I told you about?"

"Oh!" Emily's cheeks turn pink. "I'm so sorry!" Powell puts his arm around her shoulders, and, even in her embarrassment, she looks at him adoringly.

"Yeah, I'm Tanner. Tanner Smythe," Tanner says. Then, inexplicably he sings, *"That's Smythe with a Y."*

Did I miss something on the LoveMatch intake forms? Is there some sort of male singer requirement? We all look at him in confusion.

Tanner tries to explain, "Like the radio jingle? The billboards? *Smythe Family Moving and Storage . . . that's Smythe with a Y?"* Singing the jingle again doesn't help, but Emily politely tries to cover up the awkwardness.

"I just moved here," she tells him apologetically. "I haven't seen that billboard yet. But I promise I'll look for it!"

"Let me take you on the rest of the tour," Powell ends the conversation by steering her away. I bet the next stop is his bedroom. I'm tempted to yell something about this not being the seventh date, but I don't want to make Emily any more uncomfortable than she already is. Though if she spots the non-disclosure form, the one the Last Barons always referred to as a sex contract, I'm sure she'll experience another round of embarrassment.

Tanner is staring after them, gnawing on his lower lip.

"Remember what I said about you being weird?" I tell him. "You've gotten weirder."

"Have I? More like you're getting weirder. Why'd you go on a date with Jackson? I thought you said there was nothing there."

He's acting jealous, which is yet more proof that I should never have made out with him. Misguided possessiveness is not an attractive quality.

"And there is nothing there. I brought him out with Powell and Lexa because Powell told me to invite you."

"Me? And you picked him instead. That's fine, Cass, I get it." But clearly, he doesn't, because if he did, he wouldn't be so mad right now.

"Of course I chose him, given the way you've been acting lately. And when I said you've gotten weirder, I was referring to you singing at Emily. What's wrong with you?"

"My family owns a moving and storage company," he explains.

That's something I did not know about him. He doesn't mention his family much, and, given his black sheep status, I don't blame him. But there's a time and a place for everything, and his first time meeting my brother's potential fiancée isn't it.

"You chose a strange time to bring it up."

"I spent my childhood getting teased about that stupid jingle."

"And so, you provide it as ammunition so people can tease you about it as an adult? Good plan, Mr. Smythe-with-a-y."

"That's not . . . never mind. Don't you have something better to do than to harass me? Go work out or preen in the mirror or something."

What I'd like to do is throw a drink at him. That would be satisfying and might wash that smirk off his annoying face. Alas, my hand is empty, and I don't want to make a mess in my own kitchen anyway. So instead, I just turn and walk away.

Another clue that Powell is very interested in continuing his relationship with Emily: an enormous SUV with tinted windows and bulletproof siding has pulled up in our driveway. When Powell got a meet-the-friends date with Lexa, he brought me and Jackson, a guy he hardly knows. For this one, former Last Baron of Sound Devon Malloy and his supermodel girlfriend Brixley have just arrived. They actually traveled out here from California in Devon's private tour bus, since he avoids flying unless it's the only thing he can do (and then he travels with a physician who keeps him dosed on happy pills). The bus is too large to make the turns in our neighborhood, so the driver parked the behemoth somewhere else, and a secured car service is dropping them off.

Brixley is as gloriously glamorous as always, emerging from the car in a hat so wide it puts my own sunhat to shame. She will never permit sunlight to touch her porcelain skin. Her long dress flows around her. I can't help but wonder if she changed on the bus, if she had been wearing a tank top and pajama pants like we mere mortals do on long rides.

"I'm so relieved to see you," she says, an odd choice of words as she hugs me. I hug her back, and then catch a whiff of something that makes me wrinkle my nose.

"Why do you smell like . . ."

"Avarice by Xander, launching next week at department stores across the country?"

"Oh, no." My heart sinks.

"Oh, yes. I told him he should have taken the private jet he's always bragging about, but he says it's more environmentally friendly to travel together. He spent the whole car ride on the phone with his new agent, who I presume is named 'Bro.'" I look past her at the car, and sure enough, my least favorite person in the world is paused, halfway out of the vehicle, shouting into his phone. I bet the driver is ready to place a foot firmly in the middle of his back and force him the rest of the way out.

"This day keeps getting better and better."

"Just wait," Brixley warns me. I'm not sure how to interpret that, until I spot Devon. Powell had greeted him first, and with my brother in the way, I hadn't realized how much he's changed since the last time I saw him, at Jace's tribute concert. He's letting his hair grow long, and instead of the latest fashions, he's wearing baggy white linen hippie clothes and several strings of chunky amber beads dangle around his neck.

"Wow."

"Yeah, wow. Is Tanner here yet? He promised me mojitos."

"You've been talking to Tanner?" I try not to be hurt by that, but I am. Though I shouldn't be surprised he's moved on to whomever else he can get something out of. I doubt he's trying to sleep with Brixley, but taking some shots of her can only benefit his career. And we all know that his career is the only thing that man cares about. He certainly doesn't care about maintaining friendships, or he would have kept his lips to himself.

"Of course. Who do you think has been keeping me updated on your recovery?" She gently touches my cheek with her cool hand, grey eyes studying me intently. "No scarring. Your surgeon did a good job."

"I thought I was the one keeping you updated," I tell her, stung by her words. Was my best friend going behind my back to gossip about me?

"You always say you're fine. Your hair could be on fire, and you'd tell me it was no big deal. Tanner's honest."

"And what exactly did he say?"

"That you struggle, that you hide your pain like you always do. And one night, when you were watching movies, did you fall asleep on his shoulder?"

I don't want to talk about that. I don't want to talk about anything that has to do with any physical contact with Tanner. So, I lie. "I don't remember."

Brixley shakes her head and sighs because I guess I just proved her point. "We'll talk more about this later. But for now, don't ruin this for me. I spent six hours in a bus with Devon and Xander. I need a strong drink as far from them as possible."

"He's inside," I mutter, and we hurry in, while Xander is still in his perched on the edge of the seat discussion with Agent Bro, or perhaps, Agent Dude. He's shouting both terms so frequently I can't tell if there's one or more people on the call with him.

"Tell me you made something for me," Brixley says as she hugs Tanner.

"I started mixing when I heard the car arrive," Tanner replies. Technically, he didn't hear the car arrive, he heard Powell say, 'Emily, wait in the kitchen a minute, the others just got here.' But, whatever. Let him exaggerate. He's made three mojitos, one for each of us ladies. Emily is already nervously sipping hers.

"Hi," she greets Brix in her soft voice.

"You must be Emily." Brixley looks her up and down. Calculations are going on in her brain, evaluating the cost of every aspect of Emily's appearance, from her shoes to her make-up. The number probably adds up to the price of one of Brixley's lipsticks. She's not a snob though; she doesn't judge. "Powell told me all about you. I brought some samples for you."

"Samples?"

"People send me freebies all the time." Brixley waves her hand dismissively, as though free stuff appearing on doorsteps is perfectly normal. In her world, it is. In mine too, though I think Brixley gets a wider variety of items than my brother. Nobody sends him cosmetics, and he rarely receives jewelry. "Powell said you prefer silver, so I have a few pieces for you. I think rose gold would look better with your complexion though. I'm going to need to have a serious talk with him about accurate descriptions. Cassidy, I brought you a stunning dress from Fallon Way's fall collection. You aren't allowed to wear it in public until September though."

"Thanks, Brix." That's something to brighten my day. She picks out the very best gifts for her friends and family. Other samples—that's what she calls the clothing, make-up, and 'lifestyle accoutrements' that show up at her agent's office by the truckload—are often given to charities. A select few make it to her SwiftaPic feed.

"Nothing for me?" Tanner asks teasingly. Because obviously, he always wants something.

"A belt and a couple of vintage t-shirts. They were originally meant for Devon, but his style has changed."

"Cool, thanks!" Tanner loves free stuff. Also, he loves taking advantage of people. I hate him.

"Emily, shall we head out to the pool and get to know each other better?" Brixley suggests, which triggers the reddening of Emily's cheeks.

"I . . . sure . . . I mean . . ." she stutters. I can sense the reason for her hesitation. Wearing a swimsuit in front of a supermodel with a perfect body is intimidating enough, but she's also got to face Powell—who hasn't seen her at that level of undress yet—and his famous, attractive former bandmates.

Brix can sense it too. "Don't worry, I have no intention of getting in the water. I'll be sitting in the shade with my drink, and maybe waiting for chocolate cookies? Tanner, I've been restricting calories just in case."

"I have a special meal planned," he says. "But no cookies. I will keep your glass full though." He points to a currently empty glass pitcher, next to the assortment of mojito makings.

I hear the front door open, and the former Last Barons make their rowdy way toward the kitchen. I down my mojito, fast. I'm not waiting for that pitcher to be filled; I'll mix myself something else outside. This afternoon is going to be miserable, and I'll need a steady supply of drinks to help me through. "Ladies, let's go."

I can't take it. I can't take any of this. Powell, Devon and Xander are horsing around in the shallow end, Emily is sitting with her feet dangling in the water watching Powell with rapt attention. And Brixley dozed off, leaving me with nobody to talk to. I'm not getting in the water, not with creepy Xander in there, but there's a different creep in my house. Speaking of Tanner . . .

"Cass, can you go check on when the food will be ready?" Powell asks. Except it's not really an ask. I reluctantly return to the kitchen, where Tanner is rolling out pizza crust.

"Pizza? I thought you were making something special."

"Of course, you're here to criticize." He continues efficiently sprinkling flour over the surface and pressing down hard on the rolling pin.

"Aren't you supposed to toss the dough?" I ask, because if he thinks I'm here to criticize, I'm happy to meet his expectations.

"Not for St. Louis style pizza."

"That's not a thing."

"Yes, it is."

"No, there are only three styles of pizza: Italian, New York, and Chicago. That's all." Yes, I'm taunting him. But he's asking for it.

"I'm really not in the mood to argue with you. If you want to be useful, you can set the table."

Is this grumpy jerk seriously telling me what to do in my own house? I'm tempted to tell him to set it himself and head back out to sit next to Brix's sleeping body. But I am the hostess, and I know Powell won't even think to get dishes out, so I do it. I make a lot of noise, too, slamming plates and silverware around.

Okay, maybe I'm a little immature.

"The outdoor bar is out of beer," Xander says, coming up behind me, with a towel around his waist. Usually, I can smell him in advance and escape, but the saltwater in the pool must have removed his cologne. Probably need to have it drained and replace the water later.

"Check the bar downstairs," I tell him. Neither Powell nor I are big drinkers, but we tend to keep our house well stocked for our guests.

"New chef?" he looks past me at Tanner. "Hey, man, grab me a beer. An IPA, but not too hoppy."

Tanner ignores him entirely. And even though I have a general distaste for Tanner right now, Xander is the literal worst. So, I can't let him get away with that.

"He's not our chef. He's our friend, Tanner. You've met him before."

Xander looks at him without a shred of recognition. He's faking; he must be. This is their third meeting, and one of those was an entire dinner, during which Xander kept making snide remarks and deliberately messing up Tanner's name.

Tanner gives him a polite smile. "Yes, I remember you; you're that intern from Powell's record company. We've met a few times. You have what, six weeks left? Do you think they'll hire you on fulltime?" Tanner is open, friendly, and so brilliant I almost want to forgive him everything.

"Excuse me?" Xander's outrage is loud and real. "You don't know who I am?"

Tanner shrugs. "I thought I did. You aren't the intern? I swear, I've met you before. Wait, are you from Cassidy's gym? Sorry, you don't have the build of a personal trainer, so I assumed . . ."

This has gone from the worst day to the best. Xander is purple, actually, really purple. Veins are bulging from his forehead, and for the next five minutes we are treated to a rant about how he is *Xander Fields, damnit*, and *how dare you imply*, and *I'm calling my publicist*, and *Cassidy you need to do something about the hired help*.

He storms out, presumably to order Powell to fire Tanner, and I start to laugh. I laugh until tears come to my eyes. Tanner is laughing too, and when we're able to stop, it feels like something has eased between us.

"Tanner, that was amazing."

I'm finally seeing his dimpled grin, one that hasn't appeared in weeks. "Full disclosure, I've rehearsed that exact speech in my head a dozen times. Kind of a taste of his own medicine."

"It was perfect. He's on the phone yelling right now." Xander is outside on the patio, pacing and gesticulating and informing 'Bro' or 'Dude' exactly how insulted he's been. Emily is staring, in probable horror, while Brixley is now wide awake and filming Xander's diatribe. I hope she sends the video to me later.

"Cassidy, I . . . I miss this."

My attention pivots away from the scene outside and back to my occasional arch-nemesis.

"You miss making Xander angry?"

"No, I miss *you*. I miss laughing with you and hanging out with you. Can we pretend that night at my apartment never happened? Please?"

Can we? Deep down inside, I want to. Sure, Tanner's prickly and takes offense at the most innocuous statements, and he tricked me into getting mousse on my face so he could put the moves on me. But he's also the same guy who came over every day while my brother was out of town, so I wouldn't have to be alone. He bakes me cookies, and watches movies with me, and yes, there was that one time Brixley mentioned, when I fell asleep on him and had my first night unencumbered by nightmares of having my attacker's massive hands around my throat. And he did just destroy Xander, and I do love a good Xander smackdown.

"Are you going to return the phone case I gave you?"

"Do you want it back?" He reaches for his pocket as if he's about to rip it off his phone right now.

"I just wanted to know how accurate this erasure was going to be. Let's pretend I left immediately after dinner." That feels right. I had dinner, I left, we're fine.

"That means I still owe you dessert."

"Yes." I hate this feeling. I hate this energy that surges between us. I hate that it's back, and I can't do anything about it even though I know exactly how Tanner's lips taste on mine and how his hands feel on my body. So, I shrug, tell him I'll collect on that sometime, and finish setting the table.

Dinner is ready. There's an enormous bowl of salad in the middle of the table, though not as massive as my individual LoveMatch salad. Devon does a strange little bow and refers to it as an offering. I don't know what that's all about. I'm more interested in trying Tanner's weird version of pizza.

But he doesn't make it all the way to the table, because first Brixley wants to take a pic of him holding the pizza, then he must take a close up before it's served, then Brix needs one where she's putting a slice on a plate, then Devon starts talking about how perhaps we're all too superficially interconnected and maybe we should live in the moment.

"That's enough," Brixley finally snaps, not at Tanner who is taking his dozenth picture, but at Devon. "I'm sick of listening to you complain all the time. Social media is part of my job. Yours, too. Stop acting like I'm overdoing it."

"I don't understand why you can't live in the moment, rejoice in the present. Be mindful. The last thing I posted . . ."

"Was a pseudo-inspirational quote about connecting with others. Yeah. I read it. Your new-found spirituality doesn't pay the bills, Devon."

I'm watching in amazement. The two of them never fight. Never. They've had a perfect relationship since the day they met, on a Last Barons video shoot.

"Modeling pays your bills. And you have enough money you never need to work again. You *choose* to keep posting because you get off on having so many fans."

"Says the man who performs half naked."

"I don't do that anymore." Devon's voice is dripping with contempt, but I can't tell whether it's for Brixley or his past shirtless self.

"You don't do anything anymore!"

"Hey," Powell interrupts. Emily is sinking down in her seat looking extraordinarily uncomfortable. Xander is smirking, Tanner has been slowly backing away, and I'm . . . well, I'm waiting to see if I have to jump in and protect anybody. "Can we stop fighting, try and have a pleasant meal?"

"NO!" Both Brixley and Devon shout at the same time. Then Brixley takes a deep breath. "Sorry. I've been trying. Ever since we broke up, he—"

"WHAT?" Now it's Powell's and my turn to simul-shout.

"I can't right now," Brixley mutters and exits the room. She doesn't storm out or stalk off like a normal person, no, she glides away, seemingly untroubled. But there's no way she's actually untroubled, so I follow her out and guide her to my bedroom, so we can talk privately.

"I'm so over Devon's new attitude," she says by way of apology. She throws herself beautifully on the bed. Even angry and distraught, she is stunning.

"You broke up? Are you okay?"

She lets out an unmodel-like snort. "It was a long time ago; we just haven't told anybody. You know how these things go."

Yes, I sure do. All the negotiations amongst publicists, the media statements, the discussions as to who can or should start dating again first. I've helped Powell through a bunch of them.

"You could have confided in me."

"It wasn't a good time."

That hurts. Brix is my best friend. Any time is a good time. Unless they ended it during one of my recent hospitalizations, but still, she could have told me after I was released. At a minimum, I would have taken her out for post-Devon drinks and complaining. Or maybe we'd have spent a week in St. Tropez, admiring sun-kissed beachgoers and helping get her groove back with some random billionaire. I'm sure there are loads of men out there eager for the opportunity to be her rebound, and several of them would meet Brixley's strict criteria.

"Cass," she puts her cool hand on my knee. "We broke up right before Jace died. In fact, he was the one who encouraged me to spread my wings. Jace told me I shouldn't stay unhappy, not with my whole life ahead of me."

"That was months ago!" And how tragic, to have poor doomed Jace talking about having one's life ahead of them, not knowing how short his would be.

"Yes, but he died, so that wasn't a good time to announce, and then with the concert coming up, we didn't want any distractions. Anyway, pretending is better. I'm a model, do you have any idea how many sleazy people and obsessed fans hit on me all the time? As long as I could pretend I was dating Devon, I had the protection of a relationship with a man of status. It's just been easier. Or it was."

"I thought you guys were rock solid. Brix, I'm sorry. I'm trying to be supportive, but I'm in shock. You two were so in love for so long."

"Ha! The Devon that I met ten years ago? Him, I loved. Devon five years ago, still a great guy. We encouraged each other's careers, we wanted the same things, we enjoyed spending time together. Even when we broke up, I still loved him. We remained friends, obviously. And we supported each other through Jace's murder. But Devon now? He's a smug, pretentious, holier-than-thou jackass. I can't stand him."

"Wow." I'm floored. Other than my mother and stepfather, Brix and Devon were the strongest couple I knew. To witness their collapse is shocking, especially now that they reached I-hate-you levels of post-breakup animosity. "I wish you'd said something. I would have invited you out more often, so you wouldn't be stuck with your ex all the time."

"I'm not. The house is huge; we hardly have to deal with each other. Plus, I've been traveling for work, and he's been . . . on his spiritual journey." She pronounces spiritual as though it's distasteful. Brixley has always been a smart science-minded rational woman, so I can imagine watching Devon getting in touch with his inner self might be off-putting to her.

"I have something that will temporarily help," I promise her. In my nightstand, there's a secret box, one that I keep hidden from Powell. If he knew about it, the supply of special ordered Parisian gourmet truffles would disappear. "Never mention these to my brother."

We are surrounded with truffle wrappers and fully immersed in our discussion of every single one of Devon's numerous flaws when someone knocks on my door. I half-expect Devon with an apology, but it's much better: Tanner with pizza. He's got a tray with two plates of food, plus a bottle of pinot and two glasses.

"You ladies missed an uncomfortable dinner."

"Tanner, you're an absolute sweetheart," Brixley kisses his cheek when he sets down the tray, and I inexplicably feel a surge of jealousy. I like what I have going with Tanner, our cautious rebuilding of friendship. But seeing his ease with Brix while he's still acting tentative around me hurts a little.

"Just trying to help. There's still gooey cake in the kitchen for dessert. Emily didn't want any." When he says that, he casts a look at me, as though attempting to convey a message. I don't get it.

"Thanks," is all I can say to that. I never heard of gooey cake, but the name is unappealing and I'm not going to judge Emily for not wanting to try any.

"So ... I'm going to head out. This evening's a bust. Xander left to go clubbing, and Devon said something about meditating in his sacred space. And I don't want to be a third wheel with Powell and Emily. But Cassidy, can we maybe grab lunch tomorrow, so we can talk?" Tanner gives me another of those looks. Oh, no. He wants to talk about that evening we both decided didn't happen. He's already going back on our agreement to never mention it again.

I agree to meet up with him, and when he leaves, Brix and I eat his not-as-strange-as-expected pizza and drink all the wine and continue our discussion about how Devon's probably just putting on an act, and he's going to be back on stage shirtless and dancing his ass off soon enough, but we certainly won't be in the audience to support him.

# CHAPTER TEN

Breakfast is awkward. There's Brixley, with her egg white omelet and cup of tea, glaring daggers at Devon who is consuming what looks like a plate of raw kale sprinkled with seeds and blueberries. Powell and Emily are sitting across from me acting all lovey-dovey, holding hands under the table and nuzzling each other's cheeks. I suspect there's been some fudging of the number of dates, and Tabitha is going to be mad.

And I have to sit and watch all of this while Xander regales us with the tales of his amazing time at the clubs, and the myriad beautiful fans who threw themselves at him, and how he stopped by my room when he got back, but I must have been asleep because the door was locked, and I didn't answer.

Brix checks her phone and abruptly stands up. "I'm flying to New York for a shoot. My car will be here in ten minutes." Our truffle binge ended with her making a midnight phone call to her assistant, and this is the result. It's not difficult for a supermodel to find a job that gets her an escape from enduring a bus ride with her ex-boyfriend and an over-cologned egomaniac.

"You aren't traveling to El Paso with us?" Xander asks in surprise, as though he completely missed the scene last night at the dinner table. Since Brixley announced the break-up, she doesn't need to pretend in front of us anymore, and she certainly isn't planning to suffer through another interminable trip with two awful men.

"No. You and Devon can go do your thing. Though I thought performing made your chakras misalign."

"We're doing a charity event for Jace's foundation," Devon replies sharply. "Don't denigrate my work."

"Whatever, I don't really care anymore. You go on your journey, and I'll go on mine. And mine involves getting on a terrifying airplane and soaring through the sky at a great height, protected only by an aluminum tube and the skill of a pilot who may or may not be drunk." That's the most succinct summation of Devon's fears I've ever heard. Brixley's words tear into her ex, but I don't blame her for finally snapping, after tolerating Devon's nonsense for months.

"Shut up!" Devon covers his ears and yells at her. Awesome, we're going to be treated to round two. "Stop talking about flying!"

"What? I should continue to be controlled by your phobia? We're not together, Devon. I shouldn't have come out here on your bus."

"Yeah, maybe next time you should take a helicopter. I know a company you can call. Their fleet is a little short though."

Never has such cruelty come from Devon. Never.

"This is exactly how my parents' divorce went," Xander whispers to me. He seems to be enjoying this, whereas my world is collapsing. Other than my mom and Hank, who are still sickeningly in love after sixteen years of marriage, Devon and Brixley were my strongest example of a functional relationship. If they can't make it work, who can? Especially since they've devolved into pure hatred. I am horrified watching them as they start volleying insults back and forth. Powell tries to intervene but gives up and rushes Emily out of the room, to protect her delicate constitution. I bet he's embarrassed that his whole meet-the-friends plan went so horribly.

"We have an hour or so before Devon and I need to go," Xander tells me. "Let's leave them to fight. We can hang out in your room."

That's my cue to evacuate. Alone.

I managed to get a long intense workout in at my gym to destress, and now it's time to meet up with Tanner for lunch. I'm in for an awkward meal. Things are starting to inch their way back to normal between us, but I'm not good at these post-fight conversations.

Fortunately, he let me pick the place, so we're going to my favorite diner. They don't serve many vegetarian options, but there's a salad that I love, and since I already worked out today, I don't see a problem ordering a grilled cheese with jalapeño on sourdough as well.

"Interesting choice," Tanner says as he slides into the booth across from me. I don't want to tell him the real reason I selected this place—grasping for any kind of control while going into awkward situations—so I shrug.

"I like diners. Mama Nina makes good food."

"Last time I came here, I got berated and kicked out for harassing you."

I had forgotten about that. Yes, this is where Tanner Smythe, photographer, ambushed me to pick a fight about some photos he'd taken of me earlier that morning. But I don't want to admit that our encounter here wasn't the first thing on my mind when I suggested this place.

"Yes, we're returning to the scene of the crime. Didn't you say you wanted to start over?"

"Not *that* far over. Just like, a couple of weeks."

Our waitress appears to take our order. Tanner is going for breakfast foods. I've changed my mind on the salad, but not on the grilled cheese. I'm getting my sandwich with soup instead—garlic tomato is today's special. My breath isn't going to be too pleasant, but I'm not planning on kissing anybody, so that doesn't matter.

After she walks away, Tanner's dimple appears as he teases me, "You look out of place here. You fit better in that trendy vegan café that opened last week, or maybe in a high-end bar where the cocktails cost sixty bucks."

"Wrong, as always. I'll have you know, my very first job was in a diner like this one." Well, dingier than this one.

"Really? I can't imagine you working."

I raise my eyebrows at that, and he starts stuttering. "I mean, I've seen you in conference calls with Powell's label and running his errands and whatever. And at the gym. But I meant like working a blue-collar job."

"I was six. I got paid twenty-five cents an hour for bussing tables, plus one meal per shift."

"Child labor laws didn't exist?"

"It was off the books." The diner owner was trying to help; it was back when my mother and I were living in our station wagon. Mom waitressed, and I started out spending her shifts hanging out in an empty booth with my coloring book and a few broken crayons. I was so proud when I was offered the job. My mom's boss interviewed me and made me do a test shift, and I worked my little butt off. She gave me a cupcake to celebrate my hiring. In hindsight, she was a sweet older woman who took pity on a family going through tough times. Long after we moved on from there, we sent her postcards updating her about how we were doing. She passed away a few months before mom met Hank, so she never got to see how far we came.

I don't realize it, but I am staring into space thinking about those old days. I snap out of my reverie when Tanner starts speaking.

"I like when you talk about your past. It makes you more human."

As opposed to what? A robot or a monster? I'm not going to ask, because I probably won't like his answer, and we're trying to repair, not destroy, our relationship.

"I've told you I grew up poor." I'm not ashamed of my history, but it's not something I like to bring up. My past is nobody's business anyway.

"It's easy to forget."

"Not for me."

He stares at me for a moment. "I like when you're real."

"We're not here to talk about my past though, are we?"

"No."

Our food arrives quickly, which will make things easier. I always prefer discussing emotionally laden topics over a meal—the act of having to chew gives me plenty of time to think of my responses.

"Elephant in the room?" I ask as I crumble crackers into my soup.

"Emily," he nods.

Okay, that's not nice at all.

"What about her? I thought you wanted lunch so we could talk more about the night-that-never-was."

"And I thought we resolved that the night *didn't happen* and reset our friendship. I've never known you to be one to dwell on things. We can talk about it, though, if you want, Cass. I'm sorry, and I've missed you, and I will never touch you again." He reaches across the table as though to take my hand, and immediately withdraws as he realizes he's taking action that directly contradicts his words.

That's not quite what I was hoping for. I mean, obviously he and I as a couple are absurd. And the way he reacts over *almost* having sex proves that we never should because then I'd lose him as a friend. But to never touch me at all ever again? Who's going to hug me when I need it? How will we watch movies together if I can't lean against his shoulder? Those are important elements of our friendship.

"Tanner, you give the best hugs. You're allowed to hug me."

"Thank you for your gracious permission, my queen."

I roll my eyes at him and use my fork to steal some of his hash browns. "Now that we've gotten that out of the way, did you seriously ask me here to talk about Emily? What happened? Did you recognize her from back home?" If so, I have a lot of questions. For her. Like, does she have any pictures of emo high school Tanner, and how soon can she get them to me?

"Emily is not from St. Louis. She lied. I doubt she's ever even been there."

"She grew up there, she's only been in Arizona a few months."

"No, I have no idea where she really came from, but I guarantee she's not from St. Louis."

"How do you know?" I'm willing to indulge this possibility, in part because I'm hearing Jackson's warnings in my head right now.

"For one thing, she didn't recognize the cheese on the pizza."

"So? You used a fancy cheese, big deal. I couldn't identify it either." And, not to brag, but I've eaten a lot of different cheeses.

"It was Provel." At my blank look, he elaborates. "You can only get it in St. Louis. It's our official pizza cheese. Love or hate it, everyone has an opinion, and everyone knows what it is."

"Maybe she was always on a health food diet? Strict parents?"

"Even on a health food diet. Unless she never attended a birthday party or left her home as a teenager, she should have recognized the pizza. She didn't recognize my family either."

"The Smythe advertisement? Are you sure it's that popular?"

"I was teased my entire life by people coming up to me on the playground and singing 'that's Smythe with a Y.' We—they—have billboards all over the city. You can't drive down any of the freeways without seeing an ad. But she didn't know what I was talking about."

"Could she have been from just outside the city?"

"If she'd said that first, yes, possibly. But she said she lived 'near the river.' And when I asked which neighborhood, she changed the subject and asked me where I was from."

"She was making polite conversation."

"No, she doesn't know the neighborhoods. I told her I grew up in Parkingham, and she said she heard that's a lovely area."

"And?"

"I made that up! Parkingham? Seriously? She lied, Cass. And if she'll lie about where she's from, what else is she lying about?"

The benefit of sourdough—one large bite buys me a minute to consider my response. I want to like Emily, partly because she seems sweet, partly because Powell likes her, and mostly—selfishly—because I want to be done with LoveMatch. But Powell is my priority, always, so if Emily lied about something as significant as where she comes from, we need to investigate further.

"I should call Jackson, loop him in on this."

"No, you should call Mike. Why isn't he involved? He's in charge of Powell's security."

"True. I'll do that now." I grab my phone right as a text notification arrives. While, yes, checking messages in the middle of a meal is rude, Tanner has already taken about thirteen pictures of both of our plates and posted at least two of them on SwiftaPic, so I think I can sneak a peek at my incoming messages.

I'M GOING TO KILL TANNER!

"Whoa, this one's about you," I tell him, flashing the screen at him. It's from Brixley.

"What'd I do?"

Why?????? I text back.

She responds with a link to an article on the notorious Celebutante blog.

> Breaking news: DevBrix has been over for months! Devon Malloy and supermodel Brixley parted ways in February! The truth was spilled by Brix's confidante/photographer Tanner Smythe. "They've been hiding the breakup from the media, but they hate each other," he claims . . .

"Tanner! Did you leak the story? How could you?"

He snatches the phone from my hand and skims the words on the screen. "No, no way, this wasn't me. Cass, you have to believe me! I'd never do that. Never!"

Once, months ago, he'd insisted something wasn't him, that he'd been framed, and I didn't believe him, and instead had him arrested. This time I do. But I might make him squirm a little.

"How much did they pay you?" I ask, trying to glare angrily.

"Nothing! I'll call them, I'll prove it, Cass, I swear I didn't leak anything." He's panicking and practically on the verge of tears as he watches his career and friendships crumble, so I relent. There's only so long I want to torture the man.

"Fine, I believe you. I'll have Powell's lawyer contact Celebutante and demand a retraction. Hang on."

It wasn't him, I send Brixley.

How do you know?

I'm sitting across from him and he's about to cry.

Aww, don't make him cry. Who did it? Devon is furious. He called and yelled at me. I might sue him. Devon, not Tanner. For emotional distress. His dedication to meditation isn't helping with his newfound anger issues.

No idea. Xander maybe?

Brix's response is a string of angry emojis. I suspect she's contacting him next, or having her attorney send a threatening email.

I text Devon too, but he doesn't respond. Then I try calling Powell.

"What's with your boy?" is the bizarre way he answers the phone. Clearly, he's seen the news.

"Tanner's our pet paparazzo. He'd never release a story without permission." From the grimace on Tanner's face, I doubt he likes to be thought of as anybody's pet, but too bad for him.

"That's what I thought, but you never can tell with some people." When did my brother become the suspicious one?

"Could have been Emily. She was there when we found out."

"Emily isn't capable of leaking a story. She doesn't have any contacts anywhere. And how dare you accuse her! I thought you liked her!" His outburst of defensiveness is unexpected. I'll need to tread carefully while he's in the early she-can-do-no-wrong stage of this relationship.

"I do; she's wonderful." I'm not supposed to lie to my brother, but I'm going to maintain this one while we investigate the real story behind Emily, geographical liar. "But maybe she was on the phone with a friend, or she posted something online."

"She doesn't have any friends. She just moved here. And she doesn't follow gossip sites. I trust her, Cassidy. Just because you have trust issues doesn't mean you should pin this on my girlfriend."

"Are you allowed to call her that? Has LoveMatch given you permission?"

"I don't need permission. I do what I want!"

Oh, now I've made him mad. Powell doesn't like to be told he can't do things.

"Yes, Powell, you're right. You're a superstar, you can do anything. And I'm sure it wasn't her. But it wasn't Tanner either. It could have been Xander." Actually, that can't be true. Xander would have claimed the leak, so he could get the attention. He doesn't care if his press is good or bad, as long as they spell his name correctly. "Or it could have been anybody. Devon's assistant, his manager, his bus driver, the best friend or roommate of any of those people. Tanner's an easy target because they kept tagging each other on SwiftaPic last night." An inner circle leak would definitely want to hide behind a falsehood. No sense in losing their job and access to marketable gossip.

Fortunately, Powell agrees with me. In the world he lives in, there are always leaks.

"Is he mad at me too?" Tanner asks when I hang up with my brother. He was watching my face the entire time, chewing on his lip and probably mulling over a future with no access to local celebrities he could exploit. Sigh. That's uncharitable of me. Other than that one time, when we first met, Tanner hasn't tried to exploit us at all.

"He acknowledges it probably wasn't you. What do you stand to gain from attaching your name to something dumb like that? Brix's publicist will fix everything. It will either come out that you weren't the source, or that she told you to spread it."

"But I didn't!"

"Yes, but if it works out better for publicity purposes for Brix to admit she asked her dear friend to reveal her secret, than that's what you'll agree to. This is out of your hands. Besides, we have other issues to contend with. I'm calling Mike now." I dial the number for Powell's security consultant. He handles all of my brother's security and bodyguarding demands, though when there isn't a direct and worrisome threat, the physical bodyguarding is outsourced to beefy local men.

"I hear you have a leak that needs to be plugged. Should I send some men to talk to Tanner?" Mike asks when his assistant connects our call. He must not be in his office—there's a lot of background noise.

"Where are you?"

"I'm on a job for another client. Don't worry about it. But if you hear gunshots, stop talking to me and I'll call you back later."

"Gunshots here, or gunshots through the phone?"

"Either one, obviously. Cass, are you in danger? Who has a gun? Where's Powell?" He's suddenly in protective mode.

"I'm fine. Powell's probably fine, too." Unless he's being murdered by Emily as we speak, but if she really is a LoveMatch hired hitman, she'll wait until after the wedding night. "I was wondering, though, did you happen to run a background check on his new girlfriend?"

"Emily Davis, twenty-seven, Capricorn, from St. Louis? No, of course not, because I'm terrible at my job."

"She's clean then?" I can feel relief replace the stress hormones running through my veins. After everything Powell and I have been through, what with the near-death experiences and bombings, and all the black widow fears Jackson instilled in me, this whole maybe-Emily-is-lying thing has been stressing me out. But there must be another explanation. Like perhaps Tanner doesn't know as much about his hometown as he thinks he does.

"Clean and boring. No debt, no criminal charges, no social media, nothing worthy of blackmail, nothing suspicious whatsoever. She's never even had a speeding ticket. Do you know how rare it is to get back such a blank sheet?"

"And she is from St. Louis?"

"Yes. Didn't I say that already? Hey, bad guys just showed, gotta go." And the phone disconnects.

I want to feel better. I'm relieved that Mike has in fact run the check and that it didn't come up that Emily has a sordid past or been widowed four times or anything. But something doesn't seem right. Tanner is so certain about her background, and while I don't necessarily think not recognizing bizarre hyperlocal pizza cheese is solid evidence, the neighborhood thing is pretty damning. Her possible nervousness around celebrities doesn't explain away outright lies.

Tanner has a skeptical tilt to his head. "Mike said she really is from St. Louis?"

"He ran his checks."

"That's weird, Cass."

"Yeah, I know."

# CHAPTER ELEVEN

It's stupid to show up at Emily's place and confront her, right? Like, that's an incredibly bad idea if she does happen to be a criminal mastermind capable of fooling Mike's background check, right?

But Powell sent her flowers last week, which actually means he came up with the idea and I placed the order and made all the arrangements, so I have her address. And it's not too far away from the diner. And Mama Nina doesn't mind us leaving Tanner's van in her parking lot while we drive my car over there. So really, the stars aligned, and we have to do this. It's fate.

"Maybe we shouldn't be doing this," Tanner says nervously as I pull up in front of Emily's address. She's renting the end unit of a small one-story apartment complex. The building is cute, the stucco painted a cheerful yellow, and there are flower boxes lining the shared patio. Most of the plants in them are desiccated from the heat, but they probably looked beautiful in the spring when she first moved in.

"We're just checking on her to make sure she's okay after last night," I remind him. "This is the friendly thing to do for my potential future sister-in-law." Or at least, that's our cover story.

"I'm not sure you can pull off 'friendly,'" he mutters. So, I give him a friendly elbow in the ribs.

Emily is startled when she opens the door and finds us standing there. Her hair is wrapped up in a towel, and she's wearing old sweatpants and a tank top with no bra. "Umm, hi?" she says as she steps behind the door to use it as a partial shield.

"Hi, Emily, we were in the neighborhood and wanted to stop by and apologize for what happened last night," I tell her, smiling as though this is a perfectly normal social visit. I wish we'd brought a gift basket, or her empty brownie pan, something to make this seem innocent and not at all accusatory.

"Oh, sure, come on in," she invites, as she reaches up and touches her towel. "Just . . . make yourselves at home and give me a moment." She rushes off to her bedroom.

Tanner and I look around her tiny living room. It's crowded, to say the least. Most of the space is taken up by the largest, ugliest couch I have ever seen, an old-fashioned red and blue plaid monstrosity with big bows on the arms.

"Wow," Tanner whistles as he surreptitiously pulls out his phone and takes a picture. "If she is who she says she is and she marries your brother, this thing is going to end up in your house."

"I'll get her an interior designer as a wedding gift." I wander over to check out the piano in what is supposed to be the dining nook. Sunlight is shining through the sliding glass patio door and glinting off the piano's wooden surface. It's pretty, but this must be a temporary location for it. And this proves Powell hasn't been here yet—he'd have whipped out his phone and arranged for two movers and a piano tuner to show up and relocate it far from any direct sunlight and into a safer area, where they would then verify that it was not yet damaged. Powell's a stickler for proper instrument care.

"That was my grandmother's," Emily says as she returns to the room and sees me touching a few keys. "It's the one I learned on myself, and I hope to teach my own children on it someday."

"It's lovely," I tell her, though I honestly can't tell a thing about piano quality. I can identify the showy white traveling one Powell uses for performances, and the well-cared for wooden one that sits in his music room and once belonged to his mother. But aside from those particular pianos I see all the time, they're all the same to me. I don't know what makes them good or bad or otherwise.

"Can I get you both some tea? I have a pitcher ready," Emily offers. She's changed into one of her modest dresses, and her damp hair has been combed. "Sorry, I wasn't expecting visitors. This place is such a mess." That's what every woman says when unexpected company shows up, but she's exaggerating. It's mostly neat and uncluttered. None of the evidence I'm looking for is laying around, like, say, marriage certificates, how-to guides on killing husbands, a shelf full of labeled urns.

"Tea would be wonderful," Tanner says. He's sitting on the hideous couch, trying to pretend he's not about to jump up and shout *j'accuse* and use a bunch of St. Louis slang to trap her.

I offer to help Emily, partly so I can snoop around her kitchen. It's disappointing, again, with the lack of evidence. Her refrigerator is plastered with takeout menus—Chinese, Mexican, non-St. Louis pizza, and one from the Thai place we passed on the way here, the one Tanner suggested we try next time we're in the area. Inside the fridge is sparse, just a few sandwich fixings, some fruit, and the promised tea.

"We'll have to drink this in the living room," Emily tells me as she gets out the glasses. "I sold most of my grandmother's furniture before I moved here. I did keep her dining set, but it doesn't fit in my apartment, so it's in storage while I decide what to do with it. I've been eating on the coffee table."

Tanner accepts his glass of tea politely, but the second Emily looks away from him, he mouths 'poison?' at me. I shake my head. Even if she's an intended black widow, she wouldn't be foolish enough to kill us in her home. Though I didn't tell anybody where we were going. Do I have time to shoot off a quick text to Powell? Or to Mike?

"So, Emily," Tanner seems to have decided to take the lead on the conversation. "Last night was uncomfortable, wasn't it?"

"You should have seen them this morning," she replies, while sipping the tea she poured from the same pitcher as the rest of ours, so unless this is an immunity-to-iocane-powder type situation, it should be safe. I take a cautious sip and don't immediately keel over. "I'm not used to being around celebrities, of course, but I never expected so much drama."

"That was not a normal occurrence," I explain. "But I think Tanner was talking about the food. Powell had asked him to cook you a taste of home . . ."

Emily's cheeks turn scarlet, and she covers her face with her hands. "I'm so so so embarrassed!"

That is most certainly not what I expected. I had a whole scenario in my head in which she insisted she really was from St. Louis, and the two of them got into a fact battle, shouting things about riverboats and Provel cheese and the famous Arch until she admits defeat, tells us she's actually from some foreign country, and she murdered the real Emily Davis and stole her identity.

Tanner and I exchange a somewhat confusing glance. He keeps raising his eyebrows and kind of tilting his chin at me. I have no idea what that man is trying to convey, so we continue sitting in uncomfortable silence, sipping our non-poisoned tea, and waiting for Emily to look at us again.

She finally regains her composure. "Did Powell already tell you? Is that why you came?"

"Tell us what?" Other than 'no, she didn't contact gossip sites,' and calling her his girlfriend, he's given me no new information about her today.

"There's been a little bit of confusion, and it's all my fault. I grew up fairly sheltered, I was raised by my grandparents, and because they were so old, and my grandad was always sick, I didn't get to do much. I . . . I'm kind of a small-town girl who doesn't always say the right things."

"St. Louis isn't a small town," Tanner points out, all puffed up with hometown pride.

"St. Louis, Michigan is. It never occurred to me that when I said I came from St. Louis, I should have clarified. I'm from right here," she holds up one hand and taps a spot on the palm. I squint at it, trying to see what she's talking about.

Tanner laughs at me. "Cass, that's how people from Michigan do geography. She's showing you the mitten."

Obviously, I'm going to look up the supposed other St. Louis later, find out if it's a real town or not. But for now, I'll pretend to believe her. And I may also look up Michigan sign language, make sure this 'mitten' thing isn't a practical joke they're playing on me.

"Yes, right in the middle of the mitten. We had a two-story house on the Pine River. Whenever I talked about my childhood with Powell, I guess I never mentioned the state. Tanner, I am so sorry! I thought you were such a weirdo at dinner, with your billboard song and your insistence on the pizza being normal. And the cake you brought! I'm sure it was delicious, but I've never been a cake fan anyway, and by that point I was so uncomfortable with listening to Xander and being the only woman at the table . . ."

"To be fair, Tanner is a weirdo," I assure her. My instinct is not to believe her because that's who I am as a person. But if Mike checked her out and says she's clean, and if she truly is so sheltered and socially awkward that she didn't realize we all thought she was from Missouri, then maybe this is all a misunderstanding. Maybe I've let Jackson get into my head.

# CHAPTER TWELVE

There is such a thing as angry guitar strumming. I can hear the difference in the notes, see it in the tightness with which Powell grips his pick. Also, the fact that he's glaring at me as I enter the room contributes to my analysis.

"What's your problem today? Did someone take a bad picture of you?" I flop down on the armchair across from him.

"Someone showed up at my girlfriend's house to harass her."

"That's the second time you've called her your girlfriend. Has Tabitha approved that language?"

His guitar emits a discordant growl. "I don't need Tabby's permission."

"Did Emily say we were harassing her?"

"A ha!" The guitar exclaims as loudly as he does. "So, you admit it?"

"No, Powell, I don't admit anything. Yes, Tanner and I stopped by Emily's, but we certainly weren't harassing her. It was a friendly visit."

"Can you pull off friendly?" Wow, he sounds exactly like Tanner. And that's insulting. He's seen me in action at industry events, smiling, laughing, complimenting people, not punching record execs with wandering hands. See, friendly.

"I'm always friendly, thank you for the insinuation."

"Oh, yeah? Then explain to me why she was crying on the phone?"

"I don't know Powell, you tell me. When we left, she was fine." Still shy and nervous, but definitely not in tears. She even hugged us both, so she couldn't have been too upset with us.

"She said you went over there to accuse her of lying about where she was from."

"Sort of, possibly. But she's the one who brought it up first. And she's the one who kept saying she was from St. Louis without clarifying she was talking about a tiny town in the middle of the mitten."

"What mitten?"

"This one!" I hold up my hand just like Emily had, and now my brother thinks I'm insane, since I'm obviously not wearing any mittens.

"Have you been drinking?" he asks skeptically.

"No, it's a Michigan thing. Tanner explained it."

"I thought he was from Missouri."

"That doesn't mean he doesn't know anything about other states. People travel, Powell."

"What's the abbreviation for Michigan, anyway?" His strumming has slightly calmed down now.

"I'm not a geography expert. Ask Emily."

"She'll think I'm an uneducated idiot if I ask something like that. Remind me to look it up later."

I could remind him he has a phone and is perfectly capable of looking it up right now, but I won't. I could also point out that technically, he is uneducated, having been road-schooled while on tour and barely passing his GED test. He's smart in the ways that count, even without book learning. But as a college drop-out who also spent part of my education not paying attention while being road-schooled on tour, I can't mock him for being the same. Though I did do most of my senior year of high school in person at a real school. The Last Barons were in the recording studio at the time.

"When did she tell you where specifically she was from?"

"After dinner, after Tanner and Xander left. She made a comment about how strange Tanner was acting, and I said I thought they'd get along better since they're both from St. Louis. Then Devon said something about how on the inside we're all from the same place, and I got distracted. He's gone off the deep end, hasn't he?"

"That's what Brix says."

"But anyway, later on, Emily and I were in my room, and she cried from embarrassment, and she told me the truth about the misunderstanding. She's so sweet, she was afraid everybody would hate her."

"In your room? Powell, I don't want details, ever, but . . ." My brother is a sucker for tears. They're his undoing.

"Yeah, I know, it wasn't the seventh date. But she was crying, and I was comforting her, and one thing led to another. And now I think we have to get married."

"It's too soon to know if you knocked her up. If she told you she's pregnant, she's either a liar or it's not yours." This may not be the time to bring it up, but I hope he had her sign the paperwork I left on his bed.

"No, it's not that. It's . . . it was her first time."

I laugh. I can't help it. "Powell, that can't possibly be true. She's what, twenty-seven? And attractive. And from a small town, and in small towns teenagers have nothing to do but sneak out behind the barn and have sex."

"What are you basing your theory on? An after school special?"

"Maybe. Or a book or something. I'm sure I heard that somewhere."

"She was serious, Deedee. And I have . . . reasons to believe her."

I put my head in my hands and want to shut out the entire world. Of all the stories I want to hear, anything involving my brother's sex life is not among them. "Not listening anymore."

"I wasn't going to share details. What's wrong with you?"

"Nothing. It's been a weird day. You describing your *reasons* wouldn't be out of place."

"Eww. No. You're my sister. And you're definitely not an expert. But Cass, seriously, I think I might have to marry her."

"Do you need to pay a dowry? What's the penalty for taking her virginity?"

"Not because of that. Don't you think it's possible to just sort of . . . know?"

"Know? Like she's your soulmate, and you belong together, and all that nonsense? No. I don't think it's possible. I think relationships need to be built over time, not jumped into."

"When my dad met—"

"Of course, I remember. When our parents met, it was love at first sight. I've heard the story a thousand times."

He blinks at me. "Oh, yeah, them too. I was going to say when my dad met *my* mom, it was love at first sight. She was playing piano in a restaurant, and he was dining with some work colleagues. He always said that from the moment he saw her, he knew he would marry her one day."

I remember that story, too. Hank is a hopeless romantic, and when he tells it, I swear little hearts and fireworks are circling around his head. Same as when he talks about seeing my mother at the snack counter of a Last Baron's concert when we were celebrating my twelfth birthday.

Powell plays a few more notes, softer and more contemplative. "I've been thinking about my mom a lot lately. I've dreamed about her. She's touching my cheek and telling me she loves me. It's odd; I haven't had those dreams in years. But she's just been on my mind way more than usual. Do you ever dream about your dad?"

"No. Not really. I was so young when he died." I was six years old. I remember hugging him good-bye when he dropped me off at school, and I ran off without a backwards glance. Then I never got to see him again, not even in my dreams. His funeral was closed casket, due to the severity of his injuries.

"That's sad." He continues strumming, eyes distant. I think tears are forming. Oh my god. His mom is on his mind because he's fallen in love and is wishing she was here to bless his wedding. This is the 'I wish my mom could meet the future mother of her grandchildren' moment.

Comforting people has never been my strong suit. "Are you wondering what your mom would have thought of Emily?"

"Deedee, I already know she would have loved her." He plays the opening chord to a song I faintly recognize. "When I first met her, I felt this strange connection. I had this need to impress her. Isn't that funny? All I wanted to do was make her smile, and that was after talking to her for five seconds, the night she smuggled me out in her car. It was instantaneous." He plays a few more chords, and then begins to softly sing:

*Something old and something new*
*I really want to marry you . . .*

"Stop!" I interrupt. "I remember this one. Isn't this the proposal song you wrote as a joke five years ago? Doesn't it say, 'when you leave, you'll take all of my soul and half my assets?' And isn't there a line about castration? Don't sing this now. Don't sing this to her, not ever."

"I'm going to rewrite *those* lyrics. You know, it's kind of crazy. When I'm not with her, I think about her, and it's . . . she's fine. I like her, she's pretty and she loves music, and she's so sweet. But when I'm around her, I just have this urge to try to earn her love. Like I want her to care about me and be proud of me, and I want to protect her. She makes me feel strong and needed, but at the same time, like a little boy desperate for her affection. I've never felt that way with anyone before, ever."

Is it me, or is that not a ringing endorsement? But I'm not the expert in relationships.

"What does Tabitha have to say about all of this?" The cynic in me suspects she'll start counting her bonus money. "Is she going to take you engagement ring shopping? Be careful, I've seen what's on her finger. She has expensive, gaudy taste."

"No, Felicity does." He plays another chord, winces, and tries again. "Tabby would have preferred something much smaller and more low profile, but her stepmother doesn't think that's appropriate. It doesn't sell the image of successful matchmaking. Tabby hates her ring, but she's dedicated to the cause."

"Creating the illusion of love? Is that the cause?" Lillian thinks all men are interchangeable, Tabitha flaunts a ring to pretend she's snagged a wealthy man, they coat everything in pink and charge a fortune to basically run tests through a computer algorithm and throw parties?

"Finding love is the cause," he corrects me. "And it works. I'm supposed to meet with Tabitha later this evening to discuss the last date and plan the next one, and it needs to be super romantic. But I can't tell her we already slept together."

"Yeah, you should leave that out. There's probably a clause in the contract with some kind of penalty. You'll owe her another hundred grand for violating it."

"There isn't. I called my lawyer this morning; I'm in the clear." At least he's taking those legal precautions. And I know he's a stickler for condoms; I was the one who handed them out and made groupies sign non-disclosure forms on the final Last Barons tour. Responsibility was drilled into their heads from the moment they were cast in the band. *There will be no bastards on my watch*, their manager repeatedly informed them. *And no diseases either*. That last bit was usually directed at Mason, the most reckless one, though Xander did put up a decent fight for the title.

"Do you honestly see yourself marrying her?"

"I might. She'd be a good mom to our kids. She's kind and compassionate, and she doesn't seem to be after my money. I haven't asked her yet, but I'm planning to bring her as a date to my big party."

"The launch party? That'll be filled with photographers. Is she comfortable with that?" The Emily I've met is a shrinking violet. Powell's dates to these events get swarmed by not just the paparazzi, but by lower-level record label personnel who want to manipulate their way to the top. Plus, there's the endless need to smile, wear heels, say only positive things about the new album, and simultaneously stay on Powell's arm yet remain in the background. It's exhausting work; I know, because I've done it. But when *I* do it, I don't also have to flirt with him, kiss his cheek without getting lipstick on his face, and show enough cleavage to be sexy without being trashy.

"I told her before I take her to any big events, I would hire Tanner for a session in advance so she can practice posing. She didn't like that suggestion though. She said he makes her uncomfortable. I'm sure that's just because of the whole St. Louis misunderstanding. Do you think it's a bad idea?"

"Yes. Not only the launch party, but also rushing into marriage. You're moving too quickly."

"I'm not an idiot. I'd make her sign a prenup."

"Right, but . . . you need to know her long enough to make sure she isn't planning to murder you on your honeymoon."

His jaw literally drops, and I realize how ridiculous I sound.

"You think Emily is going to murder me? *Emily*? She made me take a spider outside instead of swatting it. She's not going to kill anybody, especially me."

"Was it a black widow? Maybe she felt a kinship. Jackson said . . ."

"Jackson? The guy who spent an entire evening flirting with Lexa and flaunting his wealth? He told you Emily was plotting to kill me? And you believed him?" Powell's immediate skepticism is warranted, but only because he doesn't know Jackson's real identity.

"No, let me explain. He said he knew someone who used LoveMatch's guarantee program and died on his honeymoon, and he thinks maybe . . ."

"Maybe the whole organization is a front for a murder collaborative? They lure men in, charge them lots of money, and then kill them? Cassidy, are you listening to yourself?"

Powell's right. This is absurd. Right?

"Deedee," he sets down his guitar and moves to sit on the arm of my chair, leaning in to hug me. "I'm worried about you. You haven't fully processed what happened with Jace's killers. You barely survived the attack, and it's made you untrusting. Well, more untrusting. I want you to talk to someone about it. A professional."

"I don't need a therapist. This has nothing to do with that! Powell, I . . ." But I can't continue protesting because he's right. I haven't processed the attack. I haven't coped with my own near-death experience, nor what it was like to watch my brother's life slipping away in front of me. I like to think I'm not the kind of person to dwell on difficult times; I prefer to shove them down inside and pretend they didn't happen. Perhaps those experiences are coloring my perspective now.

"Emily is genuinely sweet, and caring, and gentle. I know it's hard for you to see the good in people. I promise, Emily is not planning on killing anybody, ever. That's not a thing most people do." He's using a soothing tone and gently stroking my hair. He's much better at the whole 'comforting' thing than I am.

"Yeah, I know. I'm sorry." I truly am. I've been acting so suspicious; I was so ready to jump all over Emily. But maybe I'm the problem. Perhaps I need to make more of an effort.

He slides down the arm of the chair until he's practically on my lap. "Deedee, I love you. You need to relax, chill out a little.

Why don't I order takeout from that awful vegetarian place you love so much, and we can watch a movie? You can even pick, as long as it's not too gory."

"I don't watch gore. I like true crime documentaries." Better than the stupid slapstick comedies he prefers.

"Maybe you need a break from crime, to clear your mind. How about we watch old concert footage, and talk about Devon and Brixley? You would not believe some of the stuff he told me. He's got issues."

Perfect. That's exactly the distraction I need right now. Also, I desperately want to hear Devon's version of the breakup. Or Powell's interpretation of Devon's side. That's probably even better. Less accurate, but more entertaining.

# CHAPTER THIRTEEN

When I was a child living in poverty, my mother always did her best to take care of me. She made so many sacrifices that I didn't appreciate until I was older. Now that I'm an adult, she still likes to take care of me, notably by spoiling me with gifts. I'm not much of a materialist, so she tends to favor things like activities we can do together.

That's why I spent the afternoon with my mom at her favorite day spa, getting seaweed body wraps, matching mani-pedis, and relaxing facials. I let her pay, so she could feel motherly and like she's taking care of me.

But I'm also an independent adult, so when we leave the spa for a trendy downtown bar, I pull out my own credit card and make her put hers away. Drinks are on me.

"What are you lovely ladies up to tonight?" the flirtatious bartender asks as he places our chocolate martinis in front of us. So far, he's winked in our direction three times, and I can't tell which of us is the object of his affections. Or if he perhaps has something in his eye.

"Just a mother-daughter evening," Mom replies, lifting her glass to toast me.

"Oh? Should I make a third one for your mother now, or wait until she gets here?" And here's wink number four, straight at Mom. He's way too young for her, and quite inobservant, given the expensive-but-not-ostentatious ring on her finger.

"We'll signal you when she arrives," I assure him as I set down a large cash tip. When he walks away, we both laugh.

"You think he was serious, or angling for a bigger tip?" Mom asks me.

"Probably serious. It's not the first time." Many people guess that we're sisters. We're obviously related, with our similar facial features, and identical chestnut brown hair—though mine is still natural and hers partly originates in a pricey bottle. The perception of exactly *how* we're related is skewed by the fact that she's only twenty years older than me and does not look close to her age. That comes from healthy living, personal training, and good genes. My mother has never gone under the surgeon's knife, never had botox, and is the envy of all her peers. I aspire to be like her, though the little crinkles forming at the corners of my eyes suggest I carry my father's aging genetics more strongly. He never had the chance to grow old, but I've seen pictures of his sister. I fear I'm going to be a wrinkly hag before I'm forty.

"Being your mother is a lot of work; I'd like to get credit for it," she teases. "So . . . tell me everything I've missed." She and Hank just got back from a six-week trip. Mom is a nurse, and she keeps her license up so that she can volunteer around the world. They spent the first five weeks helping out at a refugee camp. Hank has zero medical skills and hates needles, but he's always enthusiastic to accompany her on these missions. He's good at carrying things, following directions, and schmoozing with donors to get more money out of them. After the work part of the trip ended, they went to a beach resort, which is why my mother is well-rested, tan, and happy.

"Mom, we spoke on the phone every week, plus you were active on SwiftaPic. You haven't missed anything."

"Your brother plans to purchase himself a bride. That's something you never mentioned, and Powell has only given the sparsest of details. You need to fill me in."

"What did he tell you this morning?" My brother went over to their house for breakfast before he and his dad hopped on a plane to LA. Powell will be appearing on television tonight to promote his new album, something I normally accompany him to—he needs someone in his dressing room showering him with compliments and practicing his talking points. But this time Hank went; Powell also needs help selling his condo. Neither my brother nor I have been willing to set foot in that place since the attack, so Hank is handling the final details for him. I can't help; there are bloodstains on the floor that still haunt my nightmares. Even if they've been cleaned up, in my mind they're still there.

"Not too much, but he suggested he might have found one. Or 'the one,' rather."

"Emily. She's a piano player who wants to go back to school to be a music teacher. She's blond and pretty and apologizes constantly."

"Do you think she'll hold up to scrutiny?"

"She already has," I reply, thinking about Mike's background check and the whole St. Louis debacle. I should have called Mike back and told him he could have spared me some humiliation had he named the specific *state* Emily came from. "Oh, wait, you mean media scrutiny? She doesn't use any social media, and she lacks any desire to stand in the spotlight."

"It's not like she'll have much of a choice. Look how many times you've been profiled, and you're only his sister. And you're not after attention."

"Ugh. I certainly receive a lot of it though."

"Yes, I know. I follow your SwiftaPic mentions. You and Jace would have had either very beautiful or very horrifying looking babies." She shows me her screenshotted collection of favorites from the #BabyJace fiasco, including both gorgeous little cherubs and distorted monsters. I'm not sure I appreciate what some of the fans think of me.

"That never would have happened anyway, even if he hadn't died."

"I've always known that. You had a massive crush on Jace as a teenager, but you didn't love him. His feelings wouldn't have changed yours." My mom was as blindsided as I was by the revelations in Jace's will. We never discussed what she really thinks about the situation though, because that's a difficult conversation, and I tend to avoid those.

"I did love him!" I object, my knee-jerk reaction. You never know when someone is eavesdropping, ready to post an exposé. And anyway, it's true. I loved him. Initially it was teenage infatuation, then for a while it was hatred, but eventually my feelings for him turned back into love. But platonic love, always seeded with doubt and distrust. Hmmm. Maybe I should rethink how I characterize my emotional connections.

"Not romantically, though. Jace became a wonderful friend to you, but you never would have worked as a couple. You wouldn't want to trade taking care of one spoiled celebrity for another."

I choke on a sip of my martini. When I'm done coughing, I manage to gasp out, "Did you refer to Powell as a spoiled celebrity? I'm totally telling him what you said."

"I've said it to his face. Sure, he loves you, and you two are best friends and the closest siblings I could imagine, but he often takes you for granted. And you both know it. You have a caring and nurturing nature, Cassidy. You're the one always supporting him. Someday I'd like it to be the other way around."

"He bought me a LoveMatch membership. Does that count as support?"

"Are you using it?" Mom is surprised, which amuses me because I was sure Powell would have mentioned to her that he was dragging me on his ill-conceived scheme to find us mates. Well, I suppose I shouldn't call it ill-conceived. Powell did what he usually does: he decided what he wanted, threw money at it, and forced me to participate.

"I've reluctantly attended events. I was actually the one who met Emily first."

"You know, when I was your age—"

"Yeah, yeah, yeah," I interrupt. "When you were my age, you'd already fallen in love once and truly believed you'd do so again." She'd met my dad in college, moved in with him within months, and shortly thereafter found herself knocked up. They got married immediately and shared several happy years until he was cruelly taken from us. I'm quite familiar with this story.

"No, that's not at all what I was going to say. When I was your age, I was a widow, broke, homeless, and trying to raise a child. I envy the freedom you have right now." She almost sounds wistful. Sometimes I forget how difficult she had it, raising me the way she did. My mother sacrificed everything to keep me safe, and I don't always reflect on what that cost her.

"Oh. I thought you were going to be like Powell and lecture me about finding a partner and falling in love and having babies."

"I'm young; there's plenty of time to be a grandmother. Besides, I expect those to come from your brother first. No, Cass, what I want from you is all I've ever wanted: for you to be happy. You're fine single."

"Am I? I expected a big speech about taking this expensive matchmaking service more seriously." Then again, she has no idea how much Powell paid. If she knew . . . oh, I would love to be there when she rips my brother a new one for wasting so much money. While my mom can be spendy when it comes to some things, she's never shaken the frugality she developed during her earlier financial struggles.

"Of course not! Everything happens in its own time. I did meet your father when I was young, and we had you young, but remember, I was in my thirties when I met Hank. True love can show up at any age. And I don't think you're ready yet."

"Um, thanks?" What I'm getting from my mother is the opposite of everybody else. Frankly, it's hurtful. It's okay for *me* to say I'm not interested in dating, but for my mom to say I'm not *ready*? I went on my first date when I was sixteen! It was terrible, but still. I was ready. I could date now, if I wanted to. It's not a matter of preparation.

"This is the time for fun. Unless there's someone you have in mind, someone outside of LoveMatch. Perhaps a certain green-eyed photographer?"

I roll my eyes at her. Mom loves Tanner. She love love looooves him. I guess in part that's because he saved my life a couple of months ago. If it weren't for him, I'd be nothing more than burned and bloody scraps staining the side of a mountain road. But I don't waste much time thinking about the explosion, even though I do have faint scars on my arms to remind me.

"Tanner and I are just friends," I tell her for the hundredth time.

"I was out of town for six weeks; I didn't know if things had changed while I was away." She says the exact same thing when she's been gone six hours. This is not our first discussion about Tanner.

"Nothing changed. Nothing at all." I don't feel the need to share details about the accidental make out session that almost destroyed our friendship. Mom would read way too much into it.

She sighs, probably disappointed, because even though she says she expects grandbabies from Powell first, she does still expect them from me someday. And Tanner would father adorable children with vivid eyes and cute dimples. Though I would hope they wouldn't inherit his eyebrows. "We should head out. The show is going to be packed."

"Is it?" I check the time on my phone. The gallery opened its doors a few minutes ago. Tanner is talented, but I can't imagine there's a huge rush, unless . . . "Mom, what did you do?"

"You remember Betsy Svalbard? I gave her a personal invitation and told her not to tell anybody. I said Tanner's work is evocative and beautiful, but it takes a discerning eye to appreciate it, and not everybody will. I said we should keep the show to a more exclusive crowd."

My mother is a master of manipulation. Fortunately, she only uses her skills for good. If I know Betsy—and I do—she has bragged to hundreds of art collectors about Tanner's show, while making it sound like they won't understand the art. Dozens of people will descend upon the gallery to make purchases just to prove they have sophisticated taste. Hopefully they like the work too, but actual enjoyment is often secondary to the status symbol of having something Virginia Corbitt called exclusive in their collections.

"You are an evil mastermind," I tell my mother, raising my glass to her before finishing off my delicious chocolate martini.

"Evil? Or appreciative of the man who saved my daughter's life? I'm planning on purchasing his most expensive piece."

Mom was right; the gallery is packed. Richly garbed collectors are rubbing elbows with hipsters, art school students, and a few random guys dressed like they wandered in off the streets in search of free food. I bet those are some of Tanner's photographer friends.

I scan the room looking for Tanner. I can't find him, but I do spot Aurora Ridge. Even from behind, that matte black hair and gauzy dress is inarguably her. Speaking of from behind . . . her date. Wow. She's clinging to the arm of a man who I must have missed at the last LoveMatch event. He has . . . okay, I'm trying not to be objectifying here, but I don't know how else to say it: his ass is *fine*. He's wearing pants that look like they were made to his exact measurements, sewn on, and are grateful to be there.

"Did Tanner always have such a nice butt?" Mom whispers to me.

What? No. That man can't be Tanner. Just then, he reaches up to run a hand—the one presently unencumbered by a clinging *artiste*—through his hair, and the familiarity of the gesture confirms it. My mom is right. It is Tanner. So now I have several questions. One is, obviously, how was a man who exclusively shops in thrift stores lucky enough to find pants that fit like that? Two: Aurora Ridge? Three: *Aurora Ridge, seriously*? I swear he said there was nothing there. Four: How quickly did he jump from kicking me out of his bed to pulling her into it?

I'd like to turn around and leave, but my mother grabs two glasses of champagne off a passing waiter's tray, hands me one, and drags me over to congratulate the artist.

But his date is the one who spots us first.

"Cassidy! Oh, my darling, I'm absolutely delighted you're here!" Suddenly Aurora Ridge is exchanging air kisses with me. "I'm so glad you're finally getting involved in the arts scene."

I hear my mother snort behind me, before she is also swept up in the cloud of energy that is Aurora.

"This is my mother, Ginny," I introduce. Aurora hugs my mom, then pulls back and grips her upper arms firmly while staring into her eyes.

"You are a brave and strong woman. I would love to use you as my muse," she gushes, a compliment that is starting to wear thin. Is there anyone she doesn't want to paint? "I am so thrilled to welcome you to my friend's show. Let me introduce you to my darling boy." Even though Tanner is facing away from us and clearly participating in a different discussion, she grabs his sleeve and spins him around to greet us.

"Hey!" He exclaims happily.

"Cassidy," Aurora continues, "Do you remember Tanner from the LoveMatch carnival?" Aurora pronounces carnival as though she's Brazilian. Why does she try to sound so fancy? Does Tanner like her faux accent? Is that why he's here with her hanging off him, because she's artistic and dramatic? I thought he'd derisively referred to her as a trustafarian who was only after Swifta followers. "We exchanged our interest cards and had coffee. This sweetheart is a photographer, can you believe it? Serendipity, I tell you. Pure serendipity that we met."

"I also met Tanner due to his work," I say politely. "Specifically, he was creeping around outside my house like a stalker. Not so serendipitous, I guess."

"Hush, Cassidy," my mother murmurs before sweeping Tanner into a hug. "Tanner, it's wonderful to see you again." When he's released, he doesn't try to greet *me* with a hug. Apparently, he's sticking to his threat of never touching me again, even though I gave him explicit permission for hugs.

"Thanks for coming. And, Ginny, I haven't had a chance to write a thank you note yet, but I really appreciated the housewarming gift you sent."

"Housewarming gift?" I ask. I hadn't heard about that. I hope he accepted it with a lot more grace than when he received mine. Perhaps he set the package in a corner for a few days, letting it rest before he eventually decided to open it.

"Yes." Amusement glints in his eyes. "She sent me a bottle of wine, a fire extinguisher, and a scented candle. Which I really appreciate."

Hmph. I didn't know I needed to call my mother while she travels abroad to coordinate housewarming gifts.

"The candle smells like chocolate chip cookies, so I thought it was appropriate." Mom pats him on the arm affectionately.

In addition to loving him for saving my life, she also loves him for his baking skills. Though when she shows up at various board meetings with platters of cookies, I'm not sure who gets the credit. "Now, I need to take a look around. I've brought my credit card."

"You don't . . . you don't have to buy anything," Tanner shoves his hands in his pockets and starts acting all embarrassed. "That's not why I invited you." He is the worst salesperson of all time. Don't invite a wealthy art collector to your gallery opening and then tell them not to spend money. That's not how selling works.

"Nonsense," Mom says. "I'm not buying out of a sense of obligation. Your work is beautiful. Aurora, you're an artist; why don't you show me your favorite piece." She's purposely ditching me with Tanner, perhaps because of her earlier insinuations that I need a green-eyed photographer in my romantic life. Or perhaps because she noticed the absence of his traditional affectionate greeting and can sense there's still something off between us.

Aurora is, of course, glad to do so. She, unlike Tanner, knows how to make a living in this business, and sucking up to the people who arrive at shows ready to drop a ton of money is a good way of doing so. Not that Aurora is displaying anything in this gallery, but I imagine she's pressing her glossy business card into my mom's hand and regaling her with descriptions of her own artistry.

"I really am glad you came," Tanner tells me as they walk away. "I can't believe how crowded this place is. I never expected this."

"My mother loves you, so she may have hinted to a talkative nouveau riche collector that your work is exclusive. That's the magic word to get buyers in the door."

He almost seems disappointed to find out it wasn't his name alone drawing in the crowds.

"But you don't need us," I continue. "You have your girlfriend." I want to make a snarky remark about how swiftly he's moved on, and hey, didn't you say there was nothing between you? And also, this can't be an approved LoveMatch date, out in public like this, unless there have been several others in between that he's failed to mention.

"If I didn't know better, I would think you were jealous." His dimple is supremely irritating right now. "Besides, she just arrived ten minutes ago with an entire entourage, and they're cleaning out the hor d'oeuvres and loudly critiquing my work."

"Oh." I almost feel bad about my snap judgement. But it was within the realm of possibility, so I don't feel *that* bad. I change the subject. "I see you got all gussied up for the event."

He glances down at his shirt, a v-neck in a deep green fabric that clings to him, highlighting his abs, yet still appearing cool and professional. "Does this look okay?"

"Yes, definitely. New outfit? Did Aurora pick it out?"

"Stop that. For real, you don't know where it came from?"

"How would I? I mean, I can start naming thrift stores and consignment shops and you can tell me when I guess correctly." Honestly, he's never looked like this. Even when he dressed up in a suit for the Jace Monroe Memorial Concert, his clothing didn't fit this well.

"I got this today. It all happened at seven this morning, when someone started pounding on my door. When I went to answer, three people shoved their way into my apartment and attacked me."

"So, you were robbed? And then what, they stole all your clothes and you had to rush out and buy new ones?"

"No, they like, attacked me with measuring tapes and things. They had all these racks and boxes, and they didn't say a word, they just started stripping me and measuring me. At first, I thought you sent them."

"If I wanted someone to attack you, I'd send Mike's people, and I assure you, they would not use measuring tapes. Socks full of nickels maybe, but not measuring tapes."

"That would hurt! This is why people are scared of you." He takes a step back as if to demonstrate his fear, but I'm carrying an evening bag tonight, and there certainly isn't room in it for a sock full of any kind of coinage. "I finally got them to tell me where they came from, and they named some New York fashion house. They said, 'what Miss Brixley wants, Miss Brixley gets.' They gave me four complete outfits, three pairs of shoes, and a list of hashtags I'm supposed to use when I'm wearing them. Then they just left, saying they had to get back to the airport. She literally flew a group of designers out to dress me without asking."

"That sounds like Brixley making an apology for some of the hate you got when people thought you leaked her break-up without her permission." Brix's publicist decided it was best to claim the supermodel had asked her dear friend to leak the news because she was so tired of pretending. She's just ready to move on, you see, and it's so difficult when the world would condemn her as a cheater. She needs time away from Devon to continue her healing process, and isn't it wonderful how Tanner was willing to take the fall and possible bad press and spread the word for her?

"I lost a lot of SwiftaPic followers over that debacle," he says with a frown. "Hey, speaking of people being mad at me, is Powell still upset about the whole Emily thing? Is that why he isn't here?"

"No, he's out in LA filming a couple of tv spots for the new album. He was mad—at both of us—but I calmed him down." He's still a little salty, but mostly because he's bothered that I didn't blindly assume Emily was innocent and I actually investigated her. He's also kind of annoyed that I called Mike because *"you don't need to check up on me with* my *security guy, Cass."*

"I'm surprised you didn't go with him. Aren't you his assistant?"

"Isn't this your first Arizona show? I stayed to support you." Slight exaggeration. I didn't want to deal with the condo sale. But the gallery opening provided a solid excuse. And I did want to be here.

"Really?" He does that thing where he sort of smiles, then looks away like he's embarrassed. "Thanks, Cass."

Mom returns, a big grin on her face. "Most of the pieces are already marked sold. Great show, Tanner. I'm proud of you."

He blushes like a schoolboy. From what he's told me of his family, this might be the first time he's had someone say that to him.

# CHAPTER FOURTEEN

Tanner and I are working on repairing our friendship and getting back to the way things were without feeling awkward around each other. Step one was going over to Emily's and harassing her about her hometown. Step two was me showing up at Tanner's gallery opening and accidentally ogling his rear end, so that didn't quite go the way I planned.

And now, step three. He's coming over for lunch. I've taken some meals out of the freezer, ones our personal chef prepared. I heated them up and plated them nicely, so I can pretend they're freshly made, though Tanner will see right through the ruse. We'll be dining by the pool, so the table is ready, and the misters are on to keep us cool. I may open a bottle of prosecco and make some kind of mimosas, something light and fizzy and fun. Friendship repair requires a lot of prep work.

He arrives right on time, pulling up in his van and temporarily bringing down neighborhood property values while he parks in the driveway. I spy on him through the security camera as he hesitates, dragging his fingers through his hair and checking his reflection in the side view mirror before he grabs a cake box—cake? Yay!—and comes to the front door.

"It's unlocked, come on in," I invite him through the speaker and laugh when he jumps. No matter how many times he's come over, he always gets startled by that.

"I brought dessert," he announces when he finds me in the kitchen.

"You didn't have to bring anything." I'm the host; I'm prepared. There's a carton of vanilla almond ice cream in the freezer, his favorite flavor. I prefer anything with chocolate, but as the hostess, I was willing to make this concession for him.

"I owe you. Remember? You came over for lasagna and left before dessert." He opens the box to proudly display a raspberry cheesecake drizzled with dark chocolate. Okay, I'm not even going to mention the boring old ice cream. I'll be careful not to get cheesecake all over my face like the mousse-that-never-happened.

"That's right, you do. Put it in the fridge, we're eating outside."

Tanner, as always, is appreciative of a meal he neither had to cook nor pay for. And we're doing well. We talk about Powell's upcoming album release party—Tanner received a guest invitation, but I bet he asks for a press pass and spends the whole time hiding behind his lens.

"Oh, I almost forgot," he says after he puts his fork down and groans his appreciation for the food. I half expect him to belch and undo the top button of his cargo shorts. Why is he wearing those? Why didn't the sexy pants makers include shorts? Although I don't really care. I don't need him to wear nice clothes. I'm not checking him out or anything. "I brought over something I found at the thrift shop. I'll be right back."

I watch him as he cuts through the house to retrieve whatever junk it is from his van. Sigh. I definitely preferred the gallery show pants. I'm glad he's not wearing them.

He returns and flourishes an old magazine. "Ta-da!"

I accept it reluctantly. "*Teen Pop*, May 1998. Yay. Good job, buddy. Very topical." It still holds that thrift shop scent, a mix of disinfectant and dust that triggers childhood memories of back when all we could afford was used clothing, usually on bag days, when you could fill a paper shopping bag for three dollars. They didn't offer the best stuff on those sales, just leftover end-of-season cast-offs, or garments in too poor a condition for most people to bother with. Fortunately, my mom was skilled with a needle, thread, and stain remover.

"You have to check it out. It's vintage. And it's funny! Powell's baby picture is in there. I found it mixed in with a bunch of old *National Geographics*." That explains things; I doubt teenybopper magazines of the 90's are something he regularly searches out.

"Fourteen years old doesn't count as vintage," I inform him, but since he's so proud of himself, I oblige him and flip to the *Match the Baby Picture to the Star* game. Tanner points to a grinning blond toddler holding a toy car on an ugly plaid couch. "Nope. That's not Powell."

"According to the answer key it is."

"That's Bret from All4You. Powell is the one in the corner with the toy piano."

"Are you sure?" Tanner snatches the magazine and studies the pictures, as if he knows anything about what my brother looked like thirty years ago.

"Given that the toy piano one is in a frame on Hank's desk, yes, I'm sure. Bret is not Hank's secret love child. Also, I remember when it happened. Powell thought it was hilarious. They're all mixed up; *Teen Pop* had to print a retraction a couple of months later. They switched Xander with Vernon from Formula5. He was furious, his agent called up the editor and screamed. Honestly, Vernon's picture was better." I point out the difference. Then I take it back from him because I can't remember which one was Jace, and I want to compare his real picture to the awful #BabyJace images. I'm looking at all the smiling babies when something hits me. The couch under Bret's chubby baby legs is strangely familiar. Red and blue plaid, with bows on the arms. Why is that familiar? Wait . . .

"Tanner, look closely at the one they labeled Powell. Do you recognize the couch?"

"No, why would I? It looks like it's from the eighties. Well, I guess it is. It's hideous though."

"Right. Haven't we seen a spectacularly hideous couch lately?"

His eyes widen and he pulls out his phone, scrolling through millions and millions of pictures, so he can reach the ones from two weeks ago at Emily's house. They aren't his best shots, since he was trying not to be noticed, and he wasn't planning on posting them anywhere, but yes, that is the same couch. Same awful plaid, same enormous bows.

There's a sinking feeling in my stomach and a tingling in my fingers from the adrenaline rush. Something is wrong here.

Tanner isn't reacting the same way. Instead, he's laughing. "What a weird coincidence. Maybe these were a popular style. Didn't Emily say she got all her furniture from her grandmother? Is Bret from Michigan too?"

"Tanner! This can't be a coincidence. Don't you get it? That's marked as Powell's picture."

"Okay?"

I can't shake this strange sensation, but I can't quite figure out what's causing it either. Why would Emily have the same couch? I kind of want to call Jackson. But I need to do more research, try and confirm the nascent suspicion blooming in my mind.

"Do you think it's possible she tracked down that particular couch, thinking it was in his baby picture?" I'm still trying to formulate this into a theory. Why would she? How would that help her relationship with Powell?

"That's insane. Nobody would do that. I know you said Jackson was suspicious of LoveMatch, but that seems a bit over the top."

"There's a million-dollar bonus on the line."

"A how much bonus?" Tanner's eyes practically bug out of his head.

Yeah, I guess it might seem like a lot of money. It is a lot of money to most people. Heck, it's a lot of money to me. The majority of my assets are tied up in real estate. My bank account only has . . . well, let's say I could buy a husband from Felicity, but I couldn't afford to divorce him and buy another. Unless there's a discount on the second spouse. Buy one get one half off, maybe?

"Focus. It's not about the money. She said she inherited her grandmother's furniture, so either this is a huge coincidence, or she lied and got the couch specifically because she thought it was similar to the one Powell had as a kid."

Tanner is silent for a moment, considering. He blinks a few times, and nods, so I guess that means he's had some sort of revelation. Or he came up with some SwiftaPic tags. #uglycouches #badfurnitureofthe80s #coinkydinkormurderplot.

"What was your childhood couch like?" he asks, still doing his I-have-a-theory nod.

I close my eyes and think back. It was brown and floral, with hard wooden arms. "Uncomfortable and ugly." My mom hated it; I remember that. My dad used to sprawl across it, reclining on throw pillows and reading his big heavy textbooks. On movie nights, I would sit between them, bowl of popcorn in my lap. And when I was five and had chicken pox, I spent all my time snuggled on the firm cushions, watching television and scratching, while Mom brought me cups of juice and dabbed calamine lotion all over me.

"You're smiling," Tanner points out. "It may have been ugly, but you have fond memories. Do you think . . ."

"She bought the couch thinking Powell would recognize it and it would trigger happy childhood memories? That's ridiculous."

"No, not for the memories, for the emotions. It's subliminal. You just don't understand because you don't have emotions." Figures Tanner would use this serious investigatory discussion to insult me.

"So much for you and I resetting our friendship, Tanner."

"Sorry, I meant that as a joke. But I bet I'm right. Not about the you not having emotions part, but about the trigger. If we're going to believe your outlandish theories, that's at least an explanation. She bought a piece of Powell's childhood, so he would feel at home, so he would feel content, so he would be comfortable."

"Maybe my theories aren't so outlandish after all." I'm thinking back to my first appointment with Lillian. "His entire life is in magazines."

"What?" Tanner is confused, and I realize I've pulled a Powell-style unexplained non-sequitur.

"At my LoveMatch intake, Lillian wanted insight on how to find the perfect woman for Powell, and I told her everything she needs to know about him is in magazines." It was a throwaway line because I wasn't going to help her out with specifics.

"You think Emily and Lillian are working together? What about Tabitha?"

"I don't know. Tabitha is so . . . earnest. And dedicated to the process. She believes in what they're doing." After my French bakery talk with Tabitha, I can't imagine her being that manipulative. She truly trusts the algorithm. She's getting married because of it.

"So, Lillian went to the trouble to track down an ideal woman, and then bought her a hideous couch and told her to lie about where she got her furniture? If—and I'm not agreeing with you yet—they did this, then this can't be the only thing, right? There has to be more to trap Powell than just outdated furniture."

"You're right. Tanner, we need to investigate further. Come with me."

Lucky for us, Powell's still out of town. If he were here, and he knew where I was taking Tanner, he would insist on accompanying us. And then we'd have to listen to him tell the backstory of every single piece of memorabilia in his vault. We'd be trapped in there for days.

I lead Tanner through the house and Powell's music room. The music room is my brother's pride and joy, with his mother's old piano as the focal point. There are some comfortable chairs set up, so he can have an audience. One wall is hung with his guitar collection. And the wall across from it, the one that looks like decorative stone and displays a large artsy metal sculpture of a stylized piano, that's the wall holding a secret.

"You ready for this?" I ask, as I reach my hand under the keyboard of the wall art. I press the correct spot, hold it down for three seconds, and the hidden door swings open. As I had hoped, Tanner gasps loudly.

"That was so cool, Cass! You have a panic room?"

"Of course, but not here. The panic room is in my closet."

"What?"

"Yeah, the big mirror on the back wall is the door."

"Does Powell have one, too?"

"Same one, it connects our closets."

"Can I see it?"

"Not right now. Maybe later. I want to show you something in here first."

Tanner shakes his head, eyes still comically wide. "I find it interesting how you're all 'I grew up poor, I'm a normal person' and at the same time, you're like, 'why yes, of course I have a panic room behind my enormous closet, doesn't everybody? Anyway, let's check out my other secret room.' Do you not see the dichotomy here?"

"I live the dichotomy, Tanner." Lots of people transition from poverty to wealth. Or at least, that's the fantasy, isn't it?

This particular secret room is a Last Barons fan's dream—it's where Powell keeps all of his memorabilia. The walls are covered in posters and framed albums. A cardboard cutout of eighteen-year-old Powell stands in the corner, keeping watch over it all. Because, of course, my brother would keep that.

Tanner hefts a trophy. "Is this a Grammy? It's heavy!"

"Five pounds. He's got another over there—you can use them as hand weights. But if you drop them, he'll send Mike to kill you."

Tanner prudently puts the award down, but he can't keep his hands to himself, so he picks up the crystal America's Choice trophy. That's from Powell's solo career, not the boy band. "Album of the Year? Nice. I didn't know he was this good."

"I can give you a printed award list from his media packet. It's three pages long. I'm surprised you don't have a copy already."

"I'm a serious photographer," Tanner reminds me, an argument we've had many times. Somehow to him being serious means not researching the celebrities he stalks.

My phone buzzes with a text. WHAT ARE YOU DOING IN THERE?

Sigh. The door sensor alerted my brother to our location. I don't want to tell him the truth, not yet, in part because if we're wrong, he's going to be so mad at me.

I'M SHOWING TANNER YOUR AWARDS SHELF. HE DIDN'T BELIEVE THAT YOU'VE WON ANYTHING AT ALL, EVER. SOMETHING ABOUT BOYBANDS BEING A PASSING FAD.

Tanner's phone immediately starts going off with a series of incoming messages. He frowns at the screen. "What exactly did you tell Powell we're doing? He's sending me a ton of press releases."

"Sorry, I'll fix it."

POWELL, I WAS KIDDING. I JUST WANTED TO SHOW HIM THE ROOM. AND HE'S VERY IMPRESSED WITH ALL OF YOUR ACCOLADES. STOP SPAMMING HIM.

I apologize to Tanner for unintentionally subjecting him to my brother's obsessive need to be admired. At least I cut him off after a dozen messages, and before Powell started including video links.

Now, to get down to what we're here for: I open the file cabinet and start pulling out magazines. They're all in protective plastic covers and organized by years. "Grab some gloves and help me." I take my own white cotton gloves and pass him the box. We risk Powell's wrath if we leave fingerprints on any of these pages.

"What are we looking for?" Tanner asks, gloving up and sitting cross legged on the floor with a stack of old *Hot Teen Hits!* from the late nineties.

"Anything about Powell. Anything that jumps out at us as something Emily might be using to gain his trust or affection."

We flip through in silence. I haven't looked at any of these in years, and it's so funny to see these old pictures. Most of the articles are drivel, full of trivial Last Barons facts. Mason loves dogs! Jace is a Libra! Wow, Xander played little league baseball. And Powell . . . the only bone he's ever broken was a toe. I guess these are the things teenage fans cared about. I remember getting into fierce debates with my middle school friends about which Last Baron we were going to marry, and who was the best singer, but I never wondered if Devon liked oatmeal cookies or Jace poured the milk before the cereal.

"Hey!" Tanner suddenly exclaims excitedly. I look up, hoping he's found something that would constitute proof that Emily was somehow acquiring Last Barons knowledge to manipulate Powell. But I'm disappointed by the image he's chosen to share.

"Put it away. I don't want to see that. It's embarrassing."

"But you're so cute! What are you, fourteen? Cass, you're adorable. You had braces!" He keeps shoving his find at me, so I take the magazine. *Powell Corbitt relaxes backstage with his sister Cassidy.* It's one of the candid shots from after a show. Powell is still wearing his shiny performance shirt. I'm next to him, trying to hand him a plate of food, but we're both laughing about something off camera. I don't remember seeing this specific image before, but I must have. One of my jobs was scanning through all these articles, looking for factual errors. My stepdad paid me fifty bucks for everything I found, and then he'd demand the retractions, edits, and apologies on Powell's behalf.

"Lots of kids had braces. Can you focus?"

"Can we take these out to the patio? Maybe grab a beer?" Tanner is clearly not taking this mission seriously. He watches Crime TV with me. Shouldn't he realize that most investigative work is tedious? Also, he has no idea how much of a stickler Powell is about maintaining pristine archives.

"We're wearing special gloves. Do you honestly think we're allowed to risk liquid around these?"

Tanner surveys the stacks we've already gotten out and the filing cabinets behind me. He sighs, a photography snob conveying his boredom with looking at other people's photographs. "Fine. But this is going to take all afternoon. We should order takeout for dinner."

"Sure, whatever." I don't much care about dinner plans, other than having leftover cheesecake for dessert. Besides, I'm preoccupied reading about Powell's favorite shoes, a fluff piece that was his first endorsement deal. He didn't actually like them. They pinched his toes, and the soles weren't flexible enough.

"We could try that new Thai place," Tanner proposes, still fixated on his stomach, even though we literally just ate a full meal.

"Can't get takeout from there," I respond automatically. "Peanuts." We can't bring those in the house. I take the next one from the stack. This is a group interview where they talk about their favorite subjects in school. Music, obviously, for all but Devon who loves 'anything science related.' Given his current crystal obsession, I doubt those science lessons stuck.

Something is bothering me. A little worm crawling around in my brain. We saw the menu at Emily's.

"Tanner," I say slowly as it's coming to me. "Emily said she's allergic to peanuts."

"I think it's a common allergy. I recently read a piece about the increase in peanut allergies . . ."

"No, stop talking. She had the Thai menu on her fridge. There's no way she could eat there. Powell would go into anaphylactic shock just walking through the door."

"She lied!" Tanner's finally getting it. "Wait, why would she make up an allergy?"

"So she has something else in common with Powell? Making a connection through shared experiences?" I'm trying to think what else I know about her. She plays the piano—but that's not something she can fake. Her grandmother died of cancer. Wait. "She said she nursed her grandmother through cancer. It started in the breast and spread everywhere."

Tanner grabs a magazine. "I just read about that. Not Emily's grandma, Powell's mom. Breast cancer that wasn't caught early enough. These coincidences are adding up."

I didn't need to read about that to know it already. Powell's mother died in hospice care when he was ten; we've talked about it dozens of times over the years. I'm familiar with every detail about the twisted path the disease took through her body, and everything they tried to do to find a cure or buy more time. Powell is still traumatized. He pays for me to get a mammogram every year, even though I don't carry the scary breast cancer gene, and I'm not at a high risk.

"These coincidences are manufactured. Hang on, I want to start making a list." I pull up a notes app on my phone.

1. Peanuts (allergic???)

2. Cancer (fake??? Ask Mike to find obituary)

3. Couch (why???)

While I'm compiling my notes and thinking about calling Jackson for advice—he's a secret agent, I'm sure he knows what to do—Tanner continues paging through old Last Barons propaganda.

"What does Emily smell like?" He's staring down at an article, finger pointing at something I can't read from this angle.

"Ummm . . . springtime, according to Powell. I think she smells like honeysuckle."

"Listen to this. *My mother was my biggest supporter, and she still is. Sometimes I get a whiff of her perfume, a phantom honeysuckle aroma, and I know that's her, looking down on me and beaming with pride.*"

"Holy crap, Tanner! Emily stole his mom's smell."

He's staring at me, mind working. "Scent is the strongest memory trigger. If she is deliberately wearing perfume to smell like his mother . . . that's gross."

"No, that's safety and security and comfort. He told me he feels oddly secure with her, he said she brings up strong emotions and a sense of connection. She's manipulating him on a subconscious level!"

Everything about her is suspect now. I bet Prokofiev isn't her favorite composer, I bet there's an article out there saying he was Powell's mom's favorite.

"Cass, this is evil!"

"We need to call Jackson." Our secret agent friend needs to be aware. He can add this to the mountain of evidence he's been collecting, pass it on to his superiors, and then we'll sit back with popcorn and watch LoveMatch implode. I just have to hope he doesn't want Powell to keep dating Emily to gather more intel. I don't want to put my brother at risk.

The basement bar contains a selection of top shelf liquors, so that's where we retreat after taking pictures of the relevant interviews we've found so far and carefully repackaging the magazines in their archival envelopes.

"Gin and tonic?" Tanner suggests, and helpfully goes behind the bar and pulls out the bottles. He's been here often enough to be perfectly comfortable back there.

While he pours, I set my phone on the counter between us, dial Jackson, and turn on the speaker. But he doesn't answer. Figures. I'll text him instead.

Hey! Got some evidence Emily isn't who she says she is and is lying to manipulate Powell. Call me!

My drink is half-consumed before I receive a response.

In middle of something now period space bring Eva dance tomorrow my place sent I said sent hey watch what you're doing dammit wait sent sent

"Use your superior texting skills and tell me what this is." I shove my phone at Tanner's face.

"Jackson uses talk to text and doesn't pronounce send in a way the AI can understand," he interprets. "And either you guys are going dancing tomorrow, or he wants you to bring the evidence to his place. How do you know where he lives? Do you go over there often?"

It's not just idle curiosity prompting his question. I sense a hint of jealousy as well. Ha! Didn't he accuse me of jealousy for merely asking about Aurora? That's called projection.

"I'll call him later for the address. But I'll get it directly—who knows where his talk to text will send me?"

# CHAPTER FIFTEEN

I called Jackson last night and gave him a preview of what I'd be bringing over, and he was thrilled. But we couldn't get together right then because he was on his way out. According to him, he's found a weak link, someone he can exploit. They'll be meeting up, and he will be bribing his way into the LoveMatch computer system. This investigation is progressing nicely and will hopefully conclude before Powell drops a bunch of money on a non-refundable diamond ring.

Jackson also said he'd text with updates but didn't.

That's why I'm still worried now. He hasn't gotten back to me yet. Either something terrible happened, or he got distracted and forgot. And since he's a secret agent working a murder investigation, I'm going to guess distraction isn't the issue.

After six unanswered phone calls, I'm done. I'm heading over to his apartment. I put the address he gave me into my GPS and listen to the disembodied voice direct me to a trendy high-rise near the Salt River, where I park right next to Tanner's van. Ha! They're neighbors!

But Jackson's apartment number is several floors higher, and there are fewer doors on this corridor. It makes me wonder again who is paying his salary. I'd ask, but he's not home. I try pounding on the door, loud enough to make a neighbor stick their head out and glare at me, but Jackson doesn't answer. I'm getting suspicious.

Fortunately, I have a friend nearby.

Tanner, at least, opens the door to my polite knocks, but for some reason, he seems annoyed. Also, he's shirtless. And he's standing in such a way so as to block me from seeing inside his apartment. Does he have a woman over? It's afternoon, too early for a booty call, which means he had a hook-up last night! I try to bite back my annoyance.

"What are you doing here?" he asks me in surprise.

"Turns out, Jackson is your neighbor on the penthouse level. I need to borrow your lockpicking tools so I can get into his apartment," I tell him.

"Why would I have those?"

"What happens when you lock yourself out of your van?"

"I call a locksmith. Cass, what's going on?"

"Can I come in to talk about it?"

He looks over his shoulder and frowns.

"This isn't a good time."

"Is it Aurora?" I try to peer around him. I assume there's a half-naked woman lounging around, about to sexily call out something like 'babe, come back. I miss you already!'

"What? No, nobody's here, I just ..." he reluctantly lets me in. The furniture is shoved aside, and one wall has been transformed with streamers and a 'Happy First Birthday' banner. Colorful confetti litters the floor, and several jumbo-sized wooden blocks are strewn about. "I had a couple of shoots this morning."

"You're doing first birthdays? You had toddlers here?"

"This place is expensive, and I haven't gotten any magazine jobs lately. You know I'm a portrait photographer, this is the kind of thing I do." He's defensive.

"Did you do the session shirtless? Because that hardly seems appropriate. Unless that's part of your schtick." Though that gimmick is more suited for a boudoir shoot. I sneak a glance at his bed; it's neatly made, with no evidence that a lingerie-clad woman was posing on it while a half-naked Tanner stood over her with his camera.

"I ended up with birthday cake smeared all over me. Can we not talk about this? Why are you trying to break into Jackson's place? I thought you had a meetup scheduled."

"He's not answering my calls or texts. I'm worried about him. I told him about the magazines we found, and he was going to do some kind of clandestine operation in the LoveMatch offices. But I can't reach him."

"I'm not going to help you commit a felony." Tanner is the most stubborn person when it comes to what really should be classified as a misdemeanor anyway.

"Fine. I'm calling backup." I plop down on his couch so I can call Agent Cassidy Walters. Tanner watches me for a moment, then gets back to cleaning up his toddler mess. He doesn't put a shirt on right away, and I sort of don't mind. But I sort of do, because I almost feel like he's trying to create a deliberate distraction for me. Jerk.

"Your friend is missing," I tell Walters as soon as his groggy voice answers. He knows the day starts before noon, right?

"Who is this?" Ooh, he's cranky.

"It's me, Girl-Cassidy. Don't you store my number in your phone?"

"I told you not to call me on weekends."

"But this is an emergency. Jackson is missing."

"Who?"

"Your buddy, Jackson Shih, though apparently you know him by a different name."

There's a confused pause before Walters figures out who I'm talking about. "He's missing? For how long?"

"A couple of days." Slight exaggeration. "Can you help me and Tanner break into his apartment?"

"I need a warrant."

"To check on a friend who could be bleeding out on the floor? It's extenuating circumstances."

"I wish you'd stop watching crime shows. Where are you now?"

I give him Tanner's address, and he agrees to meet up with us. Excellent, we have an FBI agent on our side. A reluctant one who might yell at me, but whatever works.

Agent Walters takes his sweet time. I guess he doesn't agree with my 'bleeding out on the floor' assessment, or he figures we're already too late.

"Finally," I say when I open Tanner's door and invite Walters and his enormous cup of coffee inside. So not only is he so unconcerned he stops for a drink on the way, but he also doesn't think to offer to pick us up anything?

"It's early," he complains, though it's midday. "Besides, I took some time to look into a few things. Our mutual friend hasn't been online in almost twenty-four hours."

"Like I said, this is an emergency." I'm surprised Jackson's supervisor hasn't raised an alarm. Don't they monitor their people? "Percival, this is Tanner." Who is now, thankfully, fully clothed.

"Agent Cassidy Walters," he corrects as he shakes Tanner's hand. "And I remember you. We haven't been properly introduced, but I helped tear apart your van a few months ago. You came up with some great hiding places. I almost missed a couple of them."

"You did, actually," Tanner replies, looking at Walters with distaste. "At least three."

"Really? Nice. Maybe someday you can show them to me, so I know where to look next time I'm searching a bomber's mobile workshop."

"After all the damage you did? Forget it." Tanner is usually much friendlier, but he was pretty upset about what the FBI did to his van. The work to repair it took weeks and cost a lot of money—though Powell paid for it, as an apology. Technically, I suppose the FBI was supposed to fix it, but who knows how long that takes? Filling out the requisition forms alone would probably take longer than the time it took for the private company my brother hired to complete the repairs.

"Okay, can we get this over with? Where's the apartment?" Walters guzzles down some more of his coffee.

"Upstairs." We take the elevator up to the expensive level. Luckily, this floor doesn't require special elevator keys to access. Though if it did, maybe Walters could have used those hacking skills he's always bragging about to short circuit the electronics.

Walters knocks on the door, as if that's something I hadn't thought of. Then he tries calling, again, just like I already did.

"Have you verified it enough yet? Kick the door down," I encourage.

"There are security cameras," Tanner warns. "Don't get me evicted."

"Block the camera view of my hands." Walters pulls out what I can only assume is a lockpick kit out of his pocket. See, that *is* a thing people carry around with them. I try to signal Tanner to point that out, but he ignores me.

Tanner and I position ourselves on both sides of Walters, so the cameras can't tell it's not a real key going in the lock. A few seconds of jiggling, and the door opens. And we are all hit with a rotten stench that physically propels us backward and makes me want to vomit.

"Get behind me," Walters orders, even though we already are. He reaches into the back waistband of his pants, drawing a gun.

"Whoa," Tanner backs further away.

"Do you know how to use that?" I ask.

Walters fixes me with a withering glare. "I am an FBI agent. Of course, I know how to use this. Stay behind me, and if I say run, you run."

I'm going to guess it goes against protocol to take civilians into a possible crime scene that smells like dead bodies. But breaking into a crime scene is probably against protocol too.

Walters' feet crunch on broken glass as he makes his slow way into the apartment. Tanner and I tag along behind, crouched slightly, as though Walters' body will protect us. I'll be honest, I wish Agents Johnson and Benitez were here. They're much more intimidating to bad guys.

In the kitchen, we find the source of the smell and all the broken glass. Walters immediately holsters his gun and lets out a string of swears.

"Is that . . . kombucha?" Tanner asks, as we assess the destruction. There is one intact growler sitting on the counter, surrounded by glass shards and rotting fermented liquid. I can spot at least two swing top lids amongst the debris. My stomach churns again. This is what Jackson drinks? And *enjoys*?

"Those were going to be for next weekend! One was supposed to be mine!" Walters surveys the mess in disappointment. He sighs heavily, perhaps imagining how delicious his promised drink would have been. Or maybe that's a sigh of relief that he doesn't have to fake like he's enjoying the smelly beverage.

"Wow, check this out!" Tanner calls from the living room. This apartment is much bigger than his tiny studio downstairs.

I rush over to him, thinking he's found evidence, maybe blood or something, but no. He's staring at the wall of flatscreens and all the gaming equipment. There are only two pieces of furniture in the room: an elaborate futuristic looking chair with a built-in massager, and a table next to it with a selection of controllers and a couple of headsets.

"Don't sit in that," I tell Tanner, as he's about to try out some of the chair's features.

Walters examines the television screens, something akin to envy on his face. "No wonder he's so good, his system . . . this is amazing." When he's done admiring the wall, he shrugs. "There's nothing wrong here. Don is . . . I mean Jackson isn't home, that's all. And he failed to burp his bottles to let pressure out. When he gets back, he's going to have a lot of cleaning to do."

"Assuming he's not dead somewhere in the apartment. We haven't checked out the bedroom or bathroom," I remind him.

"Fine, I'll do that real quick; then we'll get out of here. And maybe let's keep this little exploration between us." But after Walters goes to search for bodies in the bedroom, he emerges with a concerned expression. "Blaine-Corbitt, I think you need to see this."

The room is not what I expected. It's screen-free, for one thing. For another, there are at least six framed pictures of me, including an 8x10 on the bedside table, encircled by candles, lotion, and a box of tissues. Oh, so gross. So much creepier than I could have imagined.

"What is this?" I ask, partly because I'm horrified and shocked, and partly because I'm hoping someone will reassure me that those are actually stock photos of a woman who looks just like me who came with the frames. Everyone has a doppelganger somewhere, right?

"That looks like . . ." Tanner steps closer to look at the contents of the table. "Hey, I took that picture! He stole it from the gym's SwiftaPic. He can't print that! It's copyrighted!"

Glad to hear this stalker-esque self-pleasure display isn't what's bothering Tanner. Yes, friend, let's fixate on whether he had legal rights to print my image.

"Cassidy, did Jackson ever give you any hints that he might be obsessed with you?" Walters is doing his professional FBI investigatory thing, examining the photos wearing a pair of latex gloves that appeared seemingly out of nowhere. If I ask where he got them, he's going to shoot me another glare and again remind me of where he works and what he does for a living.

"No. He didn't like me like that. He only gave me an interest card because he wanted to talk to me about his LoveMatch investigation." Stalkers are common among Powell's crowd, and I've had one or two mildly obsessed fans over the years, but nothing like this. I'm profoundly uncomfortable now.

I back away from the bedside table and collide with Tanner. I wasn't aware that he was behind me, and I didn't know how badly I needed his arms to wrap around me until they don't. I sense their absence. Even though hugs are his standard form of comforting, he limits himself to giving me an awkward shoulder pat.

"It'll be okay, Cass. We'll get the cops involved. Don't worry." He ceases his patting and steps back, keeping distance between us.

"There's nothing illegal here," Walters corrects. "This apartment needs a deep cleaning, and the pictures of Cassidy are disturbing, but no laws are being broken, aside from us breaking and entering. We're not reporting this to the police. Or anyone else, for that matter."

"But this guy is a psychopath. He needs to be stopped!" Tanner says, demonstrating that he, at least, is on my side.

"He hasn't done anything wrong. Being a gamer who made a brewing error and has a fixation on a beautiful woman isn't a crime."

"Copyright violations are a federal crime," I point out.

"Civil. They're a civil matter. Sue him. For now, we need to go. We're the only criminals here. We need to leave before he returns. Unless Tanner wants to go back to jail. Cassidy, I assume you can make bail."

"I'd cover yours too," I promise Tanner. And I direct him to take photos of the room, over Walters' objections.

We regroup downstairs at Tanner's.

"You realize what a crap show this has become, don't you?" Agent Walters asks me. He's acting like I'm somehow at fault. Meanwhile, Tanner is getting me a glass of water and putting cookies on a plate. I know which man I prefer.

"We had reasonable suspicion. That's a police term."

"A police term, not a civilian on a wild goose chase term." Walters seems awfully angry with me. "You goaded me into committing a crime."

"Jackson is missing. Even you said it's odd he went offline. And he was really interested in fermenting things. Do you honestly believe he would have let his kombucha go so long it would explode and contaminate his pristine apartment? If anything, that's concrete proof something bad happened to him." I don't know why I'm still insisting on this, given our recent discovery that Jackson is a creep who had ulterior motives to talk to me.

"I'll call around to hospitals, see if he was in a car accident or something. Okay? Will that make you feel better?" Walters is acting a bit condescending now, which I don't appreciate. And he took one of the cookies, even though I'm pretty sure Tanner intended for this entire plate to be mine.

"You aren't worried? Don't you think we should report him missing? Maybe call the police? The FBI? Some other agency?" *Like the one that sent him into danger in the first place?*

"What other agency? You think this is suddenly something for the CIA? Like every time a Canadian national goes off the grid, we need to bring in the experts?"

"He's Canadian?" That's new info for me. "What's their spy network called?"

"The CSIS, but why would we call them? This isn't an international incident."

"Can you call his supervisor?"

"Supervisor? He doesn't have a *job*. Cassidy, where exactly do you think Jackson works?"

"I thought he was a spy. He told me he's investigating LoveMatch, and he goes on raids with you."

I certainly do not expect Agent Walters to react by laughing so hard. He sprays cookie crumbs all over, something that does not endear him to Tanner.

When he finally composes himself, he manages to choke out a few words. "Jackson Shih is not a spy. He's a gamer who calls himself Don Toronto. We go on raids together *online*. I'm surprised you don't think he's an orc hunter or a dragon master. Did he tell you he's a sharpshooter with a laser gun?"

"But he's doing an investigation! And you told him to trust me, and he knew my secret nickname for you!"

"You gave him a secret nickname?" Tanner interrupts. Great, now he's all offended.

"I . . . Cassidy, I thought when you called me Percival von Sharkington it was hilarious, so I started using it as my gamer tag."

"That's a stupid name," Tanner mutters under his breath, apparently jealous that I bestowed a joking name on someone who isn't him. He's so weird sometimes.

I put my head in my hands and wish I could dissolve into the cushions. Am I really so gullible? I swear Jackson all but stated that he was a secret agent, he had all these ideas about LoveMatch, and . . . what? It was all to trick me? It was a way of getting close to me? I don't like this feeling of having been manipulated, of having trusted someone and then getting betrayed.

"Cassidy, I'm sorry I laughed," Walters says, and his pitying me now is somehow much worse. "Jackson misled you, likely intentionally. He went a little off the rails when his cousin died."

"His cousin?" Tanner asks. He sounds like he's talking around a mouthful of cookie. Is he eating those too? I lift my head from my hands to verify. Yep. Everyone in this room but me is a thief.

"Yes, Lester Zheng. He died on his honeymoon a few months ago. Jackson inherited his billion-dollar fortune—that's when he quit his job. But Zheng's widow is suing him for a marital share. Jackson is convinced that she murdered his cousin for his money. He's been fixated on LoveMatch and blaming them."

"What? That's what this was all about?" I sit up straight. "That liar! He made it sound like he was hired to investigate it. He's just trying to prevent a bereaved widow from access to her husband's estate?" And that means the car, the apartment, all of the finery I thought he borrowed for his cover story actually belongs to him. As revenge, I should give Lexa his number. She'll milk him for all he's worth.

I expect Tanner to join in on my outrage, but he looks thoughtful. "What if Jackson was right, though? He is missing, isn't he? And what about the LoveMatch stuff? Even if he is creepily obsessed with Cassidy, we did find evidence that there's something going on there."

Walters lets out the most exasperated sigh I have ever heard, which is really saying something since I am often surrounded by divas. "Fine. Show me this 'evidence.'" He helps himself to the last two cookies, as though stealing my treats will fortify him for the monumental task.

Tanner sets up his laptop and opens the files for me to explain to Walters. I point out all the coincidences linking the old magazine articles and Emily's possibly fake personality and life story.

"This is fascinating." He's finished reading and is sitting back rubbing his eyes. "I never thought he'd find anything; I thought he was just looking for someone to blame."

I refrain from shouting *I told you so,* and instead calmly ask, "What's next? You go undercover to a LoveMatch event? You pose as a billionaire looking for love, try and see if they off you?"

"They don't ever give me undercover assignments. Benítez gets them all the time. Oh, she's *soooo* good at it, she speaks five languages, she's a chameleon. It's not fair. Even right now, she's . . ." he cuts himself off before he violates FBI rules and reveals where his fellow agent is currently disguised. "Um, anyway, no, this one wouldn't go to me."

"So, what do we do?" I'd like to establish a plan.

"*We* don't do anything. *You* are no longer involved. *I* will report this to my superiors, and *they* will determine the next steps."

"But LoveMatch kidnapped Jackson!"

"How did you make the leap from Emily might be a hired actress to LoveMatch is kidnapping people? I will concede that perhaps Jackson is missing. That doesn't necessarily have anything to do with them. He could have gone off on his own, family emergency or something. And if he was taken, for all I know, it was someone from another guild—we do have a tournament coming up next weekend. Evidently without the kombucha I was promised. My girlfriend is going to be so disappointed!"

"You're rather nonchalant about the idea that your friend was kidnapped." Is this something that occurs frequently in the gaming world, holding players hostage to keep them from participating in tournaments? Will Jackson be found stumbling through the desert, his game-playing thumbs broken as a warning to others?

"Because we have no proof!" He turns to Tanner for support. "Would you please stop her from watching so many crime dramas? She has a misguided idea of how many missing people cases are actually kidnappings as opposed to guys who freaked out and left town because the woman they were enamored with was coming over to their apartment."

"Fine!" I snap. "We'll acquire proof. There's a LoveMatch Millionaires' Circle event tonight. I'll go, wearing a wire." I'm going to be a spy, a real one, not a fake one like Jackson. Tanner has a van; he and Walters can park outside the venue in it and monitor me.

"And where are you planning on acquiring a wire?"

"Well, Percival, I assumed you would lend me one. After all, as you keep reminding us, you are an FBI agent."

"I am a *good* agent, who will not be handing out our equipment to random civilians, especially untrained ones who think they're going to go solve a crime on their own."

"In the movies—"

"Any rogue FBI nonsense you see in the movies is fake, Cassidy. If agents did that in real life, they'd get fired. I'm not going to risk my dream job and my pension for you. Proper channels. If I, a highly trained investigative agent, am not allowed to do undercover work, I'm certainly not going to assist you."

I throw my hands up in defeat. "Do it then. Go through proper channels."

# CHAPTER SIXTEEN

I don't know what Agent Walters is up to, but *I'm* attending an exclusive LoveMatch event. Unfortunately, since he wouldn't lend me any equipment and no spyware stores are within a reasonable driving distance, I'm completely on my own. Tanner tried to stop me, repeatedly making the argument that I'm putting myself in danger, but I think I'll be fine. I'm not planning to stay long, just long enough to mention Jackson's name to a few people, see how they react, and later tell Walters which of the LoveMatch employees have accidentally revealed themselves to be potential kidnappers.

Maybe—as Tanner kept saying—this isn't the best plan, but I'm the best person for the job. I'm too high profile for them to harm. They don't want to risk losing my brother and his big fat bonus check. Besides, people know where I am; if I go missing, they'll search for me.

This particular event is another semi-formal one, which I suspect is designed to impress the red-bracelets and demonstrate what kind of glamourous life they'd be getting if they manage to snag one of us silvers. I weave my way through the crowd, searching for Jackson. I'd really like to be wrong. I don't even mind apologizing and telling Walters he was right. I'll tolerate his gloating, if this whole thing turns out to be just the I'm-a-spy fantasies of a wealthy man-child. Maybe Jackson did go off on a bender or was called away on a family emergency and lost his phone.

I move through the ballroom giving friendly nods to the faces I recognize. Several of these people attend every single event, which doesn't bode well for LoveMatch's success rate. Though one or two guarantee bonuses is really all they need to keep afloat.

Lillian catches up to me as I'm helping myself to a ricotta stuffed squash blossom at one of the buffet tables. One thing this company has going for it is the food; I should ask who they use as a caterer.

"Cassidy, wonderful, you made it." Lillian surveys me and smiles her approval. "That's a great dress. You'll definitely draw some eyes tonight. I have personally selected six eligible bachelors for you. I'm not allowed to give hints, but I did suggest to each of them that they wear a necktie with purple in it, just to give you a clue. They don't know who they're looking for, of course. They just know they match—somewhere between 76 and 84%—with one of the beautiful young women here."

"I'll certainly seek them out," I blatantly lie. "I'm also looking for someone else. Is Jackson Shih here, by chance? I was hoping to speak with him about . . . an investment opportunity."

"An investment?" Lillian raises her eyebrows. "If it's a hot tip, my ears are open. I haven't seen Mr. Shih myself, but if I do, I'll tell him you're looking for him. But don't waste too much time on that man; he's not a match." She is as calm and collected as always. She didn't even flinch when I brought up Jackson.

"I won't." Instead, I'm going to pause at this table to update Tanner. And, while I'm here, I may as well eat my weight in these delicious treats. I'm a fan of all things cheese, and there's enough on this table to maintain my interest.

Jackson isn't here, I text Tanner.

He responds immediately: I ASSUMED NOT. WOULDN'T THAT BE A LETDOWN?

ARE YOU HOPING SOMETHING BAD HAPPENED TO HIM?

I'M HOPING THAT FBI AGENT WAS WRONG. I HATE THAT GUY. HE SLIT THE CUSHIONS IN MY VAN!

POWELL BOUGHT YOU NEW ONES. CHILL OUT.

MAYBE THEY HAD SENTIMENTAL VALUE.

DID THEY?

NO. BUT HE DIDN'T KNOW THAT.

OK, STOP TEXTING ME. I'M GOING TO CONTINUE MY INVESTIGATION.

I pause for a moment, phone in my hand, to see if he follows instructions and stops, or if he disobeys in order to respond that he *will* stop. Nothing. Good.

My next destination is the bar. I'm going to ask Isaac if he's seen Jackson. As the fiancé of the stepdaughter of the founder, he's high enough up in the rankings to know if the agency is involved in kidnapping and murders. And, no offense, he hasn't seemed too bright, so he's the most likely person to give it away. His face will turn red, he'll stutter, maybe even bolt.

"The usual, Miss Blaine-Corbitt, or would you like something stronger this time?" Isaac asks as I take a seat. So far, no purple-tied men have molested me, though I think I did spot one of them. He has an obnoxious laugh; I could hear it from across the room. No thank you, buddy.

"The usual. I'm not in an alcohol mood," I tell him.

"Are you sure you don't want something to help you relax, make you more comfortable talking to some of the other guests?"

What? He thinks I'm not interacting enough because I'm shy? No, pal, I'm just picky and uninterested. And currently investigating a kidnapping.

"I'm fine, thanks." I watch as he starts mixing my mocktail. I need to come up with a natural sounding way to ask about Jackson.

"Excuse me," a tall dark-haired man sits down next to me. "I have a red bracelet."

"That's not the best pickup line I've ever heard, but it's not the worst." Ugh, he's got a tie with grey and purple stripes, one he keeps fidgeting with as though trying to draw my attention. Did Lillian send him directly to me, or is he waggling his tie at all the rich girls? Either way, he's interfering with my investigation.

"A classy gal like you would see right through any pickup line I tried," the man says. He's right. However, while I, in general, find pickup lines annoying, I do appreciate something more than describing an article of clothing that the man is wearing. Low effort.

"Yep." Now I wish Isaac had put something stronger in my drink. It tastes good, and . . . oh, maybe he did spike it. I'm hit with a little rush of dizziness.

"Not much of a conversationalist, huh?" The stranger is unable to take a hint.

"Nope." I take another cautious sip. He must have slipped in some vodka. Fine, I suppose one alcoholic drink can't hurt me.

"Do you like my purple tie?" He continues to shove it at me, expecting admiration and possibly a lap dance.

"Nope."

"Whatever, it must not be you, then." He storms off. His ego must be huge if he expects that anyone he approaches and shows off his I'm-not-a-millionaire bracelet to would automatically be interested. How did I match a man like that? I guess vanity and temper aren't properly identified by the algorithm.

"Awkward," Isaac mutters. "You finished your drink off quickly. Let me get you another."

"No, I'm good." I try to stand up, but my legs go all wobbly and my head starts spinning.

"Cassidy," Lillian appears from out of nowhere. "You look like you aren't feeling well. Let me take you somewhere quiet so you can sit down."

The tile is cool under my face. I wake slowly, with my head pounding and a sick gurgling in my stomach. My body aches.

"You're awake," a man's voice says, and I turn my head so fast I may have disconnected my brain from its stem and sent it spinning in circles. It's Jackson. I blink at him, trying to process this moment. Did I rescue him? Wait, no, did he kidnap me? Where are we?

"Whoa, don't sit up yet. You're going to be dizzy and off-balance," he warns as I try to push myself up.

"Where am I?" My voice is croaky and hoarse, and echoes in my throbbing skull. Since the bottom of a toilet is directly in my eyeline, I'm clearly in a bathroom, but where? This is not his apartment building.

"I hoped you would tell me." He stands up, and I'm suddenly afraid he's about to attack me. I'm too out-of-it to fight back, so I sort of scrunch against the wall behind me. This is ineffective; I'm about to die. "Are you scared of me? Can you see? Cassidy, it's me, Jackson Shih."

"I recognize you." Now I need to think strategically—do I tell him I've been to his apartment? That I've seen the creepy shrine? "How did I get here?" I remember looking for him at the event last night—was that last night? But I don't remember actually finding him.

"Someone carried you in and dropped you on the floor," he says. "At first I thought you were dead, but I guess you were probably drugged."

"Who was it?" His attackers? Or his co-conspirators? I carefully ease myself to a seated position, using the wall for support. I massage my temples, but it doesn't relieve the pressure.

"Here," he passes me a bottle of water. I accept it hesitantly, but upon determining it is still factory sealed, I crack it open and take a drink. The liquid is lukewarm, but still the most refreshing beverage I've ever consumed. "I don't know who they are. The last thing I remember, I was at a bar, waiting for my contact, the one I told you about. I woke up here, with the worst headache I've ever had in my life. Whoever it is has brought me food twice, but they're always disguised and armed. The one carrying you wore a ski mask, and the person with him pointed a gun at me and made me stand in the corner while they dropped you off."

Well, that answers my unspoken 'why haven't you escaped' question.

"Who was your contact?"

"Isaac."

"*Isaac?*" That information would have come in handy yesterday. "You asked Tabitha's fiancé to help you break into the LoveMatch computer system? What were you thinking?"

"He was the weakest link," Jackson tries to explain his ineptitude. "He's only worked here for less than a year, so I figured he wasn't involved. And he's not very smart, so I thought he'd be easy to manipulate."

"Jackson!" If I weren't suffering so badly, I'd be yelling at him. While he's right about Isaac's intelligence level, the guy is marrying into the family that owns the business. He's far from the weakest link. He's more of an unbreakable link, dangling from the strongest. Mention potential crimes to see if he flinches: good idea. Invite him to privately meet, so you can secretly discuss those crimes: terrible idea.

"What? It was a solid plan. Have you heard the rumor he's cheating on Tabitha with Lillian? If bribery didn't work, I was going to try blackmail."

I cannot believe I put any faith in the competence of this man. Even through my pounding headache, I can see the foolish mistake he made. When he said he'd found someone, I assumed he meant a janitor or receptionist, someone whose head could be turned by the promise of money, and who wouldn't have a future familial interest in keeping the files secret.

"Alright, that was Friday. They took me on Saturday night," I say slowly, since figuring our situation out is more important than berating Jackson for his mistake. Moving my mouth makes my headache worse. "I went to the LoveMatch event. I was looking for you. Tanner and I found evidence to show you, and then you were missing . . ." And I asked Lillian where he was and drank the drink Isaac made me. All of this could have been avoided if Jackson had disclosed the name of his informant earlier.

"It's Sunday morning? I missed practice! We have a tournament coming up!" He's focusing on the wrong details. I wonder if I should let him know his tournament play will not be fueled by kombucha.

My entire digestive system suddenly rebels at the water. Fortunately, despite my sluggish state, my disgust for vomit is strong enough to launch me across the room to the toilet. I feel a little better after everything I've eaten for perhaps a month is forcefully propelled from my stomach.

"The same thing happened to me," Jackson's voice is too close behind me. Maybe we really are kidnapped by someone else, but I saw the shrine on his nightstand. I'm aware of his disgusting fixation. He's as much a danger to me as the kidnappers.

"Please back off," my voice sounds too much like begging. I don't want to appear weak and vulnerable, not to a man obsessed with me. I need to be strong and intimidating, which is difficult in my current condition.

"Sorry. Cassidy, I'm so glad to see you, but at the same time, I'm not. I don't know what's going to happen to us. I've never been kidnapped before. I don't even know where we are."

If Agent Walters hadn't already told me Jackson wasn't a secret agent, this is the moment I would have discovered that for myself. Secret agents possess basic observation skills.

"Look around, Jackson. Pink tiles, pink toilet, pink heart shaped bathtub. We're in the LoveMatch offices." I can't believe he didn't realize it. I didn't, not right away, but that was because my head was foggy, and I was lying with my back to the enormous pink tub, perched on its two-step high tile pedestal in the middle of the room. No place but LoveMatch or an eccentric pinkophile's mansion would have a monstrosity like that.

"That's great! That's the proof we needed! Kidnapping is a bad enough crime that the police will have to investigate my other allegations." He holds up his hand to high five me, as though we're somehow winning here.

"They're going to kill us, Jackson." Saying the words out loud makes it real. It's true. They have to; we know too much. "They wouldn't have drugged us and brought us here together if they planned to let us go. Once you can identify your kidnappers, ransom is off the table." Although technically, we can't identify them yet. That's a point in our favor.

He obviously never thought of the possibility that this might end in anything other than hearty handshakes and apologies from the LoveMatch murder cooperative. His knees give out and he drops heavily next to me. "They are. They're going to murder us." He reaches to hug me, and I edge away. Even on the verge of death, I'm creeped out by him.

"Don't touch me," I warn him sharply. "Or I'll be the one to kill you." This is a large room, for a bathroom, but there's nowhere to hide in it. Nowhere to go to escape him. And with this headache, there's no way I can fight him off either.

"I thought we were allies! Cassidy, we're in this together."

"I thought so too, until I saw my pictures."

"What pictures?"

"The ones in your bedroom. And your creepy altar."

"Cass, maybe whatever you were drugged with caused hallucinations. Don't take this the wrong way, but you aren't my type. I don't have any pictures of you, and I certainly don't have an altar."

"Don't lie to me. I saw them. Tanner, Percival, and I broke into your apartment looking for you."

"You did? Did you burp my kombucha?" A sudden hope lights up his face, which I'm going to extinguish.

"No. And we didn't clean up the exploded mess either. Sorry." I've just realized we should have taken measures to protect the unbroken container. Too late now, it's probably all over the walls and ceiling too. "I'm still more concerned that you had framed pictures of me . . . and the one with the lotion and the tissues. Jackson, that's gross and disturbing."

He shakes his head. "I still don't know what you're talking about. I have a picture of my Nana on my nightstand, and one with my cousin on the dresser, but those are the only photos in my room. I'm not much into decorating."

So, two possibilities here. The easiest one is that he's lying, but what does he hope to gain by that? We're likely to be killed anyway. The other possibility is that he's telling the truth, and someone else put those photos there. Someone who wanted people to think Jackson was obsessed with me.

It hits me.

"Murder-suicide!" I've solved the mystery. I don't feel better about it, but at least now I know precisely how I'm going to die.

"I hope that's not a suggestion." Jackson edges a couple of inches away from me, as though I announced my intentions rather than my realization.

"No, that's their plan. Our kidnappers put those pictures there, so you look like a stalker. They're going to deflect blame by making it look like you killed me, and then yourself. Or maybe I kill you in self-defense but die of my injuries before I can get help."

Jackson puts his head in his hands and lets out what might be a sob of fear. Oh, no. He's breaking down. Yet another clue to his lack of secret agent-ness. Looks like I'm on my own. I wish I had called Mike and told him what we were doing. But I did tell someone!

"Tanner will come looking for us!" I trust him, and unless the kidnappers took my cell phone and texted him hourly, he'll realize something was wrong. But they could have sent him misdirections. When I was drugged, would they have been able to make me enter my passcode? All it would take would be them texting him that I'm on my way to some desolate location. He'd show up in his van, and they'd get him too. Okay, no, I am on my own.

Think Cassidy.

List of assets. What do we have? One sobbing man who probably can't handle himself in a fight. Or can he?

"You don't happen to be a black belt in anything, are you?" I ask hopefully. This could be the moment he reveals himself to be a ninja warrior.

"Why, because I'm Asian? That's racist!" He gives me a brief glare before returning to his misery. I'll take that as a no.

Other assets? Me. I've been in exactly one fight, and I won. Broke my cheek, almost died, but still won, mostly due to my brother's assistance—Powell would be a lot better to have with me than Jackson. Of course, right now, in addition to being hampered by an unhelpful companion, I'm wearing a slinky sequined cocktail dress and stiletto heels, which is not ideal battle apparel. Wait, these heels can be weapons! I'll give one to Jackson too, and when our kidnappers come back, we'll stab them.

What other potential weapons do we have? I scan the room. Nothing, nothing at all. This bathroom has been cleaned out since we were here for our double date. There's a bathtub, a sink, and a toilet. No decorations, no towel racks. Even the lid for the toilet tank is missing, which is a shame—heavy porcelain would make for an excellent head smashing device.

So, our list of available assets is me, a pair of shoes, and I suppose some plastic water bottles. But they're the super cheap flimsy kind that definitely won't hurt anyone.

How long do they plan to keep us here? It's daytime on a Sunday, so the building is probably empty, meaning they may come in soon to finish us off when nobody can hear us scream. However, it's more likely they'll wait until nighttime, so they can smuggle our bodies out easier. That's if they're smart, and they must be. This can't be the first time they've done this.

We need to get out of here early. I assess the room. Toilet, tub, sink. Toilet, tub, sink. This is hopeless.

Wait! No! I have an idea that might work.

"Jackson!" I shake his shoulder. "I think I know how we can escape!"

"You do?" His tear-stained eyes fill with hope.

"Yes. If you need to pee, do so now—I'll look away—and then I'm going to destroy this toilet."

He winces. "How very lady-like of you."

"Not . . . eww, Jackson."

After we both take turns standing in the far corner and facing away while the other does their business, I demand his shirt.

"Why do you want my shirt?"

"Because I'm wearing a dress and a thong and nothing else. I need it to help us escape."

He reluctantly pulls his shirt over his head and gives it to me. "Careful. It was expensive."

"I'll buy you a new one," I promise, then jam the shirt into the toilet and flush. The bowl fills quickly and starts overflowing onto the floor. Next, step two. I reach into the open tank and pull out the rubber stopper, disconnecting it from its little chain. I learned how to do the opposite at my gym once when there was a little incident in one of the locker rooms.

Step three, I remove my thong, and even though I'm an expert in changing without showing any revealing flesh, Jackson's eyes still nearly bug out of his head. This little bit of fabric is enough to stop up the sink, which I turn on at full blast.

I survey my work in satisfaction. Jackson is less impressed.

"What's this going to do? Besides ruin our shoes?" He edges away from the overflowing water.

"Whatever's below us is going to flood, building maintenance will investigate, and we'll be saved."

"Yeah, sure. Except LoveMatch takes up two floors. That's who's below us."

"They can't all be in on the kidnapping scheme. And they aren't here on weekends. I'm hoping the water company sends someone out or we short out the power or something." I hope my optimism isn't misplaced.

"And we're just supposed to sit in this water?" Jackson is so lucky I'm here. I can't believe I ever thought he was a secret agent. He's painfully incapable of taking care of himself.

"You're welcome to sit wherever you like. I'm going to wait where it's dry." I clamber into the tub to avoid the toilet water, and Jackson follows. This was definitely built for two people. It's actually quite comfortable, shaped at the perfect slope for relaxation—or awaiting death. And since it's centered, we have a good view of the entire room.

I undo the straps on my heels and hand one to him. Now we're both armed and ready to go. Soon, the water will flood whatever room is below this, and will ideally trip some kind of alarm, bringing some non-kidnapper type person to come fix the leak. They will discover us, we'll escape, find a phone, and call the police, Powell, Tanner, and Mike, in that order. And when I get my phone back and have his number, I'm calling Walters and gloating.

# CHAPTER SEVENTEEN

My purse and phone are missing, so I can't keep track of the time. All I can say is that it's been four inches of rising water, and still nobody has come to our rescue. This is an older building, so there's a slope to the floor that you don't notice until you flood it and watch the angle of the water. Unfortunately, the door is at the highest part, so it's not flowing outward into the bedroom area of this suite as fast as I would like. There must be a leak below us though. This is an office building; no matter how much faux-marble and gilded edging decorates the place, most of the ceilings are the standard acoustic tile found everywhere. And I know those can't support the weight of hundreds of gallons of water.

Jackson has given up. He's been suffering and hungry and scared for almost two days, and I made his mental condition worse by reminding him that kidnappers generally have an end goal. He had hoped that his massive inheritance made him a ransom target, but my arrival dashed that hope. And his trauma response? *Talking*. And talking. And talking. I may now know everything there is to know about what it's like to grow up Chinese-Canadian, the cheat codes to dozens of video games, and how pretty Lexa is, and maybe he should have accepted her interest card.

Despite the ramblings of a defeated man, my headache is starting to ease. I keep my eyes closed, resting up for battle, wishing Jackson would shut up, and hoping Tanner comes through for me. He will, I trust him. We've had our ups and downs, but there's nothing I wouldn't give to see his face come through that door right now. I direct my limited mental energy toward sending out a plea to the universe. *Bring me Tanner, now, please.*

The sound of a key in the outer deadbolt makes me sit up and take notice. Huzzah! It has worked! I summoned Tanner, and now we are saved!

It's never that easy.

The door opens, water rushes over the threshold in a wave, and we are met with an angry Lillian, Isaac, and . . . Emily! While there's a modicum of satisfaction in being proven correct, I'll have to hold off on the gloating. Especially since their unmasked state suggests we're in grave danger.

Jackson and I scramble to our feet, somewhat ready for the confrontation. I'm realizing now that instead of waiting in the dry tub, we should have been next to the door poised to attack. Maybe next time I'm kidnapped, I'll do that.

"What happened here?" Lillian screeches, outraged at the damage we've caused. She was the one with the key, but she quickly shoves it into her jeans pocket and draws a gun from her purse. There's a gun in Emily's hand as well, pointing directly at us. Truthfully, if I had ever thought to make a list of possible causes of my death, 'shot by brother's girlfriend while standing in a heart-shaped bathtub with a shirtless faux secret agent' would not have made the cut. But here we are.

"Toilet's broken," I say cheerfully. Must keep them off-guard. I've got my left shoe at the ready, a terribly paltry weapon against those two shiny guns.

Emily snorts. "What exactly do you think you're going to do with that? Put it down!" She's nothing like the woman she's been pretending to be. This version of Emily is calm, confident, and armed.

"Are you going to shoot me? That might put a damper on your relationship with my brother. He doesn't like people who shoot me." I keep ahold of the shoe, a feeble act of rebellion.

Emily throws her head back and laughs, and Jackson does not take that as an opportunity to charge her and grab the gun. I really am on my own here. "Cassidy," she says, in a voice dripping with contempt. "He's not going to blame *me*."

"Such a tragedy," Lillian adds. "I wish we'd done a better job with background checks. I had no idea Jackson was obsessed with you, Cassidy. He's going to kill you and then himself." Another triumphant moment for me and my detective skills. I would prefer to be wrong, though.

"I thought we were ..." Isaac is not the brains of the operation. He takes a moment before nodding. "Never mind. I get it."

"I hope you're good at dismembering bodies. I hope that's not too hands-on for you," I say, hit with a sudden inspiration and hoping Jackson follows along. "We had so much time, we figured we'd leave notes, just in case. These shoes carve flesh very well. In my autopsy, the examiner is going to find a message, identifying Emily and Lillian."

"She scratched Lillian L'Amour killed me and was involved in Lester Zheng's murder into my back," Jackson says. Good, he caught on. And this would have been an excellent idea, had we actually done it. And it would have been even better if Jackson had a shirt on, so his perfectly smooth unmarred back wasn't readily available for inspection. *Please don't turn around.*

"Isaac," I'm warming up now. "We didn't mention you. This could be your chance. You could be the hero that saves us."

"I'd pay your attorney fees when these women throw you under the bus," Jackson promises. "I'll testify that you had no idea what was going on, and you rescued us." The wheels in Isaac's head turn far too slowly. He doesn't accept our offer.

Lillian thinks faster than him. "Bad idea, Cassidy. Trying to appeal to the one person who isn't armed?"

"Trying to appeal to the one who probably hasn't committed murder before," I correct her. "I assume you both have."

Isaac doesn't say anything; he shifts uncomfortably in his wet sneakers, looking back and forth between the guns and us. He's in over his head; he must be. Anyone who algorithmically matched up with Tabitha can't be too terrible of a person. Of course, he is here and is rumored to have been sleeping with her evil stepsister, so I guess he's not a good person either.

"What's the point of all this anyway?" I continue, still trying to keep them talking. I want them off balance, confused, and easy to overpower. Also, it'd be nice if they turned on each other.

"Money." At least Emily-as-a-villain is honest. "We'd have been able to stop if we'd gotten Lester's trust fund. All that effort, wasted."

"Wait, you . . ." Jackson gasps, which is probably the effect Emily wanted. She's cruel, she's trying to hurt. Perhaps that's her way of keeping him off balance. "But his wife was a brunette!"

Every single person in the room with the possible exception of the slightly moronic Isaac does a mental forehead slap.

"You have heard of hair dye, right?" Lillian asks while biting back a laugh. "And cosmetics?"

"Are you serious?" I whisper to him. I don't know why I'm whispering; this is not a private conversation.

"I never met her in person. I only saw pictures, and she was always wearing big sunglasses. I would have recognized you in court, you know."

"Yes, which is why we had to move on to this stage of our plan earlier than we intended. I didn't want to eliminate the two of you until after I had the engagement ring on my finger. You should have heard from your lawyer; the date's been moved up. But you won't be there."

"Why me?" I protest. "I have nothing to do with Lester Zheng's money. I never even met him."

"Collateral damage," Lillian says.

"Trauma bonding," Emily corrects. "Powell will be so devastated. And when he finds out that I also lost a sister to gun violence, why, that's just going to strengthen our relationship."

"You did?" Isaac is again demonstrating his role as only-here-to-move-heavy-objects.

"Your other lover is an idiot," Emily tells Lillian. Now in addition to the fear-based adrenaline filling my body, I'm feeling a tinge of sadness for Tabitha. She lost her first love so tragically, and now she's going to find out her computer-selected one is a no-good cheater. At least, I hope I live to tell her about it.

Emily's finger starts to tighten on the trigger. "Thanks for standing in the bathtub. It'll make it easier to clean up the blood."

"I still think there are alternatives to killing us," I object. I'm stalling for time. Maybe I should throw my shoe? Emily is steadier with the gun; she's likely more experienced. I'll need to take her out first.

Salvation almost comes in the sound of the outer door to the suite opening. Both Lillian and Isaac turn, but Emily does not. She starts moving sideways, so her back is against the wall and her weapon is still trained on us. I wish this bathtub weren't in the center of the room. We're exposed no matter what.

"Lil! Did you get the call too?" It's Tabitha's voice.

"What call?"

"About the leak. Our conference room ceiling collapsed. Isaac, why are you here?" Now Tabitha has come into sight, and she's not alone. Tanner is with her—phone out, as always—and so is Agent Walters! Yes! We are saved by a real actual hero.

Lillian, who had temporarily lowered her weapon, brings it up again, training it on the newcomers framed in the doorway. Tabitha gasps in shock. It sounds genuine. Perhaps she didn't know about her stepsister's murderous tendencies. Though surely, given who she showed up with, she must be aware something strange is afoot.

"Put that phone away," Lillian warns Tanner. "Actually, no toss it right there." She points to the tile nearest her. He does as she asks, and winces when she stomps on it.

"Drop your phones, too," Emily adds, aiming her gun toward Tabitha and Walters. They both slowly remove their phones and drop them on the floor, to be stomped by Lillian. Emily promptly moves her gun back to Jackson and me, and we missed a chance to disarm her. I'm bad at this. So is Jackson, but I wasn't counting on him for rescue.

"What in tarnation is going on?" Walters finally speaks, and he's using the worst attempt at a Southern accent I've ever heard.

"Who are you?" Lillian moves her barrel from Tanner to the FBI agent and back again. She can't seem to decide who might be a greater threat.

"This is—" Tabitha starts to introduce him.

"Who am I?" Walters loudly interrupts before she can reveal his true profession. "Why, I'm Percy the plumber, dagnabbit. I'm here to fix yer leak." If this situation weren't so scary, I would laugh at the absurdity. Now I understand why he's never given undercover assignments. He's terrible at it.

"Where are your tools?" That question came from Isaac, and I don't know if it's because he suddenly grew a brain, or if he just wants to get a hand on a pipe wrench and fix the toilet himself. May as well do some repairs while we're all standing around a bathroom.

Walters hooks his thumb in his belt loops and jerks his pants upward. "My tool is in my waistband, *ifyouknowwhatImean*." He delivers a lascivious wink with his clue—Walters is armed. He saunters past Lillian and enters the bathroom. "Let me git my good eye on this here running toilet, then I'll pop on down to my van and grab the whole toolbox. But I think I done spotted the problem. Some idiot done gone and flushed a shirt."

"Make him get in the bathtub," Emily orders Lillian. "The photographer too."

"Why are you holding people at gunpoint?" Tabitha asks warily.

"Protecting LoveMatch," Lillian replies. She motions with her gun. There's a pause where Tanner seems to be considering taking off and running, but he looks at me, and makes the wrong choice.

"Do you really think we haven't already called the police?" Tanner asks as he approaches the tub. His arms are raised in the air, but he's acting like he's on a casual stroll, not a forced march. "They'll be here soon." Good. I knew he'd come through for me.

"So, you're saying we need to do this fast?" Emily's finger is still trigger ready.

"I'm saying you'll be caught soon. Might be best if you're charged with kidnapping rather than attempted murder." He's calm and almost cocky about it. All I feel is relief. Our ordeal is almost over. "Less time in prison."

Now would be the time for Walters to whip out his gun and badge, but I guess the fact that it's two guns to one is holding him back. He's waiting for the reinforcements to arrive.

Both men join us in the tub and there's a bizarre mini-shoving match as they try to stand directly in front of me. Chivalry isn't dead, apparently. Tanner wins with a hip-check.

"Are you okay?" Tanner whispers over his shoulder to me.

"Not really," I reply honestly. All I want is a hug from him and to wake up safe at home and realize this was all a nightmare. I dig my fingers into the back of his shirt, seeking some kind of security in this bizarre situation.

"Lillian, would you please explain what's going on?" Tabitha asks. She is the only one who hasn't entered the bathroom, remaining on the squelchy carpet. She keeps glancing at Tanner's phone, lying partially submerged on the border between Lake Toiletwater and Threshold Beach. If they still have a business after this, they're going to need to talk to some contractors about the angle of this floor, maybe have some repairs done. "Why do you and Emily have guns?"

"I told you, we're protecting the family business," Lillian says, rolling her eyes as though clearly, hostage taking is a normal everyday occurrence for matchmakers.

"I didn't realize the business was in danger," Tabitha sounds more annoyed than angry. "And if it were, murdering clients is not the way to fix anything!"

"You know, Lil, maybe your sister should join them, too." Emily doesn't move her gun toward Tabitha, but Lillian pivots hers, and something flashes across Lillian's face, something that might be guilt. Is there a sisterly bond? Could she possibly be regretting this decision? Could *she* be the weak link in this trio of criminality?

"Isaac?" Tabitha appeals to her fiancé. "Why are you involved? Would somebody please tell me what's going on?"

"Tabby, you're great and all," Isaac starts the universal break-up speech. "But I think maybe I'm just not good enough for you. What I have with Lillian is different."

"You're sleeping with my stepsister? But we're a 94% match!" Somehow, she's more outraged by this than she was by the whole 'we're about to murder a group of people in a heart shaped bathtub' issue.

"You think I didn't tweak the algorithm?" Lillian laughs cruelly. "Isaac has been keeping tabs on you for me. You're so easily manipulated."

"Enough!" Emily cuts them both off. "Tabitha, bathtub, now!"

"Ew!" Tabitha is wearing flip-flops, not the ideal footwear for wading through toilet water. "Why don't we all sit down and talk this out? Together? I'm sure we can come to some kind of resolution." I hope Walters is taking notes on hostage negotiation, since he's failing so far.

"I'm sorry Tabby, but the business is more important than you. We need a high-profile success story. Go." Lillian gestures with the gun, forcing her stepsister to take careful steps through the puddle. It's getting awfully crowded in here. This was built for two, not five.

"We have plenty of high-profile success stories. We were about to have another one. Maybe two, if Cassidy and Tanner work out," Tabitha protests as she climbs over the rim. What? I'm briefly distracted from my impending death by the fact that she thinks LoveMatch somehow brought Tanner and me together.

"Right, we were going to. And we still can, we just need to eliminate a few problems first."

Tabitha must not realize that she's now considered one of the problems that's about to be violently eliminated. She continues trying to negotiate. "Lillian, is this about running the company? I do think I'm better suited, but I'm willing to take a step back and manage one of the branch offices. Send me back to Chicago; I was happy there."

Walters does his duty as an FBI agent and nudges his way in front of Tabitha, causing her to stumble into me. "You git on behind me, li'l lady," he says, continuing to use his awful accent. "Let me help handle this. I'm a plumber, I solve problems. And whoo-wee we've got a doozy. We've got three people considering murdering five innocent people, to cover up a massive conspiracy to murder more people. Have I got that right?"

"And a prostitution ring," Jackson adds. "The LoveMatch company fulfills their guaranteed match service by hiring hookers who pretend to be someone they're not, who then kill their new husbands on their honeymoon. Emily here murdered my cousin. She admitted it."

Tabitha is shaking her head in denial. "No, no, we would never—"

"I'm not a hooker, I'm a bereaved widow, and that was a tragic accident," Emily interrupts to mockingly correct Jackson. "If only he'd better understood how to use scuba gear. He wasn't prepared for an emergency, like his wife accidentally turning off his tank. And if you had just given over the inheritance, none of us would be here today."

"Emily!" Tabitha is scandalized. "How could you? And Lillian? You knew about this?"

"I'm surprised you didn't." Lillian shrugs, as though killing husbands is an everyday occurrence. Although maybe for her, it is. "It's nothing new. How do you think we make so much money? My mother paid for your education this way."

"Can we end this now? I want to go home and change out of these wet shoes." Emily asks Lillian. "I claim Jackson. Who do you want to do first? The obnoxious plumber? Cassidy? I was hoping to do her myself, but I'll let you, if I can shoot St. Louis boy. His stupid pizza almost blew the whole thing. Or how about Tabitha? You've never liked her."

"My pizza wasn't stupid. It was Provel. Maybe all I did was expose the holes in your story." Tanner's pride has been insulted, and he's seizing on that as another delaying tactic. "You should have picked a different city to begin with."

"Whatever, we made a planning error and stole the wrong identity. I think I fixed it nicely with my Michigan pivot." Emily's cheeks turn pink, and tears appear in her eyes. "Oh, I'm so sorry, I'm just so embarrassed."

Damn, she's good.

"You should be an actress," Tanner tells her. "You sure can fake being human."

"I am an actress. And when I'm Emily Corbitt, I'm going to start auditioning. My new name is going to open a lot of doors, especially when I'm a widow. Cassidy, that was your mistake. Imagine all you could have done if you'd fully embraced what it means to be Jace's lost love. I'd say learn by watching me, but you won't be around for that."

"This has gone far enough. Put the guns away, and let's discuss this like adults," Tabitha tries to resume control of the situation, a control she's never had.

"I don't . . ." Lillian begins but freezes, head cocked. Someone is opening the suite door. Finally! I was getting worried that the promised police assistance would arrive too late. "Nobody move. I'll handle this." Lillian passes her gun to Isaac and steps out of the bathroom, shutting the door behind her.

"Time to be a hero, Isaac," I suggest. But one little flick of Emily's gun in his direction and he's a coward instead. He takes a shooters stance aimed at us, though he's shaky.

"Everybody be quiet," Emily warns.

"Screw that," Walters shouts. "Iffin y'all are gunna pop us, we's a gunna make some noise." Yeah, he's definitely never getting an undercover assignment. He's right though, we need to attract more attention. I scream as loud as I can, like I'm a teenage girl at a Last Barons concert. Tanner covers his ears, poor guy.

And Tabitha . . . instead of joining me in screaming, she steals Walters' gun from his waistband and points it over his shoulder at Emily.

"Drop it!" she commands. She's steadier than I would expect. My screams cut off immediately.

Walters reaches behind his back and realizes that she stole his gun. "Hey! I need that!" The accent is gone.

There's an argument outside, and what sounds like a scuffle before the door opens, and it's Felicity L'Amour herself. She's clad in yoga pants and a tank top rather than her usual gown, and her face is make-up free. There's a man with her, this one wearing a AAA Plumbing, Inc T-shirt, carrying a toolbox, and gaping at the scene in front of him.

"Tabitha! What are you doing with a gun?" She surveys the room. "And Marjorie! Lillian, why is she here? I told you so many times . . ."

"Mom, you said we needed another cash infusion," Lillian whines. She's always been so composed, but I guess all of us revert to childish whining when trying to convince our parents we're doing nothing wrong.

"Who is Marjorie?" Tabitha asks, though the answer should be obvious. If Emily lied about every aspect of her personality, it shouldn't be a surprise she lied about her name.

"Lillian's girlfriend," Felicity points. "But Lillian, I told you not to involve her anymore, at least not until the lawsuit is settled."

"She's been matched up with my brother," I speak up, peering out from behind Tanner. Felicity blanches when she spots me.

"Miss Corbitt! Darling, I don't know what's going on here, but I'm sure it's all a terrible misunderstanding."

"Mom! You know we needed the money after what happened in Miami." Lillian is still trying to argue her case. She's not very good at being a co-conspirator, or at least, not very good at hiding the conspiracy in front of witnesses.

"I assigned Powell to Tabitha for a reason. He's more valuable as a spokesperson. I thought you understood!" Felicity's harsh whisper carries, and hits like a punch. She knew all along.

"Wait!" Tabitha shoves past Walters and climbs out of the bathtub, gun still pointed at Emily. "You knew they were killing clients?"

"Are you naïve?" Lillian answers on her mother's behalf. "How do you think the business started in the first place?" Felicity tries to shush her, but it's too late.

"With an algorithm! We find true love! It works!" Tabitha's hands are starting to shake as her rose-colored glasses shatter. This is getting more and more dangerous for all of us.

"Oh, honey," Lillian has mastered contempt. "It works sometimes. But you know what's easier? Pretending. Anyone can be someone they're not long enough to receive an expensive ring and a spousal inheritance interest."

Emily speaks up to make things worse. "Besides, we weren't necessarily planning to kill Powell. At least, not right away. He's a multi-millionaire with a deadly peanut allergy, so obviously he's not going to last. But we were going to wait until after his new album drops; death always boosts sales. And I'm so good at playing the tragic widow." Emily directs that last part at me. Tanner shifts his body, because he feels me about to launch myself out of this bathtub to scratch her eyes out, and probably get shot in the process.

"Girls! Not in front of the . . . who are these other people?"

"I'm going to head out now," the man with Felicity says, backing away from the doorway.

Isaac has chosen sides. He swings his gun toward the man. "I don't think so, buddy. Toss your cell in the water and get in the tub."

"I'm just the plumber," he protests, but drops his phone in the shallowest spot and squelches through the water to join us.

"I thought *he* was the plumber," Isaac is targeting Walters now.

"I'm not territorial. We plumbers can work together. Maybe he and I can take care of that clog now?"

"What happened to your accent?" Emily's focus turns to Walters. If we survive, I'm writing a letter to his boss. No undercover investigations, not ever.

"Isaac, give me the gun back," Lillian holds her hand out expectantly toward her sometimes lover.

"Why did your mom say you have a girlfriend?" he responds. It's taken his brain this long to process that revelation. He doesn't hand the gun over, which is what leads to chaos. She tries to grab it, and in the ensuing struggle it goes off, the bullet whizzing past all of us and causing a portion of the wall plaster to explode. My instinct is to get out of the way, so I dive into the wading pond behind the tub, grabbing Tanner and pulling him over with me. We hit the tile floor with a splash.

Jackson sees us bail on the tub and splashes down next to me, as does the other plumber. I peek over the top to see Walters prying his gun away from Tabitha.

"I am an FBI agent. You all need to put your weapons down right now!"

They do not obey, possibly because his obnoxious accent already made them think he's an idiot, and possibly because he hasn't produced a badge. Emily puts her fingers back on the trigger. She's in a firing stance, holding the gun with both hands, pointed directly at Walter's chest. Isaac won the battle for the other weapon, and Lillian is holding her ears in pain. Her head must have been close when it fired. Too bad she wasn't in front of the barrel.

Okay, now what? Time for another asset check, quickly. I have . . . not much. We're barely sheltered behind a tub that may or may not protect us from a barrage of bullets. Still no weapons. Why don't plumbers wear toolbelts? A giant pipe wrench sure would come in handy. What can I throw?

"We have to get out of here," Tanner whispers, as though that wasn't at the forefront of my mind.

"We will. Isn't help on the way?" Any minute now, right? Since I won't be able to lead an escape, I'm kind of counting on the police.

"I was bluffing."

"What? But you can't . . ." Oh no. I've pinned all my hope on the wrong person. I misjudged Tanner's ability to control his dimple. Walters is outnumbered and outgunned, there are four people and two guns in between us and the door. Felicity is old; she should go down easily. But I imagine that the ones with direct murdering experience will put up more of a fight.

"Give me your shirt," I whisper to Tanner. I'm not going to wait around for help that isn't coming. It's time to take action. I expect an argument, but strangely, he doesn't even ask why. He takes it off and hands it to me.

I soak the T-shirt in the water, making it into a heavy wet ball, and stand up. I launch it using my best tossing-swag-into-the-crowd throw and manage to hit Emily in the face. She staggers, and in the fraction of a second that her gun is off Walters, he fires. Emily goes down, Lillian screams, and another gunshot deafens us. The water surrounding me is running red with blood.

"Ouch," Tanner says in mild surprise. He puts his hand to his neck and his fingers come away dripping blood.

"Here," Plumber Number Two whips off his own shirt, wads it up and passes it to Tanner. "Press this against the wound." Tanner's face is already turning pale, and rivers are pulsing from his wound and pouring down his chest. We need an ambulance, now.

"I got this," Jackson says, holding the shirt firmly against Tanner's neck. The white fabric is changing color far too swiftly. He's not going to make it if help doesn't arrive soon. I'm not letting Tanner die. I sneak another peek over the edge to take stock of our circumstances again. I can't tell who fired that last shot, but I'm guessing Isaac, since he still has ahold of the weapon. I'm not sure where Emily's gun ended up.

Walters is shouting commands, Lillian is kneeling next to her apparent girlfriend screaming, Felicity fainted into the water, and poor Tabitha is standing in the middle of it all, in complete shock. Isaac is moving the gun around, alternately pointing at his fiancée, his lover, and the FBI agent.

"Lillian, you're cheating on me," he shouts, finally determining who he wants to target, and full of outrage that someone would do to him the same thing he did to someone else. Guess he never learned the golden rule. When he appears ready to pierce his girlfriend's body with a series of bullets, Walters slowly approaches, still trying to deescalate the situation with soothing words, but with Emily/Marjorie turning the water red at his feet, Lillian's hysteria, and Isaac's inability to mentally focus on more than one thing at a time, this is a losing battle.

What are my assets right now? I'm with three shirtless men, one of whom is bleeding to death. I dropped my shoe when I took my backwards dive out of the tub. But Jackson has my other one in his lap. I snatch it from him, stand up and take aim at Isaac's head. My skill with a high heel is not as good as my skill with a wet T-shirt. I miss entirely, but I've created enough of a distraction that Isaac's brain can't process the happenings and he momentarily lowers the gun in confusion. And then Tabitha—Tabitha, of all people—comes unfrozen and tackles him to the ground.

Walters does not have handcuffs, or anything else that would help keep the criminal gang subdued. Fortunately, one is badly injured and unconscious, one fainted at the sight of blood, and Walters is smart enough to use the butt of his gun to pistol whip Isaac unconscious as well. That leaves Lillian, and she's too hysterical to fight back.

After Walters collects all of the now water-logged guns, he turns to the huddled mass of victims. "We did it!" he thrusts one gun-toting fist into the air, triumphant until he sees the tableau behind the bathtub.

"Tanner's been shot," I reply, my voice far calmer than it should be under the circumstances. I take over from Jackson, cradling Tanner's head and pressing the bloody shirt to his neck. "Someone call for help, now!"

Tabitha scrambles for a phone. Hers and Walters have been rendered useless by water, but Tanner's is functioning perfectly. The bomb-proof case proved its value, protecting the phone both from Lillian's foot and the several minute long soaking.

"Ambulance, now!" Tabitha yells into the phone, before calmly and rationally giving the address and a detailed description of exactly how much assistance we need. It can't come soon enough.

I'm holding Tanner in my arms, whispering supportive things in his ear. Things like *don't you dare die on me*, and *please stop bleeding, damnit*. He's blinking at me weakly, barely conscious. His lips move, taking the shape of my name, but no sound emerges. His pulse is weakening. I cannot believe he's dying here today, the last victim of the LoveMatch International Murder Network.

"I hear them arriving," Jackson tells me. "He just needs to hang on a little bit longer."

The police storm in, led by Tabitha who went to unlock the front door and guide them to the carnage. Walters holds up his badge, to assert his authority, and summons the officers to Tanner's side. His eyes are closed now, and his breathing is so shallow I can't feel it, even when I put my cheek right next to his lips.

"Ambulance is on the way," the first officer assures us, and starts describing the scene into his radio, using police secret code language. I hope some of those numbers mean *get a blood transfusion team here immediately*.

"Second gunshot victim," another officer calls out from the other side of the tub. "Still has a pulse. Hey, let go of me lady!" Lillian, in her my-lover-was-shot madness has attacked the officer, clawing at him and screeching, knocking him down into the pink water, the blood contaminants making it blend in with the awful office decor. A third officer joins the melee to subdue her. I hope he doesn't use a taser; the electricity will zap all of us, since we're all in the same puddle. Lillian is no match for the police, within less than a minute, she's cuffed and sobbing.

"It's a thong!" A triumphant voice cuts through the chaos, and we all look to the sink, where the real plumber is holding up my underwear. He'd already removed Jackson's shirt from the toilet and stopped the flow of water. "Sorry," he mutters, when he realizes he's the only one who cares about the pipes.

"In here, in here," Tabitha comes running back in. I hadn't noticed her leaving again, but she's now bringing us the people I want to see most in the world: the paramedics.

"He was shot in the neck," I tell them, relinquishing my hold on the blood-soaked shirt to the first one who reaches me.

"Carotid artery," he informs the others as they place him on a stretcher, start an IV, and roll him away at a sprint. I'm left huddled on the floor, soaking wet with water and blood. As the adrenaline leaves my body, I'm starting to shake with stress and fatigue and my worry for Tanner.

"Come on, Blaine-Corbitt," Walters gently grips my shoulders. "Let's get you checked out."

# CHAPTER EIGHTEEN

I'm developing a great deal of animosity for this hospital.

First, I was transported in the back of a police car looking like a criminal, and garnering stares as we pulled up to the emergency room doors.

Then, upon arrival, I was shuffled off to an exam room, rather than being taken directly to Tanner, as I demanded. Despite my loud protestations, the nurses—under the direction of Agent Walters—did a complete physical examination of me, even though I am uninjured. No matter how many times I told them none of the blood on my dress was mine, they still insisted on checking. And then I had to wait nearly a half hour for a phlebotomist to arrive and take blood samples—from my veins, not my clothing. They're collecting evidence and need to find out what Isaac slipped into my drink.

Just when I think it's over and I can be released to find my friend, a police officer with a recorder and notepad shows up, all set to question me and take my statement. The officer, who initially tried to sound friendly but is quickly losing patience, will not accept *I'll tell you later* as an answer.

He's starting to glare at me, and mutters something about obstructing an investigation.

"I'm the victim," I remind him. And, in a flash of inspiration, "I know my rights. I want a lawyer."

"You aren't under arrest. You don't need a lawyer," he tells me through gritted teeth. I don't appreciate his approach toward dealing with crime victims. Where's the sympathy, the compassion? The cup of coffee and donut?

"I will only give a statement with my attorney present." I clamp my lips shut to demonstrate how difficult it will be to pry any information out of me.

The officer sighs in frustration. "Ma'am, as the victim, you don't need an attorney, nor do you have the legal right to one. I'm going to find someone else who will deal with you." I'm not sure if an unspoken threat lurks behind his words, or if he's going to go find a sweeter, kinder officer, one who plays the good cop to his bad cop. Most likely he's looking for a doctor to inject me with something to make me more malleable. Some kind of sedative/truth serum.

But I'm not going to wait around to find out.

With a minor lie—a claim that the doctors told me to find him—a nurse gives me Tanner's room number, and I track him down.

There's another obstacle though: rampant sexism. That's right, this hospital is sexist. Apparently, if an ambulance radios ahead that they are bringing in two gunshot victims, one of whom was shot by an FBI agent while holding a group of people hostage in a bathtub, and the other is an innocent victim, it's the male who ends up in a room blocked off by a security guard, while the wounded female is tended to by a team of worried doctors.

Tanner's door is blocked by an immovable object.

"I'm sorry, ma'am," he repeats, looking at my disheveled appearance. I'm still in my cocktail dress, now dry, but I have an FBI sweatshirt from Walters' trunk on over it. My shoes are part of the crime scene, and I was not allowed to take them, so instead I'm wearing a pair of thick white athletic socks that one of the responding officers kindly gave me.

"I swear, if you do not let me through that door . . ." my threat is empty. What am I going to do, scream? Call his boss and complain?

"Ma'am, not without permission. This man is a criminal under investigation. Are your doctors looking for you? Do you need me to call someone?"

I hate being one of *those* people, but I'm going to pull the name card. Upstairs there's a wing called the Rebecca Corbitt Memorial Cancer Ward. Powell and Hank made a massive donation a few years ago. That familial connection to major funders might give me enough clout. I draw myself up to my full height—not impressive without my heels. "Do you have any idea who I am? My name is Cassidy—"

His eyes widen in recognition before I finish my sentence. "You're Agent Cassidy Walters? You were at the hostage situation. Wow, sorry, I didn't mean to block you out. Of course, you can enter."

He opens the door for me, so I'm not going to correct his mistaken identity.

"By the way, ma'am, I've been trying to get into the FBI. My application has been on pending status for months. If there's anything you can do . . ." He presses a card into my hand.

"I'll pass this along," I assure him. Probably to the real Cassidy Walters. Or the trash can. I'll decide later.

Tanner is sleeping. His left arm has IV tubes leading to it; his right arm is handcuffed to the bed. I try to be quiet in my approach, so I can study him. Poor guy. His neck is bandaged from the surgery to repair his carotid artery. They didn't clean him up well—there is still dried blood on the underside of his chin and on his chest.

"Oh, Tanner," I sigh, as I pull up the guest chair.

At the sound of my voice, his eyes open wide from his fake sleep.

"Good, it's you. Help me, I don't know what happened!" he rattles his handcuff at me.

"Isn't it obvious? You were arrested for trying to murder me again. You've really got to stop doing that." I expect him to laugh, but the aftereffects of the anesthesia are addling his brain. He gets defensive instead.

"Cassidy, I didn't, you were with me! I swear, I didn't! Get me out of here!" He tugs on the cuff again, but weakly. He's still pale from all the blood loss, though it's all been replaced. Twelve units, more than an entire body's worth, according to the gossip I overheard from some passing nurses. It's possible they were talking about some other patient, but given that they used the terms 'carotid artery,' 'gunshot victim' and 'heart-shaped tub,' I doubt anyone else fits that description.

"I will," I promise, leaving off the fact that I need to figure out how. He and I are both kind of trapped here. I don't have my phone, so I can't call Powell for help. He won't answer numbers that aren't in his contacts. And I don't remember my parents' numbers, which is the big problem with depending on cell phones. "But while I'm working on that, you need to rest. You've just had major surgery."

"Blaine-Corbitt!" The door to the room flies open, and Walters has no qualms with disturbing an injured post-op patient. His voice is inappropriately loud for a hospital, and he is angrier than he was when I encouraged him to break into Jackson's apartment. "You cannot impersonate an FBI agent!"

"Evidently, I can," I correct him. "But it wasn't intentional."

"That is a violation of federal law," he snaps. Then he finally notices the patient whose healing he is disrupting. "Hey, Tanner. You're looking better."

"Can you get this off of me?" Poor miserable Tanner shakes his cuffed arm. He's going to end up bruised if he keeps doing that.

"Sorry pal, I'd love to help you, but you've been arrested, and I can't release the local PD's prisoner."

I am about to start yelling at Walters when he grins and whips a key out of his pocket. "Just kidding."

"Why do you have the key? Are you the one who did this?" I smack him in the arm, slightly harder than intended. But he deserves it.

"Ow! Assaulting a federal agent is getting added to the list of charges against you!" He proceeds to unlock the cuffs and leaves them dangling from the bed. "And just so you know, all handcuff keys are the same. If you're going to try and steal my identity, maybe you should do more research for your role."

Tanner is dramatically rubbing his wrist, as though that's where his main injury is located. I reach out and stop him. "Don't move around so much. You'll pop your stitches."

"I can't believe I was shot," he reaches for his neck to probe at his surgical wound. I intercept his hand before he can touch his bandages. He's worse than Powell.

"You weren't," Walters informs him, pulling up a chair to the other side of the bed.

"Yes, I was," Tanner squeezes my fingers. Once I blocked his hand from his neck, he clung on to me and won't let go. It's a trauma response after the day we've had.

"No, you actually weren't." Walters is smug. "You were shrapneled."

"What does that mean?"

"When Isaac fired that gun, the bullet clipped the bathtub on the way to the wall, a piece of porcelain went through the air and sliced Tanner's neck as it passed. Shrapnel. A pink heart shaped bathtub almost killed you."

"That's not nearly as cool," Tanner says. He almost sounds disappointed. I bet the story of the time he survived a shooting would have earned him a lot of free drinks at his favorite bar. 'Part of a bathtub cut me' lacks the same cachet.

Tanner needed more rest, and the nurses kicked Walters and me out, so we head down to the cafeteria for coffee. He said he contacted my parents, and they're on their way to pick me up.

"You have to pay for this," I tell him when we place our orders. "My purse is still missing."

"Tabitha is looking for it, and you can pay me back," he assures me. He buys me a coffee and an egg sandwich. I didn't realize how ravenous I was until I take the first bite.

"You want to tell me how you ended up held at gunpoint in a pink bathtub?" he asks, when I'm halfway through ravaging my meal. Ah ha! He's the one they sent to question me. At least he plied me with food first.

"I'd rather you explain how you and Tanner ended up there with Tabitha."

Since I'm eating, he decides to go first. "Tanner called and told me about your idiotic decision to investigate. He figured you'd been kidnapped too."

"How?" I grunt. I'd ask a more complex question, but my mouth is full.

"Apparently, you responded to his increasingly frantic texts from another phone—one I bet we'll find somewhere in the LoveMatch offices—claiming that your battery had died. You told him you were going out of town. He made some . . . rather sexual remarks, you flirted back, and assured him that you'd be down for some dirty action when you returned."

My eyebrows fly up, and Walters laughs at me.

"Yeah, that's how we knew it was fake. I assume they couldn't unlock yours to reply, so they couldn't access your message chain and see what you were really talking about before. We met up with Tabitha this morning to confront her. And we were with her when she got a call from building security saying that their offices were flooding. Good job doing that."

I swallow the last morsel of food and wonder if Walters will buy me a slice of cake. "I was hoping security would arrive, not a bunch of matchmakers with guns. Have you apologized to Jackson yet? For not believing him?"

"I never told him I didn't believe him, I only told you that. So, no. I don't need to. He's happy now. He's got the proof he needs. Tanner's phone was recording the whole time, so we have Emily's confession to murdering Lester and planning to kill Powell. She's going away for a long time, after she gets out of the hospital. Lillian, Isaac, and Felicity are already in holding cells, awaiting transfer."

"What's going to happen to Tabitha? Was she in on any of it?"

"I think she was innocent. She's cooperating fully with investigators. Later today I'm going to go through the computer systems with her. I feel bad for her. In one day, she lost her family, her fiancé, and her business."

"She's smart. She'll land on her feet."

"So will you, Blaine-Corbitt. You did great in there. You kept your cool, and if you hadn't thrown—what did you throw?—at Emily, she would have shot me. Thank you."

"It was Tanner's shirt, soaked in toilet water."

"Classy. And the plumber's was used for Tanner's blood? And Jackson's must have been the one you flushed. I was wondering why all of the hostages were half naked."

"My underwear was in the sink."

"I'll note that in my report." Walters laughs again. I've never seen him in this good of a mood before, but I suppose I've never seen him in the immediate aftermath of a successful mission either. "You know, this was a great day. We broke up a crime syndicate, saved a superstar from a future murder, and successfully defused a high-stakes hostage situation with minimal injuries."

"It'll be a better day once I've showered and slept." And once I've got complete and full confirmation that Tanner is going to be okay. I may spend the night here tonight, just to keep an eye on him.

# CHAPTER NINETEEN

The flight attendant welcomes us with a tray of champagne and a great big smile directed at my brother. I'm not entirely certain she noticed my presence at all. We help ourselves to two of the glasses and greet our parents, happily ensconced on the large couch near the front. Hank always likes to sit as close to the pilots as possible, just in case he gets called in to land the plane and save the day. He took flying lessons a decade ago and still hasn't had his chance to be a hero.

"This is disappointing," Powell says, fortunately not in the hearing of the cheerful alcohol distributor. "I wanted the one with the white interior."

"Are you seriously complaining about the color of the upholstery in the private jet your label sent to take you to your launch party? You don't get to be that big of a diva until we land." I select one of the tan leather seats surrounding a conference table, and he takes the one across from me. Despite his aesthetic complaints, this is a very nice plane. After we take off, there's going to be a fruit and cheese course. That's why I sat at the table.

"I'm not a diva," my brother protests, while simultaneously allowing the second flight attendant to dab moisture off his face with a towel.

I take his champagne from him. "You're singing tonight, so you're only allowed to have honey tea. You know that." Before

I'm finished speaking, my words magically conjure a small teapot and a mug on the table between us. Okay, fine, they were set there by the flight attendant, once she finished making sure the diva wasn't too sweaty from walking across the hot tarmac to board.

Powell sighs. "It's my party. I should be allowed to have whatever I want." He makes the same complaint every single time, and it never works. I down his champagne before he can try to take the flute back.

"This is awesome!" Tanner drops down into the seat next to me, filled with enthusiasm. "Thank you so much for inviting me! Smile!" And here comes his ubiquitous phone, and before I can stop him, he drapes his arm around my shoulders and takes a picture of us.

"It's not awesome. Someone doesn't like the color of the interior. Someone wanted white." I give my brother a pointed look.

"Easier to meter off of tan," Tanner mutters, messing around on his phone. I peek over his shoulder. He's already posting on SwiftaPic. *Thanks @CassBC for saving me a seat on the private jet to @PowellC's album launch party #Duality #newrelease. I swear, I would take a bullet for this woman. #notjoking #privatejet #milehighpics #launchparty #howdidIgetsolucky*

"Actually, you'd take shrapnel for me," I correct, and Powell snickers. Easy for him to laugh, he wasn't there.

"True, and it nearly killed me. So, I guess I wouldn't take a bullet for you. Like if one skimmed me, that'd be okay. But I don't want actual holes shot in me."

"Can we not talk about this?" I ask. I don't enjoy rehashing the events of the kidnapping, and Powell definitely doesn't want to, either. He's been having a tough time since the whole Emily thing blew up. Tabitha kindly tried to keep his name out of the news, but *Powell Corbitt, Superstar, Caught up in Matchmaking Scam* has been a trending topic, so he's both heart-broken and embarrassed. His publicist is setting a good spin on it though, pop star ready to settle down. So far, I've seen about a thousand marriage proposals on his Swifta feed.

"While you're at it, can you get me?" Powell is always willing to have a professional take his social media photos for him. He passes Tanner his phone, and they start a mini shoot with my brother trying to look relaxed, ready to perform, and like he didn't just pull out a compact and powder his nose.

While the boys are playing, I idly flip through my own phone, and take a moment to carefully examine Tanner's latest post.

The picture isn't too bad. At least my eyes are open, and my mouth isn't. I can kind of make out the wound on Tanner's neck. The puckered skin was red and raw for days, but it's looking better now. Brixley sent him a whole case of creams and ointments to reduce the scar tissue and help it heal faster. He can thank her for them at the party tonight, where she'll be on the arm of an NBA player. He's much taller than Devon, as she has gleefully pointed out. Devon was never sensitive about being shorter than her, until now.

"Alright, folks," the pilot's voice comes over the intercom. "We're about to take off. Please fasten your seatbelts." The two flight attendants disappear behind a curtain where their jump seats are located. Hank is seat belted, but he's also poised to rip it off and dive into the cockpit if needed. Mom looks over the back of the couch to roll her eyes at me. We both hope Hank's dreams of heroism never come true.

"This is the life," Tanner sighs happily as we roar down the runway and lift off into the cloudless sky. "Is this how you always travel?"

"No, we usually fly commercial," I assure him, to avoid another of his anti-rich people digs. My brother likes to sit in first class, head turned toward the window, but always listening to the boarding passengers and hoping to hear excited whispers as he's recognized. I take the aisle seat and count how many people try to bribe me into swapping.

"The jet is for the publicity shots when I land," Powell adds. He will be the first to deplane, greeted by press and a few lucky contest-winning fans. I'll be following with his garment bag and suitcase. Life as a star's assistant is so very glamorous.

As soon as we reach cruising altitude, the food and a second round of champagne arrives, though this time Powell is not offered a glass. He scowls, but continues sipping his tea, all the better to protect his precious voice. But then he makes another attempt to violate his show day diet and helps himself to a slice of cheese. As his assistant, I do my duty and slap his hand.

"What did Valissa say about consuming dairy on show days?" He is already under the supervision and control of his lifestyle coach. She's bossier than me, and when we start the tour next month, nothing enters his body without her express permission. He's supposed to adhere to a specific and limited pre-tour diet as well, but he cheats.

"I'm performing one song tonight. I can have some cheese." When I move the plate out of the way, my whiney spoiled brother shouts toward our parents "Dad, Mom, help! Cassidy is trying to starve me!"

"What are you, five years old?" I throw a slice of Havarti at his face, so maybe I'm five, too. He peels the cheese from his cheek and shoves it in his mouth before I can stop him. Our parents ignore us both, perhaps because they know we're adults, or perhaps because they're used to our occasional immaturity. Rather, Powell's occasional immaturity. I am a paragon of adult behavior at all times.

Tanner decides to interfere with our petty skirmish by sliding the plate to his corner of the table. He places a piece on a cracker, takes a bite and smiles. "Provel? This is meant to be melted on pizza, not served on crackers."

"That cheese saved my life; we can put it on whatever we want." Powell sneakily takes a slice, and I let him get away with it, partly because of the disgusted face he makes when he eats it. From my lofty pedestal as a cheese connoisseur, I should have warned him: it's an acquired taste.

"Tanner's pizza was merely the first clue. I think *I* saved your life," I point out. Give credit where credit is due.

"And Tabitha saved everybody else's." Powell nods in satisfaction. "She's amazing."

Wait, what? She gets all the credit? I did the throwing, and Walters did the shooting. All Tabitha did was disarm her ex-fiancé. Granted, he was the last criminal standing, but still.

"Powell . . ." I begin, but he's already done with this conversation and stealing bites of non-Provel cheese.

Tanner grins at me. "Technically, he's right."

Fine, nobody thinks I'm a hero. Next time, I'll let Tanner bleed out, see what he thinks about that. Just kidding, I would never let that happen, and there won't be a next time. I think I've reached my lifetime maximum on exposure to people trying to murder me.

"I'm so glad we're hitting the road soon. The tour is exactly what I need to take my mind off everything," Powell tells us. Of course, he'd think that. He has one job: show up where he's told and perform. Sometimes that performance is musical, sometimes it's him smiling for cameras and signing autographs. The rest of us behind the scenes will be doing all the real work. "You're coming, right?"

"Um, yeah. I'm your assistant, of course I'll be there."

"I wasn't talking to you." He's looking to Tanner for an answer. It takes Tanner a second to realize that.

"What? Me?"

"Yeah, you. I already know Cass is coming; who else would I be talking to? I'm not inviting my parents. They've aged out of living on buses."

I hold back a laugh. Mom and Hank loved traveling with the Last Barons of Sound, but once Powell became a legal adult, he started rebelling at the idea of having parental supervision on the road. They always fly out to join us for a couple of shows though.

"What would I do, be your personal photographer?" Tanner is warming to the idea, an idea I should have been consulted on first. When will Powell learn that things need to be planned and organized in advance? He shouldn't be spontaneously adding people to the tour.

"I want a coffee table book," Powell says. That's not, for once, a non-sequitur. Apparently, it's been a thing lately, and superfans love them. And I can predict next year's Christmas gift for everybody on my brother's list.

"Hold on. Are you sure you can make him that offer?" I don't want Tanner getting his hopes up yet. "There are logistics involved in this."

"I told Liam about it a while ago. He says it's fine. My lawyer drew up a contract. I just forgot to ask Tanner. I've been busy." Yeah, busy writing a series of unmarketable angry songs about lies, betrayal, and how he wasn't really fooled by Emily and maybe he was going to dump her anyway, so stop rubbing it in, Cassidy.

"A four-month tour?" Tanner muses. He's seriously considering the offer. "I don't know. There's nothing on my schedule that can't be changed. Could be fun. What do you think Cass? Should I take it?"

Our eyes meet, and I feel a little fluttering in my stomach. Four months on the road together, working together? Sharing a bus?

"You realize I'd be your boss, right?" I ask him.

"I thought Powell..."

"Nope," my brother confirms. "Cassidy is the boss of my entourage. She's the boss of everybody except me." Actually,

I'm sort of the boss of him since I enforce his nutritionist's rules and block people from slipping him unauthorized food. Plus, I manage his schedule, and if he annoys me, he ends up with very early predawn photo shoots.

"Still interested, knowing you'd be under my supervision?"

"Maybe I'm even more interested." His smile seems like a challenge.

"Tanner, you have absolutely no idea what you're getting into. I think . . ." I hesitate, and his smile falters. This feels like one of those falling-off-a-cliff moments, where the decision I make now might change everything. *Deep breath, Cassidy,* ". . . I think you should take the offer. Join us on tour."

"Nobody will try to kill anybody, and you won't get arrested again," my brother adds helpfully, his method of convincing Tanner. Mike is head of security, so that's probably a promise Powell can keep, except for the arrest thing. That part is really up to Tanner.

"Since I've met the two of you, I've been blown up, arrested, and shrapneled, so I don't think you can make a promise like that." Tanner's dimple appears, and his eyes meet mine again. "But I'm in. What's the worst that could happen?"

# Also By Sara LaFontain

**The Corbitt Calamities Series**
Unexpected Encore
Concerted Chaos
Matchmaker Mayhem
Tour Saboteur (coming Fall 2022)

**The Whispering Pines Island Series**
That Last Summer
Say the Words
No Longer Yours
Cherry Christmas, Baby!
If This Were a Love Story

# Acknowledgements

This was not originally the second book in this series. But as I was trying to write the other second book, this one kept interrupting me. Powell is ready to settle down, and he kept whispering in my ear that he wants to start a family. Too bad for him, I don't obey my characters.

I had fun with this. I hope you enjoyed reading it. Ryan did. He's the first to see anything I write, and the first to give suggestions. I don't always listen to him either; he wants me to slip in humorous sci-fi references that only he would get.

I do listen to—and greatly appreciate—my beta readers. Thank you Lynn Curry, Katherine Caldwell, Carly Margolin, and Red L. Jameson. Your suggestions and guidance helped shape this into what I hope is a fun read.

Thank you to Rowan, who likes to look over my shoulder and point out perceived errors, and Willow, who does the same. You aren't always right, but you are always eager to help. Someday, you will both be editors.

Thank you to all of the online support I receive, through the Every Damn Day Writers group (you've read snippets of this every Wednesday), and the Women's Fiction Writer's Association.

## About the Author

Sara LaFontain writes books featuring unreliable narrators, flawed characters, and things working out in the end. Prior to embarking on a writing career, Sara held a variety of jobs including wildlife tour guide, purveyor of fine chocolates, cafeteria worker, ESL teacher, domestic violence victim advocate, and family law attorney. She currently lives in Tucson, Arizona with her husband and two children. When she isn't writing, she's experimenting with new crafting projects, knitting, gardening, and bragging about desert winters.

The Whispering Pines Island series of standalone novels is about love, healing, and finding happiness.

The Corbitt Calamities series is a fun chick lit series featuring explosions, attempted murders, invasive photographers, and, at the heart of it all, an unbreakable sibling bond.